The Martyring
World Fantasy Award Finalist

"Thomas Sullivan is a master of description. Even readers who are not scared by things that go bump in the night may tremble as the most ghoulish creature since Hannibal Lecter stalks the pages of *The Martyring*. A tale of murder and unholy family relationships." —William X. Kienzle

"A compelling read and the seed of nightmares. Classic Sullivan." —Fred Bean

"Trying to pigeonhole Thomas Sullivan would be like calling Hemingway an outdoor writer or Fitzgerald the king of glamour and glitz. He's that good, moving effortlessly from one literary landscape to another, his cast of wonderful characters in tow." —Lowell Cauffiel

The Phases of Harry Moon
Nominated for the Pulitzer Prize

"One is convinced that an outsize performer is trying his wings—a John Barth or a John Irving, with a touch of William Gaddis and maybe a touch of Kurt Vonnegut, Jr." —*Chicago Tribune*

"Once in a blue moon, modern American literature captures lightning in a bottle, producing a work that is both important and entertaining. *The Phases of Harry Moon* is just such a work. In the hands of Thomas Sullivan, it is a serious character study as seen in a funhouse mirror. The reader will look, laugh, and come away changed." —Loren D. Estleman

SECOND SOUL

Thomas Sullivan

AN ONYX BOOK

ONYX
Published by New American Library, a division of
Penguin Group (USA) Inc., 375 Hudson Street,
New York, New York 10014, USA
Penguin Group (Canada), 90 Eglinton Avenue East, Suite 700, Toronto,
Ontario M4P 2Y3, Canada (a division of Pearson Penguin Canada Inc.)
Penguin Books Ltd., 80 Strand, London WC2R 0RL, England
Penguin Ireland, 25 St. Stephen's Green, Dublin 2,
Ireland (a division of Penguin Books Ltd.)
Penguin Group (Australia), 250 Camberwell Road, Camberwell, Victoria 3124,
Australia (a division of Pearson Australia Group Pty. Ltd.)
Penguin Books India Pvt. Ltd., 11 Community Centre, Panchsheel Park,
New Delhi - 110 017, India
Penguin Group (NZ), cnr Airborne and Rosedale Roads, Albany,
Auckland 1310, New Zealand (a division of Pearson New Zealand Ltd.)
Penguin Books (South Africa) (Pty.) Ltd., 24 Sturdee Avenue,
Rosebank, Johannesburg 2196, South Africa

Penguin Books Ltd., Registered Offices:
80 Strand, London WC2R 0RL, England

First published by Onyx, an imprint of New American Library,
a division of Penguin Group (USA) Inc.

First Printing, August 2005
10 9 8 7 6 5 4 3 2 1

Copyright © Thomas Sullivan, 2005
All rights reserved

 REGISTERED TRADEMARK—MARCA REGISTRADA

Printed in the United States of America

Without limiting the rights under copyright reserved above, no part of this publication
may be reproduced, stored in or introduced into a retrieval system, or transmitted, in
any form, or by any means (electronic, mechanical, photocopying, recording, or otherwise),
without the prior written permission of both the copyright owner and the
above publisher of this book.

PUBLISHER'S NOTE
This is a work of fiction. Names, characters, places, and incidents either are the product of the author's imagination or are used fictitiously, and any resemblance to actual persons, living or dead, business establishments, events, or locales is entirely coincidental.
 The publisher does not have any control over and does not assume any responsibility for author or third-party Web sites or their content.

If you purchased this book without a cover you should be aware that this book is stolen property. It was reported as "unsold and destroyed" to the publisher and neither the author nor the publisher has received any payment for this "stripped book."

The scanning, uploading, and distribution of this book via the Internet or via any other means without the permission of the publisher is illegal and punishable by law. Please purchase only authorized electronic editions, and do not participate in or encourage electronic piracy of copyrighted materials. Your support of the author's rights is appreciated.

For Glenn Frey,
who never hit a sour note

ACKNOWLEDGMENTS

Thanks to Jim Hornfischer, who inspires new paths, and to Todd Cook, who grooms them, and to Rich Lehman, who watches over them. Likewise, my gratitude to Jan and the gang at Gear West, whose expertise always enriches, and to Ginny Malikowski who provided the atmosphere. Jordana Whyte and Katie Hilpisch are my indispensable muses as always, and many debts are acknowledged to Fred Bean for his faith and friendship. He is sorely missed. Last but not least, thanks to my son, Sean, for his insightful proofreading and to my daughter, Colleen, for throwing more titles at me than I have in my library.

1

I am Waterfall Man.

The sketchy accounts I gave the docs about what happened November 10, 2000, were true as far as they went, but this is for me. Even though I'll write it to a stranger. Because that's what I'm becoming.

I remember how the magic started. A road smoking with frost, trees trunks like naked thighs in a steam room, the sky just a rumor of light smothered in oily clouds, and the ditches like dirty moats full of melting snow the color of old soap. It was insane to try to ski the narrow band between the road and the creek. Every time I thought about it, the phrase "seriously dumb" ended the urge. But here was the magic all around me on the heavily wooded slopes outside Sheshebans, Minnesota, and magic makes me feel invincible. So I leaned a little. At the top of the mountain I leaned, recalculating the odds. I never did decide to go. My skis just slipped past the point of no return and gravity did the rest. Coming down, the hiss of acceleration rose like applause.

I guess I knew from the start I wouldn't make it, because I kept pushing off the right ski, feeling for the edge of the road, so that if I wiped out, it would be in the shallowness of the ditch. The baskets on the ends of my poles were punching through into sheer nothing. At the least, I was tearing up the bottoms of a new pair of Fischer cross-country skis, and I didn't care. If it hadn't been the first outing of the season, if I hadn't been intoxicated with the mist and all that crystal magic, I might have cut across the road and leveled off. But what I did was skate blindly into the descent.

Speed focused my field of vision, because trackless skiing through low-slung branches is like a grand slalom where the penalty for missing a gate is decapitation. I lost sight of the road. I lost sight of the creek. As the snow deepened on the lee side of the mountain, I carved my way faster and faster until I seemed to be skiing on light itself. The sound of the waterfall crept up on me too late. By the time I knew where I was headed, there were no more exits. I couldn't wipe out, because boulders were popping up like army helmets out of trenches. If I went down, I would break something. But there was a slim hope that I could skirt whatever lay ahead. And hope is part of the thrill you take to the White Room.

Nanosecond hope bursts over you, then fades. It sprints in your adrenaline, then drowns in your perspiration. And there is that oddly cool moment when you know you've lost control, when the looming tree or the precipice or the glare ice inform you that you have to abandon yourself to fate and faith. I've thought a lot about those odd moments, and I still don't know whether they represent remorse or arrogance. But they measure how close to death you come, and somehow that makes you more alive.

I went over the edge of something into the sanctuary of air. Boulders boiled beneath me. I didn't actually see the water. It was just the filler between the stones, the oily black background that took the place of the snow. My feet pushed as though my skis were levers, searching for a brake. My poles braced like Lilliputian pikes prodding a Gulliver of a mountain. The dance was short. A clatter of graphite and plastic, and a rough pirouette that shattered ice. The applause this time was the water cascading over me. Thinsulate and Gore-Tex, polypropylene and spandex, human flesh—all failed to stop the cold that squeezed me to the core.

My instinct was to scramble forward. I was still breathing, so the waterfall must have been ragged with air, veiling me but not forcing me underwater. That seems important now that I'm struggling to believe I'm really alive. The cold was something else. Those first sharp gulps of air stabbed at a glacier inside me with the ferocity of an ice pick. After that, I was numb. Likewise, the struggle to escape was brief. My left leg was wedged hopelessly in something that seemed to be chewing on it. Call it a maw, because by rights I should still be moldering into that mountain. Mercifully, the leg too went numb.

I was a dead man. Despite what I said about fate and faith and hope, I was a dead man and knew it. Faith has always been my weakness. I don't think I struggled at all after the first few seconds. Whether it was seconds or minutes, time became one more item added to things lost. And eventually in that limbo of lost time and paralyzing cold, a question formed dimly in my brain. Why was I still dying? Why was I still thinking? I didn't believe that this was actually death, that I had crossed over. I could see the world—murkier than before, a grotto of millennia-old boulders and silhouettes, sounds and smells—even with torrents coming down around me.

They tell me there was a bear. I never saw the bear. If it came there for me, it must have been very discreet about it. But I heard the bus whining down the grade, and the bus hit the bear. That's what sent the vehicle hurtling off the road and into the trees. Nineteen of the twenty-two aboard, including the driver, were killed. Unbelievable. Two life-and-death dramas in one hour in one little patch of mountain. That much, at least, was coincidence.

There was no feeling in me at all when I heard the crash. I don't mean just physically; I mean emotionally. A total contrast to what must have been going on in the bus. The passengers would have had time to react. All those people coming back from an outing at Mille Lacs, the icy descent, the curve, then the bear. They would hear brakes squealing and feel the surge; they would know what was happening; and even after they hit the animal and spun out, they would be flung around like screaming rag dolls until the yellow school bus broadsided against two trees and burst into flame. Then the sudden extinction. The nineteen died at the scene. Ironic that so many were perishing in a fiery holocaust while twenty yards away a man was freezing to death in a waterfall.

It has been suggested to me that I could not have seen the molten glow, that my eyes probably weren't working at that point. So why a memory of reds and yellows? Peter Max rainbows throb in my memory. It must have been the bus. The waterfall may have distorted it, but if I did in fact still exist, it was in a taffy-pull twilight where everything looked like a Lava lamp. And there was more. The burning bus isn't what I remember most. What I remember most is a hole in the sky.

I don't know what else to call it. It was an absence of light, and it rushed at me as if it were a figure, as if it had a will. It *did* have a will. It hung there, and I knew that something extremely perceptive swarmed within it. I stared into its silhouette, which kept changing shape—if that wasn't also a refractory trick of the waterfall—and I sensed a malevolent joy pouring out of it. There are moments when you transcend verbal communication, when you know that five senses and a bunch of grunts can't contain the universe. Such was this moment. A coherent presence faced me, and it was absolutely and utterly commanding. My intelligence withered before its depth and intensity. At the same time, I knew it lacked whole dimensions of the human heart. Whatever it was, it had no compassion. It was feral. It had discovered me in my hour of agony, and it was delighted. My bones were cold enough to shatter, but the chill I felt went even beyond that.

Hallucination, you say? My whole life has been a hallucination since that day when my identity as Michael Bowden Carmichael ebbed close to—and maybe beyond—extinction. Maybe Michael Bowden Carmichael is the hallucination. Maybe what I saw was a glimpse of the true universe beyond the regional physics of a small planet around a hospitable star. Maybe the virtues and vices of Local Planet Number One are just vanity and folly when you put them up against the cosmos. Give Bogart and *Casablanca* credit for the metaphor: Worldly destinies don't amount to a hill of beans in the vastness of the universe.

So what did it want, this thing with no eyes and no substance? Why had it been attracted to me? I wondered, and at the same time I knew. I stood on the brink of an eternal night that crackled with furious things—spirits, urges, demiurges. The lightless specter was master of that domain. It radiated a passion for chaos, a joy over death. Nineteen souls were being dramatically extinguished a few yards away; that was why it was there.

But why this feeling of extraordinary discovery over me?

I wasn't dead. If snuffed-out humans are what excited the specter, there was no reason to be exhilarated at finding just one still hanging on. What pierced my dulled awareness, and what still troubles me fifty-one days later, is that the only remarkable thing about me is that, if I wasn't dead, I wasn't really alive either. I was somewhere in between. And in the last stages of consciousness on November tenth, the coherent hole in the sky moved directly between me and the burning bus. Suddenly the translucent waterfall vitrified completely, and I saw straight through the silhouette as if it were a tunnel filled with stains moving toward me. For one brief moment, the bus of the dead and my suspended body were connected.

2

When the final curtain comes down, you lose the audience and the light but not the play. Even if you suffer sudden and massive extinction, you awaken again at some level of awareness. I know you do because of what is out there now. A busload of them. Silhouettes and shadows who have reached the vestibule of my mind and are waiting for me to make a mistake.

They are homing in on the fact that I am lost and isolated. There is no one I can turn to. Writing this is my attempt to reach out. Maybe only to a saner version of myself that existed before, but I'll grab any hand in this storm. Almost any hand.

Who am I kidding?

I don't know how to take a hand. This is a hell of a time to have to learn how to trust.

Everyone calls me Michael to my face here at the hospital, but behind my back they call me Waterfall Man. No one calls me Bowie, which is what I was before November tenth. And the news media can't get beyond the bouncy sound of my full name: *Michael Carmichael is a dead man walking. . . . Michael Carmichael is recovering at Mayo Clinic.*

Recovering. Right. As if the fracturing nightmares represent progress. Nightmares like the magic mirror in the bathroom. Or the microhells writhing in the corner of my room that suddenly take on color when I stare into the shadows. I don't think I'm recovering at all. I think the long slide in my life that began before November tenth has detoured through another dimension.

Like I said, when I had friends, they called me Bowie. I'm burning bridges, I guess, so I don't have friends anymore. Some of that happened before the accident, because I was cleaning up my act; some of it is happening now, because I refuse to see anyone or answer the phone. I don't want to hurt the people from my past, but I don't want to be seen like this.

If I look the same in the huge mirror in the bathroom, it's because what's changed is so deep it may never show on the surface. I remember my dad saying he changed suddenly. He just told me one day that he'd lost it. He knew his memory was going, and that he couldn't react the same, couldn't find the precedents and the links that held his life together. And more and more after that he spoke in a different tense. He didn't "want" things anymore; instead he had "wanted" them. He spoke so sadly that I knew he really had changed. His attitude went south, and that dulled his effort to live, and that made him age rapidly. I guess that's what I'm afraid of finding in the bathroom mirror at Mayo: the past tense.

This particular mirror is one of those incredibly clear silvered layers with very thick glass over it that make the world behind you look dimmer and deeper. You'd swear your image was a distinct and separate person. And you'd swear there were eyes glittering out of the gloom behind you. And there was this one time—perfectly explainable, I'm sure, when you consider the condition I was in—but this one time when it got very, very crowded in that glass.

It was maybe the second or third visit I made to the bathroom by myself. I was unsteady on my feet, and the nurse hung around the outer room, telling me to leave the door open a crack.

"Don't you be modest now; I seen everything you got. And you ain't ready to solo yet."

I closed it, because I *was* ready to solo, and they had to understand that I didn't belong in a hospital. It would have been okay, too, but the light in the mirror immediately began to fade and the air stopped moving. I'm very sensitive to moving air now, and at that moment I felt like someone had stuffed a rag down my throat. I fell forward, planting my hands on the edge of the sink. I *thought* I planted my hands, but it seemed like I was still rocking forward, my face continuing toward the glass. The light went rosy, a deeper red with each thud of my heart, as if my pulse were gushing into the mirror. The image—I can't call it *my* image—began to bunch at the throat and under the eyes and around the mouth. Veins throbbed at its temples. I tried to call out, but all I got was the gurgling of lungs filling with blood.

And then my forehead touched the mirror. In fact it passed through the mirror—passed through and met cool, moving air. My lungs filled with vital, healing oxygen and my vision suddenly cleared. I say it cleared, but what I saw was like broken glass picking up multiple images. I was inside the mirror—inside the image or inside myself—and I saw my face catenated in an endless chain.

If I tell you the aftermath, that the nurse heard the mirror crack and barged in to find me with a gash in my forehead flowing like a bloody cataract, you might logically conclude that what I saw were reflections in the broken shards that rippled from the wall. But the memory is vivid and nonnegotiable, and it wasn't just clone-perfect images—they weren't *exactly* the same. It was me in uncountable different moods and expressions.

What the hell was I looking at?

They sewed me up, but the wound isn't healing. A maintenance man came to replace the mirror, and I watched him take out the pieces of the old one.

"Man, how did you do that?" he wondered aloud. "It's jigsawed like it's been twisted. Must have been a flaw in the glass."

There was no spidering from a simple point of impact. Like he said, jigsawed. I've scrounged paper and pen from one of the orderlies, cheap reading glasses from the hospital pharmacy, and I'm writing this down. There's nothing else to do here. They tell me I'm convalescing great, while I choke down the upheavals.

So now you know why I don't want to see anyone who knew me before. I have to sort this out among strangers whom I can leave safely behind. Once upon a time, before divorce and booze and pills and unemployability and fatherhood interruptus, I liked me. Now I'd sell my soul to get back to being the cliché I was. Make that souls. Maybe I can hold an auction.

When Admissions caught up to me with the registration form a week out of the coma, I told them to put down "no living relatives," which is a triple-decker lie. I have three living relatives. My sister Laura works for a right-wing lobbyist on the left coast; my kids are seven and nine and live in the Twin Cities. I saw all three of them in September at Dad's funeral.

Jessica and Danny were there courtesy of Dolores, my ex, who made no pretense over the fact that she thought I was using the funeral to manipulate the terms of custody. I'm not supposed to love my kids anymore. Dolores whisked them away at the end of the service before we could get reacquainted. She figures the sooner they forget about me, the better. Even though I've been basically clean for eleven months and off probation for six. In her report to the judge, the outreach officer said that I was always in the gym or out on the trails and that I've become "a model for physical rehabilitation." She didn't say much about my psychological state, but you could infer that I was ready to pick up the pieces of my life. Sound body, sound mind. All before the accident, of course.

Dolores practiced extinction on me, but there's no way she can have missed all the news about the accident. I made the papers for a week straight in Minneapolis after the details of my hypothermia were known. *Time* and *Newsweek* had snippets, and NBC's Tom Brokaw tacked on a piece about me at the end of the story about the bus. Peter Jennings skinnied my saga down to a couple of lines, as if to say that ABC had seen NBC's feature and deemed it not that important. Listen up, Peter. No one has ever been that far through the long white tunnel and come back before, no one has ever brought consciousness of death back with them, no one has ever pumped warm blood again after having their veins turn to slurry and their heart stop. Stay tuned and maybe I'll give you the scoop when I figure out exactly what else happened to me while I was on the wrong side of the River Styx.

I saw a videotape of the ABC newscast. They wheeled in a TV with a VCR that they use for presurgical orientation and showed it to me. The nurse said someone left the tape because I wouldn't accept any visitors. I finally figured out it was Sam. Sam always tapes the nightly newscast while he closes up his ski and outdoors shop. I guess you could call him my friend, despite what I wrote about burning bridges. Funny, the farther I get from other people, the closer we get. Sam is half Ojibwa, half Norwegian—Simota Ingmar, if you can believe that. We both know skiing, and we both know silence, and that puts us in the same church if seldom at the same service. He must have left the tape.

There was a helicopter shot of the waterfall, and then another of the hospital where I was lying in a coma. Jennings told about the accident and that I had been cross-country skiing. Mainly he focused on the bus and the fact that it was an unusually early storm that had come out of nowhere. Nowhere. I could have told him where it came from. I've prayed for storms enough times. Winter is what I live for: the white cathedral . . . tabula rasa. Nature puts on Her holy vestments and wipes away the whole cruddy earth, absolving all sin. The trees go naked before Her, and I write upon the sacred snow with my feet shod in Salomon boots mounted on skinny boards. I punctuate the text with Exel poles, and I leave runes that only a higher power can read. That's how I pour out my confessions. That's how I flash-freeze my miserable, burning soul.

. . . Well, a little self-hate there. Indulge me, please. I've changed so much in the last year, sometimes I forget I'm not the loser I was. Not that I'm where I want to be yet. For sure I've got to get back into the lives of Jessica and Danny before it's too late, and in order to do that I've got to make some kind of breakthrough with Dolores. She won't even let them come to the phone. I don't think she'd wish me dead. Too much guilt if it came true. But I'm not expecting a get-well card, and she'll flat-out lie to the kids about what happened to me. I figure when I'm sure the courts will grant me parental privileges, I'll just talk to her, lay it on the line and suggest we go about this amicably instead of paying lawyers to throw paper at each other. She gets pretty emotional, but there are times when she does the practical thing too. I've never been able to predict her.

No known case of hypothermia has ever survived with a core temperature as low as mine was. 55.1 degrees. You're supposed to be dead when you drop down to the low eighties. There have been a couple of recoveries whose core temps dropped into the high fifties, but the doctors don't know how I hung on. One of them called it a mammalian reflex. The medics airlifted me off the mountain and jumped me downstate to Mayo, where a team worked on me half the night. They even had a live Net exchange with some experts at Tromso University in Norway. I was clinically dead, circulation zero. My brain was so cold that it essentially didn't need any oxygen, and the doctors used a cardiopulmonary bypass to warm my blood outside my body. I was partially paralyzed and on a ventilator for three weeks, then intensive care for another six.

So of course I'm changed. Even though they can't find anything wrong with me, I've got to be changed psychologically. The shrink—Dr. Anthony P. Weibens—just keeps nodding his head and saying I've been through an incredible trauma and it will heal. Like he deals with people who were clinically dead every day. I don't dare tell him the details of the accident or about things like the mirror. I've fed him a couple of see-through nightmares just to seem cooperative, because if he knew how delusional I am, I'd never get out of here. As it is, if Dolores ever gets a court order to look at my treatment records, I'll be back sitting in the supermarket parking lot, hoping to catch a glimpse of my kids coming out of Cub Foods with her.

Something is wrong, all right, but it's physical. Believe me, I'm not a hypochondriac. By the time I visit a doctor voluntarily, it's a toss-up whether he or the mortician will get my business. Extreme jocks tend to develop a rapport with what's going on inside them, and they know if there's a physical change. When I'm in shape, I'm like that. I take a breath and feel it in my toes.

I was in shape before I lost my kids. Then I fell off the deep end. Divorce wasn't that big a deal, a couple of strangers coming together, then becoming strangers again, but when society steps between you and your natural-born flesh and blood—well, for me it rendered my contract with civilization null and void. No stranger with a gavel was going to hear a few minutes of frantic pleading and then decide that my major role of fatherhood would snuggle right in there between lunch and dinner for a few hours every other weekend.

I couldn't handle it. Self-destructive between visitations, yeah. Jack or Jim from the bottle before noon; prescriptions and aliases off the Web. The first time I didn't bring my kids back from a parental visitation, I got the benefit of the doubt and probation, but the second time was totally unambiguous. Airline tickets in my pocket, alcohol and drugs still in my blood from the in-between days when I was forbidden parental rights, the kids in the backseat. I was two hours away from becoming one of those quasi-kidnappers on a milk carton whose last name happens to match the kidnappees. So that's why Dolores is afraid. They could have put me away solid. They should have put me away solid. But it would've killed me. Some people absolutely cannot live without freedom, and I'm one of them. I think everyone recognized that—even Dolores. So, that was when I understood that the stranger with the gavel *was* going to get between me and my kids, and I promised not to defy a new court order. I got off with three months' jail time and more probation.

Jail focused me. The only way I was going to have contact with Jessica and Danny was to get clean and in shape again. Not that hard, if you want to know the truth. The hard part is convincing the judicial system that the little aberration they saw was just a blip reaction to what the court did in the first place. So, I got in shape. I've never been in better shape than I was on November tenth. And since I've gotten the rapport with my body back, I know unfailingly when something is wrong inside me.

I try not to stare at the mirror in the bathroom now, and I shave with the door open. This morning I filled the sink with hot water without looking up. I tried to concentrate on the shaving gel, but already I sensed the expansion in the glass. I made myself into Santa Claus before I looked up, but instead of comic relief, the white beard just made the red gash in my forehead look like a bullet hole.

"You're a fraud," I said to the image. Or the image said to me.

We raised our silver-handled Gillettes to our sideburns, observing mirror protocols—my left, his right. A thin mist came between us. Whose breath? Steam began to close in from the corners.

I leaned back. Dangled the razor in the water. Not possible there could be that much steam from just the sink and my breath. It would take a roomful of breathers to make the mirror look like that, like a daguerreotype photo, all grainy and imprecise. The shaving foam blended with the steam, so that all I saw was the gash that won't heal. Ugly. Red. The mark of Cain on my double.

I was getting as fuzzy as the room, but don't tell me the face in the glass was just an obedient doppelganger. I saw the asymmetry. And it wasn't just a mirror anymore;

it was a separate and distant universe. On my side I had steam—thin as a waterfall. On the other side it was dust and fire. The festering redness on my forehead was the only connection. Only, in the mirror, it looked like something raging in hellish exile a million parsecs away. A buoy. A beacon in a nether ocean.

The door reverberated as I bumped into it, but I couldn't turn my back on the mirror. Fumbling, I raked the jamb across my shoulder. I don't know, maybe in my terror I was somehow marching in place, but I couldn't seem to leave the bathroom. It was as if the walls were made of distance, and I didn't find myself in the outer room until the steam dissipated and innocence rose up the glass.

A doctor once told me that the reason men sometimes get dizzy when they shave is because the way they move their neck can shut off the blood supply to the brain. That's the rock I've been clinging to all day.

3

Finally, a few more sheets of paper. The orderly brought them to shut me up. I keep asking why everyone is acting funny, but he won't say. No one will tell me what happened. They want to know about the IV. Did I put something in the plastic bag? Did I fool with the drip rate? I tell them I didn't, and I get reassuring pats. They think I'm incompetent. Incompetent or not, my hearing is so acute since the accident that I pick up scraps of conversation from the hall.

"He must have had a flashback," one of the nurses said.

The person she was talking to answered: "Either that or he thinks he's Jack Frost. Lucky if he doesn't come down with pneumonia."

I guess they mean about finding me in the shower this morning. As if I were trying to go back to the waterfall. And I guess that means they know less about what happened to me last night than I do. That's what this is really all about. Last night. I didn't have a flashback. The nurses don't know about the wheelchair or the elevator. The things I remember from last night . . . they were real.

Sometime after I drifted off cold hands jostled me out of bed and forced me into a wheelchair. My eyes weren't focusing and the walls were spinning, and whoever was pushing me stayed out of sight. It wasn't until we got to the service elevator at the far end of the hall that I understood: If there was anything at all behind me, it wasn't an orderly or a nurse.

The door rolled open with a hollow boom—hollow, I remember that. It should have been muffled. Because the inside of the elevator was crammed with bluish figures. The wheelchair glided toward them, and I braced for collision. But it was like becoming part of an X-ray. There was no contact at all. The blue began to fade, and I realized there were no lights on in the car. The door was sliding shut. An overpowering dread iced the pit of my stomach. I did not want to be in the dark with those filmy presences. I struggled to rise and stop the steel door, but the nurses were right; there must have been something in my IV. Liquid cobwebs fed my blood. I fell back in the chair, and the little steel car got darker than the inside of a crocodile's stomach.

And then the whispering began. Different cadences, different registers, but each one invasive and intimate. A chain of pleas and threats came at me that were trumped suddenly by a child's shrill denial: "I am *not* dead!" Then the voices rushed together and nausea overwhelmed me, because the elevator was falling, and it wouldn't stop, an endless descent, faster and faster, that must have beat Jules Verne silly for penetrating the Earth's core. The crescendo of whispers rose as if acceleration were squeezing the pitch. And the mounting g-forces seemed to separate my body from my mind. I must have passed out. Tell me it was the compression in a dream, and I'll believe you, because the next thing I remember was coming to with a gentle nudge when the elevator bottomed out.

I expected that we had arrived at the gates of hell, but the door slid open and there was a great chill. The chill sharpened my perspective, and I saw that all the whirl and the blur of descending in the elevator had ended in some kind of freezer. It must have been a lab. A forensic or a research lab, judging by the horrors that the bluish figures showed me in the faint light. Vats of cadavers hung like sport jackets in ordinal rows. Discreet items of human anatomy floated inside glass decanters. The ensemble of silhouettes who came off the elevator with me flitted in an overwrought dance around the sinks and tables, their whispers oscillating like the gain on a badly tuned radio.

I don't know what they were trying to show me. Death per se? Hell's morgue? Were they the spirits of the things there in the formaldehyde?

Whatever was coursing through my veins from the IV must have taken majority control then, because my neck began to feel like pasta and my head lolled to one side. The next thing I remember is the nurse finding me in the ice cold shower back in my room. I was sitting on the tile floor in the soaked hospital gown. They said I wasn't even shivering.

It's not fair that I'm being held to blame, that they think I'm acting out delusions of a troubled mental state. I didn't seek this out. The drama came to my bedside. I want out of here, and this has set me back. The nurses are checking on me every fifteen minutes.

Weibens, the shrink, is trying to be casual about it, but I can see he's just about wetting himself with excitement. Here is two plus two. Here is something he can add up without any help from me.

". . . and yet you *were* in that cold shower," he said

when I gave him a blank look and a shrug. "Ice-cold . . . with your hospital gown on."

"The label said 'wash in cold water only.' "

He smiled his studied little smile and asked me to think about the shower and how I felt about surviving the waterfall. I conjugated guilt for him with so much sarcasm that he brought up my family. He knows I don't want to go there. He'd be glad to speak to my ex, he said, if I thought that might help. The insecure bastard. He's checked up on me completely. Maybe even talked to Dolores and told her juicy details about my mental condition.

"My ex is the reason I take cold showers," I confessed.

He looked at me, hopeful that I wasn't yanking his chain again. "You miss her?"

"We were like rabbits. She's one of those . . . watchyacallits?"

"Nymphomania is a myth," he said dryly.

"Yeah? I'm really glad she didn't know that when we were boffing our brains out."

"Sexual addiction is another matter."

"That's it. We met in group therapy for sexual addiction."

We met at a wedding—friend of the groom, friend of the bride. The reason I said hi to her was because she was overweight and miserable-looking at the reception. The only woman under twenty-five not dancing. But she understood the mercy rule better than I did, and three minutes into the conversation excused herself to the bathroom. Dolores Carmichael, née Burke, is the smartest woman I've ever known, the most insecure, and now the only one who has power over my life. But I'm counting on Jessica and Danny making my case. Contrary to what Dolores says, they want to see me—that's for sure. She hopes they'll take to her new boyfriend like he's their father, of course, but I don't think that's going to happen.

Weibens sighed.

"I'd like to see my kids, Doc," I said. "But not here. Not like this. Sign me out of Mayo and I can go see them."

"We're making progress," he said, smiling tightly.

Which is practically an admission that I'm not in here for physical reasons any longer.

4

Nightmares. Did I mention the nightmares? The reason I haven't gone into detail is because they don't want to leave the stage when the houselights come up here at the Mayo Theater of the Absurd. Why should I give them encores? Weibens, the shrink, says I shouldn't suppress them. He says writing them down might purge them. Okay. I've never heard of anyone dreaming in sequels before, so maybe this is a world premiere.

The central theme so far is that I keep discovering body parts in my apartment. I open a drawer and a child's fingers begin to flex in the light. They are smooth and perfect—not at all gory—and I'm wrung with pathos as I see that they are from more than one child and that they were clinging to one another when I opened the drawer. Again, I open a can of olives and it's full of eyes. Brown, green, blue. Without eyelids, they convey terror and stark pleading. I try to fit the tin lid back over them, but it keeps sliding off, like a magnet repelled by another magnet. Then I'm lying in bed, and I can't get comfortable. The mattress is lumpy as I toss and turn, and the bottom sheet is warm when it should be cool. I turn on the light and paw away the sheets and the mattress pad, exposing human thighs and knees and hip joints. There are females and males, taut limbs and flabby, smooth and hairy. There are human heads in the refrigerator, and I don't dare imagine what I'm handling when I reach into the dishwater. Weibens loves these nightmares. They so obviously represent my guilt over the bus victims, he thinks, but he won't come out and say this, and I play dumb.

Guilt isn't part of it, as far as I can see. This all has something to do with my identity. I'm searching for myself, maybe because deep down I accepted that I was going to die in that waterfall, and I can't quite recover from that. It's a tremendous psychological defeat to accept death. You don't just blithely go back to coffee breaks and routines after you've crossed the void. There are other nightmares—lots of nightmares—that seem vaguely associated with discovery or identity. I've been holding out on Weibens.

Take the scavenger hunt. I travel from house to house. Very specific houses. When one looks familiar, I go up to the door and knock and wait with great trepidation for whoever will open it. Sometimes it's a man, sometimes a woman; sometimes they are very young. I'm always relieved when I see them. Relieved that it isn't me and repelled because they look at me so hungrily.

There is one dream where I'm digging in a cemetery, first with a shovel, then with my hands, frantically clawing away sand, then clay, then rich loam. When I clear the coffin lid, I scrabble to my feet and wrench the thing open. The faces are always bloated, ghastly green, suppurating. Some have been eaten by insects or rats. Some are in midfeast, with glittering winged things wriggling into their nasal cavities and behind torn lips. None of this distracts me. I view the ruins of each face with supreme foreboding until I see that it isn't me. I didn't die. It's the same as with the houses. I'm relieved and repelled.

The most symbolic of these sequences takes place in a church. I'm lighting candles at the altar. There are a dozen, maybe two, and I get them almost lit when a draft drives the flames horizontal. They snuff out one by one while I frantically try to relight them. There is a second dream where they are all lit, and I am trying to extinguish them with a metal cup on the end of a long rod. I begin this systematically, starting from the left, but every time I snuff the last one, the first flame pops up again. It goes like that—flames trailing ragged smoke and blinking back on like oversize gag candles on a birthday cake.

There is one more nightmare, more horrifying than the others.

I see myself sitting in a chair, staring off into space, grinning. I never grin. But now I'm grinning, and that's what makes it so unreal. The terrible comedic aspect of my expression makes me look like a mannequin. The dreaming me can't stand this, and I grab up the metal candlesnuffer, which has somehow migrated from the dream about the church, and I start whacking away. There is so little resistance that I cleave off part of my face. What is revealed sickens me, because where my face is torn away there are cells and galleries, like a beehive. And in each cell there is a squirming larva.

Sometimes I can't keep my meals down, because it feels like I'm feeding a metamorphosis inside me. Those dark weeks in November when I was in and out of coma were an incubation for whatever followed me back from the waterfall. It took me somewhere. Coma dreams. If I could remember the details, I think I could untangle the reality. But it's like coming back from a long trip and finding a massive tree in your front yard whose roots are inaccessible.

The first night of consciousness that hangs together

from the lost weeks of coma is even more disturbing, because I know it really happened. There are voices—two nurses—and a sense of formal geometry. I notice the walls, the floor, the ceiling, as if they've just arrived. I feel like I'm coming out of anesthesia—a little jolt, nausea. My nose burns; my eyes smart. The voices are piercing, and the bedsheets feel like sandpaper when I move my hands. I ache with acuity, but it's a delicious pain, like scratching an itch until it bleeds. The nurses speak to me as if they've spoken to me before, but I don't recognize them.

"My, my, aren't we active tonight," one says. "What have you been doing, trying to get out the window?"

I squint at the long pane that spans one wall. There are orange lights on the roof of another wing that catch the glass in such a way that you can see finger smears and palm prints from one end to the other.

"In case you can't tell, we're five stories up," says the nurse.

"Are you thirsty?" the other asks. "We've got to get you off this IV."

While one checks the underside of my wrist where a needle is taped, the other gives me sips from a squeeze bottle. The water leaves me gasping.

"'Nough, 'nough," says the nurse. "You're out of practice."

When they leave, I stare at the prints that run the length of the windowpane. I feel so weak; how could I have gotten up and done that? And what was on my hands to make such smears? The orange lights from outside high up on the building neutralize any color on the glass, but here and there, with my heightened vision, I detect traces of what looks like blood. Or ashes. I want to get up and examine the smears, but I don't have the strength.

Sometime in the night it begins to snow—a wet, slushy snow. I watch it pelt the glass until dawn. And when it's dry and daylight, and a new shift has come on the ward, the window of my room is clean. The prints have been washed away... *because they were on the outside.*

5

The last moment I can trust as real is the one when I'm coming down the mountain catching "mad air" beneath my skis, which is funny, because that's the moment when thrill-skiers escape reality. But two months later it's as if I'm still in full flight and the rules of existence are suspended. Here's the catch-22: how do I go forward with life until I know it's real; and how do I know it's real until I go forward? Forward. Wrong word. I'll go forward whether I like it or not. What is the right word? Accept? I'm afraid of that. Accepting what's going on in the margins—alternate worlds in my mirror, half-waking visions, nightmares—is loaded with jeopardy. Those figures that dog me from the bus want me to accept that. It's their universe, and they want to drag me in. Or they want me to drag them out.

I'll tell you what I'm going to accept. I accept that there are at least two of me. I have a junior partner. And I'm going underground, because both of me know I'm not clinically schizo or something. In fact, part of me— the home team—has probably never been more rational. People on the verge of mental breakdowns have to deal with reality in a very precise and candid way. Survival forces a kind of shrewdness on you, a rationale that works short-term no matter how insane the larger premises. To top it off, my physical senses are suddenly hyperkeen. I can't speak for the other guy. He's all mist and snow and nightmares. Mad air.

I didn't tell Weibens about the handprints on the outside of the windows or the hallucinations in the mirror, because I hate to mess up a secure shrink (oxymoron) when he's just about to pronounce his star patient cured.

One of the orderlies brought me a potted red columbine and put it on the window ledge. He said the elderly surgery patient next door was through with it (translation: dead). I'm usually indifferent to flowers, but the moment that heady floral blend hit my nostrils I lit up. Here was something organic . . . something with earth around it. It drew me out of bed and kept me at the window ledge for long, shaky minutes. I even carried the pot back to the nightstand by my bed. But the day nurse—Marjorie—took it away.

"Michael, Michael, I can't let you keep that so close to you. We're not even supposed to allow plants past the elevator."

They're worried about bacteria, I guess (worried about lawsuits, anyway). But nothing seems more essential to me than that scent. It fires through me like bright colors or sharp sounds. Putting the plant back on the window ledge way over there is like sticking my IV into the ceiling. It cuts me off from essential nutrients.

I don't remember actually making a decision to leave Mayo after Marjorie continued on her rounds, but it was a simple expediency. I was suffocating. The things I needed were outside the building.

Wearing a pair of green stretch slippers with rubber skids, and half wrapped in the gown with the southern exposure, I stepped into the hall. Zamboni-style, I chugged along the linoleum, avoiding eye contact. Once in sight of the visitor elevators, I shuffled straight for the doors. But that took me past the nurses' station. The wizened little black lady there, who uses pouty looks as if she is your mother and you're disappointing her, called me by name. "You can't be out of bed, Mr. Carmichael."

I raised my palms, acknowledging a miracle. "Obviously I can."

"You're going to get me in trouble if you don't follow the rules, Mr. Carmichael. Are you looking for something to eat?"

"No. I want my clothes."

"Your clothes are right there in your closet in a plastic bag. I'll show you."

"Where are my skis?"

She sized me up as if sanity were negotiable. "I'll leave the doctor a note about getting you ambulatory."

The closet she mentioned is actually a honey-blond wardrobe, and I was pulling open its door before the squeak of her rubber soles faded down the hall. The polypropylene underwear that was scissored off me the day of the accident looked like a dressmaker's pattern through the translucent plastic bag hanging on a hook. I dumped everything onto the tile floor, and the smell—probably enough to make a goat pass out—hit me like a breeze from Eden. Except for the polypropylene, everything was intact.

My second escape attempt took place in full regalia, including Kombi gloves, fanny pack, and knit cap pulled down to my eyebrows. I timed it for the end of visiting hours to make me look like a visitor rushing in from an outing on the trails. A maintenance staffer, rolling his floor waxer side to side far up the corridor, was the only one who saw me step out of the room. The plastic boots, however, rang out like SS-issue at a Nuremberg rally, and ahead of me two children flanking their parents turned to stare. I mutated my stride into slides, punctuated every third or fourth glide by the sharp plant of a toe clip. But I must have sounded like Long John Silver dragging a body, because now the parents were throwing me hard looks. We were coming up on the nurses' station, and I wanted to pass them on the blind side, but the damned jackboots were going to give me away. And just at that moment, a dinner cart rattled out of a room pushed by a dietician I didn't know. With the all-American family blocking the view from the nurses' station, and the cart drowning my tread, I slipped past to the elevators just as one chimed. But here my luck ended. The door rolled back and Nurse Marjorie stepped out of the car.

"Michael?"

"Hey"—I took her hands in mine—"I'm really glad I got a chance to say good-bye."

"Where are you going?"

"I've been released."

"By who?"

"By Dr. Me."

I'd smelled my socks, and I was connected to the cosmos. You can't stay in the vapid ward of a hospital when you are connected to the cosmos. But two orderlies, summoned by a "Hey, Rube!" whose exact phrasing escapes me, closed in from opposite sides.

My Kevlar laces slapped, Marjorie's nylons hissed, our escorts' sneakers padded softly as we marched back to the room. They made me undress and return all holy vestments to the drawstring plastic bag. This time the wardrobe was locked.

"Michael, please don't do this again," Marjorie said. "Don't make us restrain you."

As soon as they were gone, I was back to the columbine on the window ledge.

A summary of my third escape attempt comes to me courtesy of Marjorie, because—red alert, red alert—I don't remember it. When have I ever lost track of time while awake? And I must have been awake, because sometime during the night I broke into the wardrobe, dressed, and made it as far as the first landing below the fire door before the orderlies caught up. It took three of them to bring me back to the room this time, and I gave the biggest one a dislocated jaw. This was stressed to me—the biggest one—as if I should explain how I could have done that in my weakened condition. They stabbed me with a hypodermic and strapped me to the bed.

There's more. I awoke prematurely from the sedative, unaware of what I had done. The early-morning brightness through the window made me squint, and for a moment I could see a terrifying silhouette standing there. It was the coherent nothingness that had rushed at me as I hung dying in the waterfall, and it lasted only as long as it took me to blink, but in the interval I knew how deeply that image was embedded in my mind. I blinked again and there were three silhouettes. A nurse and two orderlies edged toward me as if they had just discovered a rattlesnake in the nursery.

I rolled from my side onto my back. The orderlies braced. Something pressed up from the mattress, something as tangled as the severed legs under the sheet from my nightmare. The restraining straps. *I was lying on top of them.* And one other thing. I was covered with dirt. Dirt on my hands, dirt on the pillow and the sheets. Dirt was dried on my face and lips and hair. The smell of it was in my nostrils. I blinked the columbine into focus on the window ledge, uprooted now, the pot on its side, soil smeared all over the glass and the wall. A huge handprint was starkly highlighted on the window, and there was no doubt this one was on the inside. The reason the fingers were so long must have been because my hand slid slightly on the glass, leaving tracks like a kid's finger painting. I guess it isn't the fragrance of columbine that attracts me after all. It's the dirt.

6

They don't get it. They don't believe I somehow set myself free, or—and this chills me—that I had help. With so many employees, they just assume someone screwed up. But now they come to check on me in twos, with one waiting by the door, and there is a degree of vindictiveness in the fact that they haven't given me paper for three days. My store of stationery is down to the back of the dietician's daily checklist and a couple of sheets copped from a clipboard in the hall.

Privacy is not an issue here in Stalag 17. There is none. I submitted meekly to the WanderGuard they locked around my ankle, and I take oral sedatives. They communicate to each other with looks and nods over my head, while I joke with as much civility as I can muster. (". . . Who wants my frequent-flyer miles?") To me they speak too loudly, as if I'm a deaf tourist with a six-word vocabulary. The raised voices hurt my ears, and I could throw furniture without much encouragement, but I'm working on being downright personable. Because that's the only way I'm going to get out of here. Inside, I'm seething, and I would do it all again—kick in the door and dislocate a few more jaws—if I could spring myself out of this sterile place.

Each time Weibens brings up my dirt fixation, I plead for the columbine to be replaced, but when I can't tell him why, he gets dismissive. This may be part of his method, but he is also a very petulant person. He is too petty to be a shrink.

Time to write about the other reality before I run out of paper.

The blue pill I take during the day is just for a buzz, but the white one I take at night is supposed to put me out. Only it turns into a magic-carpet ride. The minister who comes into my room wakes me up every time. I uncrash to the extent that I can just see his black suit, white backward collar, and a face that never quits rearranging itself. He leans over me, and his voice tins gently, like metal drums rocking underwater. He wants to know how I'm doing, but I can't answer him. My tongue is about six inches thick and rooted in my stomach.

The room is warping like a Jell-O mold, but I can tell that the door is closed. There is something like a box in the corner, covered with a cloth. The cloth jiggles. The box giggles. I don't like the thing, and I keep trying to turn my head for a better look, but I can't move. I absolutely cannot move, except for my eyes.

The minister is carrying a Bible, which he holds up like a trophy for me to see. He opens it in both hands and reads:

" 'In the beginning God created Heaven and Hell. And darkness was on the face of the void. God said, "Summon light," and light was divided from the darkness, because the darkness was first. . . .' "

I see black spots all around him, like pixie dust, only they erode the air. He leans toward me every few sentences and I strain to unblur his features.

". . . the firmament, the firmament, the firmament is

made from missing water with here and there some AstroTurf—I am the grass—and matrix-state plasma. Do-dah . . ."

I can't remember it all. There are snatches of Dante's *Inferno*, and *Sports Illustrated*, and what sounds like *The Cat in the Hat* in Italian. All from the Bible. Sometimes he holds it upside down, and I guess it doesn't matter. He reads in Latin and Greek and languages I don't recognize. He switches in midsentence, so that he sounds like a talking Rosetta stone, rising to the speed and pitch of an auctioneer. That scares the hell out of me. The babble. Dogged by an echo, as if a floodgate has opened on some underworld chorus. I feel thunder spasming beyond the room. He walks around the bed, changing from a meek apostolic figure to a scarecrow with fluttering arms. Space is etched around him when he does this—like a mouse trail when you drag a cursor across a computer screen. He goes to the head of the bed, above where I can see, and he comes around the other side. But, of course, the bed is right to the wall.

When he's done, he sits down close in front of me and folds his hands. There is no chair, but he sits. I try to speak, and my tongue is still rooted in my gut, like a parasite that has barged down my throat to suck a meal. He leans forward, trying to decipher my faucial gasps, and each time he does this I make out different features. The eyes emerge first—soft, brown, compassionate. Then the eyes are gone, and it is a ruddy nose with hairy nostrils. The nose slides off his smooth face, and a mouth yawns, exposing yellow teeth and gray gums. His breath is dry and withering, like gummy cerements exuded from a sarcophagus. He sits back, embarrassed that he has offended me. The mouth goes away, leaving one eye and the voice.

The talking eye. But what he says is unnerving, because he's trying to persuade me to become a cat.

"You could be a cat, you know. Would you like that? Or a fish!"

—over in the corner a frantic flapping under the cloth on the boxlike thing that sounds for all the world like a fish out of water.

"No? The cat, then."

I don't see him move, but he is suddenly walking back toward the bed, carrying the boxlike thing. He whisks away the cloth, and there is the cat. No box. Just a very unordinary cat. It is hunched and emaciated, and it seems to have too many joints as it springs onto the bed. It drags toward my face, its bones working like an animated scaffolding under mangy fur. I can see notches in its tattered ears, and its eyes are either partially lengthened with scar tissue or it has some Siamese in it.

"Or . . ." blurts the minister, who has no face now, "you can take your pick of . . . these!"

Tonight (last night) he goes to the long window, which stretches like a panoramic screen, and twirls his hands.

Outside, the blackness explodes with silvery glints, and something hits the glass. I can't see what it is, except for its silhouette, which is like something spattered. Part of the sky behind it is blocked, but I can just glimpse layers of crepuscular things—irregular bodies not suited to flight—gliding around the building. There are more shudders on the glass, and the window seems about to break. The pixie-dust erosion consolidates into stains then—the kinds of stains I saw moving out of the bus. That is what is at the window.

The minister turns around, and his full face is back. Blurred features, but I can tell he's concerned for my wide-eyed terror. His nimble fingers disperse the horror outside the window, leaving moist smears and long streaks on the glass. The pixie dust reappears, a galaxy of it, falling to the floor. In a few seconds it rises again, over the foot of the bed, crawling over the sheets—*under* the sheets.

"Or . . ." says the minister softly, "you could become that wonderfully adaptable, enduring, and ubiquitous oldest-surviving species: the cockroach!"

They swarm over my feet and up my legs, a million indelible tingles, and I order my dead muscles to move. Busy signal. My heart is the only muscle that is totally online, and it is logging mega contractions. I wait for the horde to come streaming out from under the sheet and onto my face, but there is nothing. My skin is resonating from the soles of my feet to the crown of my head, so I can't tell where the crawlers are now. But they aren't coming up for air. And now I'm thinking *orifices*. Seven orifices, five on the face, two below grade. They are entering my body cavities, scurrying up the canals and through the intestines. *My tongue is a highway rooted in my . . .*

Here they come. Squeezing under my lips, bursting out my nose and ears. My eyelids are fluttering, as if cockroaches are probing the orbital ridges from within.

". . . yes, you could become a cat," the minister is saying.

He is sitting where he was sitting before—on the nonchair—and the pixie dust and the roaches are nowhere to be seen. Or felt.

". . . but it's much better to be human, don't you think? Choose life, as they say. Beats death, eh?" And he throws me an elbow. "Beats death, oh, that's funny." He starts to laugh. He rolls around in the air, like he's in a beanbag chair, and the laughter gets voluble. "Beats death . . ."

Like we share some arcane knowledge of that and therefore share the joke.

I'm starting to fade now, sleepy again. Or in shock. I look at him, and his head is missing. But I can hear the laugh, and there is his head on the window ledge. I look back, and he's got another head now, roaring with laughter like the first one. This one pops off and rolls out of sight under the bed. Only, I can tell by the increase in laughter that there are three voices. You get the picture. Laughing heads, multiplying like hydras. I hear Roman legions shouting, "BEATS DEATH!" I hear Super Bowl throngs: "BEATS DEATH!" Skulls are piling up all over the room. Like the catacombs under Paris. Like the holocaust. "*Sieg Heil!* BEATS DEATH! *Sieg Heil . . . !*"

And I've just got enough space left to write down the kicker. Which is that there were three other patients on the west side of the floor last night. Were. This morning they are all dead.

7

Quite a coincidence. They died of natural causes — if you call dying as a warning to me a natural cause. I say the minister was making his point. *Choose life ... beats death*. The triple witching hour for each of the deceased was between two and three a.m., and the immediate causes were staph infection, congestive heart failure, and an aneurysm.

You can imagine what the timing did for all the loyal employees on this floor. They are rattled, very alert. Lots of focus now. Somehow their anger at me has faded with the epidemic of dying, as if none of us is perfect and please don't die. This is not the ward for dying. I am their survivor. So things are changing. I have been given paper again.

Even Weibens started coming around a little. But if I hadn't had a panic attack, he never would have relented. I hyperventilated and asked for the window to be opened. At first he wouldn't do anything. Five stories up, and he acted like I was going to leap through the screen. The handprints obviously made him wary. So he just had a nurse hook me up to oxygen. It was the hospital air that was causing me to hyperventilate, I insisted, and why didn't he try giving me another plant? I think it was scientific curiosity that finally drove him to it. A large, potted hibiscus was brought in and plunked down precisely where the columbine had been, with the base sticking out from the ledge. End hyperventilation.

"Why do you think that helped?" Weibens asked me this morning. "Is it because plants give off oxygen? Do you feel like you're getting more air when there's a plant around?"

"I think it's the association," I said.

"Association? With what?"

I stared into his frail face that looked so eager for a genuine anomaly and felt that I should make something up. *I'm a slave to a giant, bloodsucking plant named Audrey II. Feed me, Seymour!*

"Dirt," I said.

"Just . . . dirt?"

"Dirt is the earth. Dirt gives us a place to stand."

"I see. Do you feel like you need a place to stand?"

"Dirt is night."

He didn't take his eyes off me. Stone-steady Freud eyes and neatly trimmed white whiskers, and even cigar smoke reeking from his clothes, daring to discuss pure air with me! I was sitting in the Naugahyde chair by the window, and he suddenly wrestled the hibiscus pot off the ledge onto the tiled floor in front of me.

"Go ahead," he said, "touch it."

"I don't feel like it right now."

"Are you afraid? It's all right if you're afraid."

It must have been obvious that I was pounding back a wave of nausea. Sluggishly I sat forward, tried to smile, achieved a lopsided grin. Fingers drooping, I aimed my hand at that huge pot. *Watch . . . this . . . Doc.* But as my fingers touched the soil, the dual reality that infects me made another illegal U-turn.

I couldn't stop my hand. Down, down I went, wrist, forearm, disappearing into the soft, moist soil, tearing the roots of the hibiscus. My fingertips hit bottom and kept on going. I do not remember Weibens's features, and I want desperately to conjure up his look of Viennese surprise.

I moved like some fabulous spirit, sliding along the path of least resistance through pockets of decay and vapors, beneath sunless oceans, beneath the roots of continents. The entire Earth and its history of death were connected to me, as if my skin had been flayed off and an infinite number of electrodes planted in the tender raw tissues. To be a denizen of that crushing under-earth is to instantly know that life is the surface garnish on a vast cemetery. What is the Earth except a slow collecting of the living on top of the dead? An orbiting compost pile. I do not want my corpse to molder in the earth. I want my cells torn instantly into atoms. I'll take the molecular shriek. One shriek. Done. Because, let me tell you, you don't want to go where I went. Forget RIP. There won't be any.

Not until you rot one hundred percent. As long as you have two quarks in sync, you are going to have awareness. You are going to know what's going on. It won't be over until your scattered atoms spew out of some volcano or dissipate into heat—recycle and become energy! (Now there's an understatement. Someone has not thought this through.)

I think it's geological pressure that is the great subterranean medium. It conveys images right through the earth, the same as light waves to the tender dead—terrifying images—but they come to the phantom senses of touch and hearing and taste and smell, instead of to the eyes. And that is why I felt the black dirt that encased me writhe, and why, very quickly in that stupendous architecture of granite and clay and magma, I knew that multiple things—not-yet-fully-corrupted things—were burrowing toward me.

The first one rocked my skull. I felt cheekbones press to mine and empty sockets swallow me. Behind me, bony fingers scrabbled through the earth to fasten wherever they could. Something else clacked dully and relentlessly around my legs. I tried to scream, but my mouth filled with dirt. Teeth gnawed into me, sand flowed like wind over my wounds. Through each pore in my body things entered—microorganisms, enzymes, bacteria—lustily at work. Converting me into the ambient elements of . . .

"Dirt," Weibens said close by in the mundane world. "What does it make you think of?"

Torrents of debris fell away from my mind, and whatever had seized my sensory input let go, leaving me whole again. I snatched my hand back, though it was only finger-deep in the soil. "Dirt . . ." I croaked, "just dirt. The stuff of everything that dies."

"You said that the dirt was night," Weibens reminded me.

"Did I? Very poetic of me." I felt blank, like a beach swept clean by a tsunami.

"Did you mean . . . eternal night?"

"I don't know."

He smiled and from the box on the window ledge offered me a tissue to wipe my fingers. "You seem to have a fixation, no doubt about that. I suppose it might reflect some turmoil you have about coming back from near death."

"How do you figure?"

"If you had died, you would be buried now."

I should give him credit. Someone who actually *is*

buried and who visits my mind is in turmoil. Someone is letting me see what it's like to be dead, slowly cooking in the Earth's vast, churning cauldron. If these aren't my real experiences, they soon will be. "Yeah, that must be it," I said. "Listen, Doc, I've played all the games, including mud pies, and it's time to go."

He glanced at his watch. "Yes."

"No. I mean weeks late. I want out of here."

"Do you think you're well enough?"

"I'm well enough to go home. Haven't I been making that clear? No one is listening to me."

"You think you're being held against your will, is that it?"

Was he kidding? *We're holding you against your will because you think we're holding you against your will.* It was his little bid to include paranoia in my diagnosis, and if I complained, it would prove I was paranoid. I looked at the hibiscus and resisted telling him it looked like a microphone disguised as a plant.

"You know you're milking this out of professional curiosity," I said. "If I had a heart bypass, liver transplant, and gallbladder removal, you and the insurance companies would have had me out of here before the surgeons snapped their gloves off. This hospital is what's making me sick. If you don't sign me out, I'm going to call the newspapers and the networks. Jennings and Brokaw would love a follow-up."

I could tell by Weibens's face that he is under some kind of pressure to sign a release. Every time the regular docs have come through, they've told me I'm ready for full rehab on my own. And probably the hospital is still fending off the occasional reporter. I'm guessing they could not have held me here much longer anyway. Weibens made it sound like I was accepting an enormous risk, but he caved as if he had been warned against thwarting another demand. For the first time in the new year, and for the first time since the accident, I'm going to be free. Free and alone. Then we'll see about mirrors and dirt. I'll be back in the woods. Back on skis. Catch me if you can!

8

It was snowing when I got out. Urgent swirls trying to materialize into something. I stood on the sidewalk, reveling in the air and squinting through flurries at the faint bloodstain of a traffic signal down the block.

Something has changed profoundly in my physical senses. That sterile, dead, dry current flowing through metal ducts inside Mayo kept me from recognizing just how profoundly. Breathing canned air is like drinking distilled water. You can take a mineral supplement to replace what you lose drinking distilled water, but where is the supplement to replace what gets depleted from air?

Hitching a ride seemed unlikely. Safe to say, not a lot of people check out of Mayo in a torn blue ski suit and Salomon boots. Scraping quarters out of the lining of my fanny pack, I called Sam long-distance up in Sheshebans and asked him if my car was still parked outside his shop.

"There's a pile of snow where you left it," he said.

Hard to tell if that was the dry Norwegian talking, or the stoic Ojibwa, but at least my car was still there. Considering how little parking space Sam has for his customers, he should have had it towed.

"That was you who dropped off the ABC newscast tape, wasn't it?" I said.

"Just wanted to prepare you for fame, Bowie."

Bowie. No one has called me that in two months. "What fame?"

"Someone started a rumor that you didn't make it and that your ghost is still skiing the mountain. It's going to just kill business when you show up for real."

The skiing ghost. There are worse ways to spend eternity. "Well, maybe you won't be too pissed when I tell you I don't know when or how I'm going to get up there," I told him. "The car probably won't start anyway, but there's a Hide-A-Key in the driver's wheel well, if you want to try and move it off your lot."

"Where are you now?"

"Standing in the foyer of a minimall, still wearing what I was wearing when they chopped me out of the waterfall two months ago. I'd skate up, if I had poles and skis."

"Call me if you find a ride. Otherwise I'll be down there by sunset to get you."

I shouldn't have been surprised at his reaching out. I can see me becoming a cause célèbre among a certain group of avid outdoors people, and an object of morbid fascination to the public in general, but only Sam can appreciate who I am with any real insight. He knows my story, generally. Generally, I know his.

He grew up in the Mille Lacs Kathio and Rum River state parks area of Minnesota, on the edge of the Ojibwa reservation there. Blood counts for more than land, and when his Norwegian father was killed in a tractor accident, he quit college and sold the family's extensive farm, except for that rugged piece upon which he built his outdoor enclave and trailhead. He lives in an apartment somewhere nearby. As an entrepreneur he is less than a raging success, but because his needs are simple, he hangs on when sparse winters drive other facilities under.

I like Sam. I like his witty, soft-spoken wisdom. What he doesn't know about the woods isn't worth knowing. He must be in his late thirties, like me. Twice in all the years I've been going to his shop he has lived with a woman, and both times the woman seemed to grow bored with the isolation and the store. He never bad-mouthed either one after they left, or seemed to miss them. I take that as a measure of his independence and his respect for the independence of others. He applies the same regard to pretty much everything: the environment, animals, business. With it goes a faith and trust in fate I'll never have. I have known him to leave the cash register unattended while he tried out some new ski equipment. The thing about Sam is, he never stops reading. Always a different pile of books next to the waxes—heavy nonfiction with a little pulp thrown in. It's made him a man for all seasons and explains his disdain for what he calls the "casino culture" of contemporary Ojibwas.

I killed the afternoon wandering the streets, longing for the woods. I had it in my mind that I was safer outside. Mayo loomed like towers of terror as I walked upstreet and down-alley, trying to stay warm.

I admit that what happened next was probably no more than a coincidence and a predisposition caused by the accident, but when I stepped out of the wind and turned, it was almost into the embrace of a huge brown bear. The fact that it was stuffed and behind plate glass in a Gander Mountain display case barely softened the jolt. I stared up into yellow fangs and jerked back as if I could feel the hot stench of a carnivore's breath. And before that momentary disorientation could pass, the real horror began. Because behind me, reflected in the glass, I saw a yellow bus careening around the corner. Gaping, stark-eyed faces filled the lozenge-shaped windows. I was certain it was going to pin me to the building and the bear, but as I spun around it hurtled past, raising a curtain of slush.

I wish to God I hadn't seen those faces close up, because then I wouldn't have seen that they were terrified or that they wore ski clothes or that there were long fingers sliding down the bus windows just as they had slid down the window of my room at Mayo or—and this is the killer—that the faces were as colorless as a black-and-white film. That's what sticks with me. The noir quality. The bus was yellow, the clothes vivid as rainbows, but the faces were uniformly gray.

It had to be the tinted windows. Somehow the tinting affected only the hues of skin, hair, and eyes. And the bus simply lost control on an icy corner. Naturally, the passengers panicked. All the rest of it—the bear, the ski outfits, the reprised timing of the event on the mountain, the curtain of slush like a waterfall—that was my imagination in overdrive. Imagination and coincidence.

I don't know how long I stood there, or how long after that I walked the street. Nothing comes back to me. The next thing I remember is the familiar profile of my own '95 midnight-blue Probe appearing in the streetlit afterglow of rush hour and sliding to a halt on Center Street. Sam looked across, but I took the passenger-door handle and he understood that I didn't want to drive. Plain-vanilla Sam. No uninvited questions.

"Car sounds like Chitty Chitty Bang Bang," he said when we were heading north on Highway 52.

"Hey, it's a zombie, but it runs," I said. "How did you get it started?"

"Firewater, couple a kicks."

If it's not worth telling, Sam doesn't tell it. And that

makes him someone whose take on a thing is worth noting. For the first time since the accident I wanted to share what really happened with someone, what I had seen at the waterfall and in Mayo. My Cartesian world is sacked and burning. I could use this man's perspective. But there on the highway last night, I didn't know how to begin.

"Hungry?" he asked presently.

"Naw."

"Hungry," he concluded.

"I'm broke, Sam."

"Let me spot you this one."

"After two months of not showing up for work, it's safe to assume I'm unemployed."

"Like you had the right job, anyway. Carpet installers come and go like colds. You're verbal."

This is true. I've worked in advertising, communications, copyediting. I've schlepped minor slogans for minor politicians, cobbled bulletins and press releases for a multinational, written a small-town weekly column, but after the divorce I fled into all kinds of silences.

Sam and I left the flat farmland below the Twin Cities, past neat names like Mystic Lake, Black Dog Road, Shakopee, Chanhassen, until he pulled off I-94 into a gas station and from there kitty-corner to a Chili's restaurant.

We sat in a wide booth isolated by burnt orange ceramic pots and enameled American relics from the thirties and forties and tried not to stare at each other. He looks like Dustin Hoffman. Pleasantly weathered, dark hair swept back, eyes with safe depths for whomever they invite in. I can't say what I look like to him. The freed inmate of Mayo penitentiary has begun to put on weight. My face, normally as hollow-cheeked as a POW's, is rounding out, and my eyes are a little smokier, as if they have begun to collect sediments from time indoors.

"Phenomenal winter," Sam said. "Lots of good skiing weather left. I could use some help at the shop."

"What do I know about selling?"

"What's to know? You like the things I sell, and you set up skis as good as anyone around. That's where I really get behind. Some days I'm stone grinding and base prepping till midnight. I can take you on through April—four months."

"I don't know what to say."

"Did I mention I need someone to clean the commode?"

So that's how I started working for Sam.

When we left Chili's, he tossed me the car keys. I took the wheel like it was the first day of driver's training—twenty miles under the speed limit. It wasn't the car I had to trust again; it was the road, the next curve, the blind crossing, the pothole, black ice—everything external that had betrayed me on November tenth. But gradually I gave in to the emancipating element of my life.

That would be speed.

The Probe stuttered under acceleration, grabbed and climbed. I took us onto the interstate bypass and into the darkness above Maple Grove. The speedometer needle slipped past sixty, seventy. Very quietly Sam, sensing that I was shaking off the repression of two months, said, "Go for it, Bowie." I pressed down on the pedal, and the headlights tunneled relentlessly through the unvarying night, turning the periphery into a gray wash.

It wasn't me inviting disaster this time; it was disaster inviting me. Because I've been there once now, and so the consequences are known. But tonight I would keep just enough control. That made it irresistibly exciting. And necessary. Just this once. To renew my membership in the adrenaline club. Adrenaline is the distillation of life. This was more therapy than Mayo with all its science could deliver. This would repair the roller-coaster track where it had twisted and torn away, hurling me in the wrong direction two months ago.

Oh, yes. Better than before.

The rush that first time back after so much downtime was stronger than it's ever been. Pure poetry. Glowing lights on the dashboard, asphalt and centerline, and then nothing but blackness. The car did not exist. We were simply hurtling through space. It's the blackness that sets you free. Soar past the chrome-yellow eye of the moon and you are in the wonderful-terrible universe where noxious green vapors roll in from the stars and tides of galaxies ripple across the void to smash into pale butterflies. All shadows rise. Marching in legions. Predators and prey. Leaving velvet footprints across the wastes of space or springing from behind planets to strangle light by its silver throat.

It could have been five seconds or five minutes that I felt the old familiar rapture, but I swear, I never saw the road again until that thing stepped out. And even when it did step out, I didn't react. The two planes of existence I was balancing had to form a seam before I realized that *something* had stepped across and was waiting calmly in the middle of the road.

Then I stood on the brakes, throwing Sam's palms against the dash. My elbows locked, stiff-arming me into the seat as the car began to spin. The headlights bathed trees and threw up embattlements of gritty snow where the road had been. But just before my field of vision was lost, I caught a full look at what it was that stood in front of the car.

It was a huge deer, a buck . . . a stag. Not a doe arrowing across the road, or a link in a chain of frightened yearlings bolting for the ditch, but a male, bristling with too many points to count and an attitude that said he was not frozen in my high beams.

We spun slowly toward the ditch while I tensed for the collision that never came. No more than three seconds passed as we moved laterally about a dozen feet and stopped in the far lane. Three seconds during which I lost sight of the stag. Every detail was still vivid, but . . .

"Where is he, Sam?"

Vanished. Unshakable calm and all.

We got out of the car, walked around in the steaming lights. Not a trace of the colossal animal. No sign of blood or fur on the bumpers. Nothing on the road, the ditch, the snowbanks. I was rattled. Sam focused on me as if my reaction were more of a drama than the deer's appearance.

"It was here," I chattered. "You saw it."

"I saw it."

"It wasn't moving. It just . . ."

Sam strolled to the exact spot where the creature had been, pointed to the tracks, and deadpanned, "The buck stops here."

Not funny. You could clearly see where cloven hooves had etched the snowcap. On either side of that, soft median tires had been passing all night, and the asphalt was bare. We looked beyond to the shoulder and the ditch and finally to the embankments for a sign that Bambi's patriarch had bounded that far. Nothing.

"Suicidal deer," Sam quipped.

I shook my head. He was right. If ever an animal's demeanor was readable . . . suicidal deer. "You drive," I said.

In the passenger seat, I closed my eyes, but the blackness in my mind was just as febrile as the night. It crawled with blind things that honed in on the soft thud of my heart, the smell of my sweat, the stress of my thoughts. Sam let me be, but I knew he was waiting for my confession now. I had to tell someone. In a few moments the things I had kept pent up for fear of being held in the hospital, or giving ammunition to my ex that could prevent me from seeing our children, or just plain being thought fried around the edges, all came spilling out:

"I don't know what's wrong with me . . . I'm changing. Sounds are too loud; colors are too bright. My nose takes everything apart, and I can tell the mood of people by how they smell. If senses are a committee, then my eyes have lost the chairmanship. And it's not just five senses anymore. Sixth sense, horse sense, common sense—something is picking up danger signals I wasn't picking up before. I'm like a tuning fork beginning to hum." I made my little speech looking at the passenger window, but I could see the interior of the car reflected there. Sam's eyes remained on the road.

"What kind of danger?"

"I don't know. Predators."

"What kind of predators?"

"I don't know."

The car droned along, and then he said, "I dropped out of shrink school, so I'm no kind of student of the subject, but after what you went through, it would be odd if you weren't changed."

"Two months, Sam. Nothing is going away. It's getting worse. If it were trauma related, it would have begun to fade by now."

"Most of the cookbook recipes in shrink school start with anxiety. You could be making it worse."

"Yeah, well, sometimes anxiety has a good cause."

He made a neutral sound, half uncertainty; because

without knowing what it was, he suspected that something besides the accident had happened at the waterfall. Sam Ingmar is a rationalist. I appreciate that now. He knows everything about the corners of the soul, religions, mysticism, Indian lore, but he sees all those things as a kind of test of his rationality. His premise is still that it's a logical world, and he can believe that only so long as he can chart the oddities.

"If I tell you what I saw at the waterfall, you'll think I'm still thawing out brain cells," I said, "because it's absolutely textbook in the way of hallucinations. I was flickering out, so I lost the reins a little. When the circuits start to close down, nothing makes sense."

"You had a bad dream, Bowie, and you haven't let yourself wake up yet."

"It was like I had another place to stand—watching outside my own body and all that, you know? I knew what had happened—that I was dying—but I didn't really care. I'd opened a door and stepped into another room, and the good news was that existence wasn't going to stop, but the bad news was that I was going to stop being me." I saw him nod. "And then the bus crashed. I don't know how much of it I actually saw with my eyes and how much I saw with my mind, but all that burning and death didn't have the least effect on me. Not that I'm feeling guilty about it now. It's just a revelation to me that I could have been so calm about death. You could attribute that to my own physical state, but I don't think that's what I was experiencing; I honestly don't. I think . . . it's because I'd just realized that there is no death." In the telling, it started to fall together. "And I *did* die, Sam. As an individual, I died. At least I had a foot on the other side. And if you tell me that's just a stereotypical picture of death buried in my psyche, I'll say it doesn't matter.

What matters is that wherever it was I went, there was still awareness. Where the hell did the memory of it come from, if I wasn't there?"

"Memories of imagination are still real memories."

"Imagination? I was clinically dead, Sam. No pulse, no respiration. And yet I remember. But so what if I wasn't clinically dead? What if I was only dying? Doesn't that still say something about the process of extinction? My awareness wasn't dying. It was enlarging."

"How do you know that?"

"Because I knew things were happening that I couldn't have apprehended with five senses. Like what was going on with the bus." He gave me no encouragement, but I wasn't about to hold back now. "I saw a hole," I blurted. "Some kind of dead spot in space. A vacuum—I don't know how to describe it. I knew it was there by its outline. And it . . . it knew I was there."

"Like a human knows?"

"Definitely not human. More powerful than a human."

"You know, it isn't that unusual for people in extreme physical suffering or fear of death to think they see God."

"I think of God as all-knowing. This thing didn't even know I was there. It *discovered* me. I think it came for the bus, and then it discovered me."

"You mean it came specifically for the bus?"

"That's what drew it."

"Before or after the bus crashed?"

"I don't know. Oh. You're saying it might have caused the crash?"

"Well, if it wasn't God . . ." His face was hawkish in the dash lights.

I felt as insubstantial as the shadow of a cloud. Dying man imagines he sees Satan. Guilt. Fear. And now two months later we have full-blown neurosis.

"Maybe it doesn't matter what it was," I said. "Maybe what counts is what happened next." *Tell him about the tunnel, Bowie,* I thought. *Tell him how the hole turned into a tunnel. Even if it's a cliché.* "I was connected to the bus," I said lamely. "He—it—connected me to the bus."

He waited, but I had nothing more to tell, and in a few seconds he understood that this was what I wanted him to interpret for me.

"What happened next is you lived," he said. "You came back. And since you didn't die, you may still have memories of what happened after you were connected to the bus. They may be trying to get to the surface. I turned my back on psychology and all the phonies and incompetents who take refuge in the profession, but you know, a good therapist might help you bring those up and put them to rest."

"You think that's all there is to it?"

"No. I can't tell you what the subconscious memories will be; I'm just saying you've got to connect with them. Maybe when you do, it will open a whole new can of worms. Maybe it won't have anything to do with psychology at all."

"What then?"

He shrugged. "A can of metaphysical worms."

Metaphysical worms. That's what Sam Ingmar left me with. I studied philosophy in college long before my marriage and family went dysfunctional, and what I remember about metaphysics is that it's where you dump things that don't fit neatly into reality. I've got a backlog of those things. And when I dropped Sam off at his ski shop where he had left his car, and started home at a crawl in deference to the near accident of an hour earlier, I got one more.

I can't say when the headlights started up in my

rearview mirror. Five or ten seconds after rounding one of the downgrade curves on the mountain, they were behind me. Too high up to be a car or an SUV. More like a truck. But on the next curve, the gibbous moon caught it broadside, and I saw that it was a big yellow bus.

9

Nearly midnight and a school bus was coming down the mountain behind me. Lots of explanations for that. Like an away basketball game going into quintuple overtime. Or maybe the bus broke down and instead of calling for backup, the driver had let the debate-team coach, who just happened to teach auto shop, work on it for a couple of hours. Or it could have been a swim-meet victory followed by pizza, followed by a Dairy Queen, followed by—*It's the same bus that hit the bear. The same, the same, the same damn bus. The same. I knew it then, I know it now.*

I pressed the gas pedal, and the Probe balked and surged. For a few seconds the ominous bus lights shrank, but then they were coming at me again like snowballs down a hill. More gas. I edged ahead. At fifty miles per hour and thirty feet apart, we seemed to strike a standoff. Maybe the driver was just impatient, I told myself. The old trucker's tactic. Bully the Sunday driver. I should be pissed, not scared. This was a bus. I risked a couple of quick glances in the mirror, but it was all silhouette and glare. *Give him what he wants, Bowie. . . .*

The shoulder was narrow and snowcapped. No telling what lay beneath it. Like a raised eyebrow, the top of a culvert flashed by at a right angle to the highway. So there was a drainage ditch. I couldn't pull over very far. And the bus couldn't pull out very far on those mountain curves. If he wanted to get past, we both had to slow.

I tapped my brakes to signal my intention, but it was what any good smart-ass would have done, and the bus shot closer by ten feet. The silhouette around the glare in the rearview mirror refined itself: a patch of luminescence, a vague hulk in the driver's seat, highlights of a brow and cheeks, and something my reason rejected . . . because they looked like huge compound eyes.

Had I connected the bus with daylight, I would have understood immediately. Sunglasses. But no one who needed sunglasses in the dark would be licensed to drive a bus at night, and it took me a few moments to sort out the truth. This wasn't a bus from the night. It was a bus from the afternoon of November tenth. And the driver then had been wearing sunglasses.

I feathered my foot on the brakes, but he came on with a vengeance. Too close now for even a glance in the rearview mirror to resolve the face in the luminescence. I gunned the Probe, and it was like the accelerator had been disconnected. Thunder at my back. Things began to reverberate, and the interior around me suddenly flooded with light. Brightness seared my neck. My sweating hands slid around the wheel. If he wanted me to lose control completely, all he had to do was lean on his horn. But he wasn't going to lean on his horn. He was going to drive right over me.

The Probe's high-performance tires were screaming, and each curve produced a fishtail. One nudge and I would go into a spin. Then the bus would snowplow into me and carry us both off the road. What happens to a bus that is already a burned-out shell and a driver who was cremated alive last year?

Speed seemed to be the lesser of evils, and I jammed the accelerator closer to the floor. The first sense I had that the Probe was actually pulling away was the illusion that the back of my neck, where the headlight beams touched, felt cooler. The second was that the white glare in the cab no longer washed out my orange dash lights. But there was less to cheer about ahead, because now the road was starting to snake, and we were both trying to hang on as we swung shoulder to shoulder. If anything was coming up the long, winding grade . . .

I know that route, but last night I couldn't be sure how much farther I had to go to the bottom of the mountain. And then the brown highway sign flashed by—SHESHE-BANS 2 MILES—and everything fell into place. I visualized one last steep bend, followed by a climb.

The brakes burned and the bus rushed forward, but I kept my foot down, slowing, slowing. We slingshot around the last curve like a pair of ball bearings in an oiled race, and there ahead of me was salvation in the form of a hill. Pedal to the metal now. The heavier bus fell behind. By the time I reached the top, he was still in the first half.

On the other side of the rise was sanity. Trees thinned and opened to a farm, and then some rustic storefronts, and then the broad concrete apron of a truck stop. What would happen if a metaphysical bus hit me? Would I die in a metaphysical crash, or is it all a case of the dead chasing the dead? I pulled into the truck stop and watched, but the bus never came.

Imagine that.

10

Picture this. You come home to find two months' worth of mineral ring at the waterline in the toilet, and when you turn on a faucet it spits at you and air hammers in the pipes. There is dust everywhere, the bread crumbs that are always on the drainboard are gone, and there are soft white spider casings high in the corners and along the cornices of your rooms. When you go near one of the casings, you can actually see eyes move behind the translucent silk.

Two months ago I would have killed anything with too many legs that lived above my head and spun its own bungee cords. Now such creatures recoil inside their wombs when I get close, and I ignore them. They are natural. Until they attack me, we will coexist.

But spiders and dust and plumbing aren't the problems here. The problems are the mail and the answering machine. I had zero mail waiting for me. *Nada* phone calls. I checked with the post office the next day. Zero. There was lots of publicity about my being in the hospital, so maybe some larcenous opportunist traced down my address and helped himself to my correspondence for the duration. He may still be helping himself. But what about the answering machine? I checked and it's working fine.

It's inconceivable that I would have no calls. They're being taken off the machine. It's a cheap machine—no remote access—so the erasing is done here, in this room. But there is no sign of forced entry to my apartment. Someone has a key.

I don't know what I expected coming home—sanctuary, I guess. Familiar walls, my books, the pictures I have of Jessica and Danny in frames on the end tables. The one of Jessica shows her looking surprised. She never looks surprised, never lets her guard down, but this shot catches her when she is coming offstage at her school Spring Festival production of *Johnny over the Rainbow*. The play is all about a boy who has to find the colors of the rainbow and put them together. Jessica got to play one of the colors—purple. There were lots of kids who needed roles, so there were lots of colors in the rainbow. Danny got to play the boy, but Jessica was purple. The color of suffering. Should have been Kermit green, because Jessica has never gotten over the shock of having to share half her universe with her younger brother. But when she came off the stage that night with applause ringing in her ears, she was jubilant. That was when I took the picture. She's coming toward me, and her unguarded reaction is to run into my arms all aglow. Her unabashed smile could put the world at her feet and knock flat all the walls she has built, but she doesn't know that. Like I said, she seldom lets her guard down.

Anyway, that's what I had thought about a thousand times in Mayo and what I was looking forward to when I came home to the apartment. I was surprised that everything looks and smells so strange to me. It shouldn't surprise me, given my changed orientation to the world for the last two months, but it does. I guess that's because I don't often let my guard down either.

The fact that Weibens encourages me to continue writing this is almost reason enough to quit, but I'm feeling a lot like newly discovered prey in the middle of a clearing. When I was sitting in Rochester's downtown area, I remembered reading about prisoners getting out of jail—that they can be overwhelmed by color and sound. So maybe it's going to take a little while. Have to think rationally. Maybe my landlord came in here and accidentally dumped the answering machine. Maybe it was a power outage. And these sensory flights I keep taking—I don't think my senses have become paranormal or anything; they just . . . overreact.

I smell varnish on the cupboards, wallpaper paste, dust burning on lightbulbs, and the chemical residue of a carpet cleaning that must have happened before I rented the place. I can hear bubbles rising in the toilet tank for an hour after I flush, and electric motors hum a mantra. The computer and the fridge sound like panzers, and the soft rush of air through the cold air return has a flat acoustic that gives me a mild sense of claustrophobia. Weibens warned me about depression but not claustrophobia. One foot indoors and I start looking for exits.

My occasional suicidal impulses have never been passionate, but now they are the default thought. I feel like an empty hourglass.

The mail got here today. Half a dozen flyers, a card with the picture of a missing child last seen with a kidnapper of the same last name (kill the bastard!), and the electric bill. Electrical usage down ninety-three percent from the same period last year. That's a hoot. Except . . . where is the carryover from the previous unpaid month? Deep, dark suspicion. I picked up the phone and rattled off three calls to Xcel Energy, Qwest, and Minnegasco. "The electric bill is correct, sir." . . . "There is no delinquency in your Qwest phone account." . . . "Our records show the gas was paid on December second."

So it hit me. Sam. Sam I am. There really isn't any connection between us that would explain such generosity, but then, my car has remained at his ski shop, and he may feel some responsibility because I started out from his trailhead on November tenth. He brought that TV tape to the hospital, picked me up, gave me a job. So it must be Sam. What a guy.

Not that I'm totally comfortable with that. These little surprises in my inner sanctum are like cats moving around in the dark. You turn on the lights and they are here instead of there, and you never heard them move.

Makes you want to back into a corner. So this morning I did exactly that: I retreated to the bathroom for a long, hot soak in the tub that would cut through the alienation. But—rub-a-dub-dub—guess what? There were at least three guys in there already, lost on the ocean blue.

As soon as the water cascaded out of the faucet, I felt the barrier thinning, but I let the tub fill and slipped down into the warmth and slid the glass door shut above the tub rail. You can't back up forever, and I can't control these appearances. I'm going to have to live with them. Steam rose like silver shrubs on the tile and the glass, and my eyelids drooped, and the mist shimmered into the faces of the trio. They all seemed to have something around their neck, and one of them could have been the minister who performed demonic magic in my hospital room. No threat. Just mist. I was still in control.

So I let it go on, and that was my mistake. The fact that I could still feel the wavy ridges that ran the length of the tub made me think that I had stopped sinking, but in a few moments I was at the bottom of a womb, being reborn into the same dimension as before: hinterworlds, seething plasmas, groaning gravities, unknowable voids. Not quite a nightmare. Yet. It was still a dream in the intimacy of the bath. As innocent as cosmic harmony to a Hindu knee-deep in the Ganges. But with apologies to the aesthetic path of discipline and denial, I have a shortcut in my bathroom. I, who believe in nothing in particular, can get there as easily as taking a bath.

My arms floated, my knees lifted buoyantly, the slightly soap-scented steam flowed into my nostrils like a drug. I was dreaming still, and dreaming is a memory of waking made perfect. Then, somewhere in that faster-than-light flight, a single link of chain fell soundlessly in a bottomless pit. And as if that stitch in time was really the tie that binds the whole fabric of infinity, everything came apart. Hello, universe of dust and fire.

I tried to wake up—I did wake up—I *thought* I woke up! But each time it was into another subcavern of dreaming. The pleasant imagery began falling away, replaced by ragged fulminations at inexpressible distances. There were galaxies ebbing toward extinction, transmuting into raw energy that spread like a contagion. The destiny of all things. The irreducible soup. I wanted to scream. I wanted to join the harmonic of banshees wailing across the vast transpans of space. The souls of the recent dead were all on the anvil, about to be hammered into prototype ethos, and I—minor man, minor species—hung in the portal of annihilation.

The drowning man surfaces three times, goes the cliché, and three times I broke free of the surreal fracturing, which I now believe is the prolonged extinction of the mind that occurs with every death. That's what these visions, nightmares, and hallucinations are all about. My reality is decomposing. My memories are coming apart. Except that I keep returning to life, and the pieces get jumbled together in bizarre satyrs and physics-defying melds. When I get it straight, I am fully alive again. But sooner or later I'll stop getting it straight. Then my mind will be dead, officially dead, irreversibly dead. And what about my body? Is that why the souls from the bus are intruding? WANTED: VACANCY.

But then, what about my soul? Nineteen intruders somehow directed to my body can't evict my soul, can they? Twenty souls. We are already coexisting. God save us from what we'll become if we actually share control.

The first time I surfaced, I was in the tub again. Except that I looked down and couldn't see the other half of myself in the clear water. There was just my upper torso and my arms banging on the tiles and the glass. I couldn't stand it, and I slipped back under to a place where the Sphinx babbles confessions. Up again, but my body was burned and ulcerated, and I let it dissolve in the water like brown-sugar crust. Diminished to a tenuous flow of memories, I saw the sun set twice without rising and smelled the Pacific trenches—rotting graves of all that have died in the oceans. And the third time—the third time I surfaced the water was cold and clammy.

I really was back.

That was my last bath. I'm pulling the plug. I'll live in a chimney before I'll sit in a tub again.

I think the visions have something to do with floating. Untethered feelings are a hazard. A good old nightmare inducer, the way shaving makes you light-headed. The tub doors are both bent on the tracks, and the glass on one of them is cracked. Is that from me or them?

11

It's Thursday. I don't remember where I left off yesterday, and I don't want to read what I wrote. I've put duct tape all over the refrigerator door, and I'm afraid to go to the window. There's a dog out there that hasn't shut up since I came back.

I had been living out of the cupboards for two days because I didn't want to deal with two months of refrigerator mold, but surprise, surprise—there was no mold. No sour milk, no acidic OJ. To the best of my memory, it's just the way I left it November tenth. At first I thought maybe it was just too hermetic for the air to get to it, that it shut down—like I did at 55.1 degrees. But I looked at the date stamp on one of the yogurt cartons, and it said, *Sell by 01/12*. January twelfth is tomorrow. Friday. Either they're doing a hell of a lot better preserving yogurt at the Dannon company these days, or it isn't the same yogurt I left in there two months ago.

I checked every item. I don't know what I was looking for—tampering, sabotage. Everything was sealed. Now why would anyone go to all the trouble of replacing my food item by item? I don't like this Goldilocks stuff.

There's something wrong with the whole neighborhood. A tension, a hostility. I knew it as soon as I left the apartment, headed for the supermarket. The damn barking dog knew it too. I could smell him from the lower entrance. Wet fur, carnivore breath, a full-throated male who had marked out his territory. I turned in the other direction.

It had snowed. I saw squirrel tracks as tight as zipper teeth, which meant the ground cover was soft and deep. Nothing else out there that wasn't always there, except a line of cars and a snowman across the street. The snowman looked new, but there was no sign he had been rolled up recently, so it must have been because of the fresh coating. Someone's red glove lay palm up in the street, pleading. Up close, I could see that the snowman's eyes had been dug out in finger-sized tunnels.

The car coughed bronchially as I scraped the windshield. *I* coughed bronchially as the blower blasted my face. We crept off for the mall. Rainbow Foods is in a side court, and the milling crowd between Menards and Sears seemed purposeless as I marched down the promenade. I was feeling my way back into the world, and for once in my life I wanted to be like everyone else. Borders books caught my eye—a Plisson print of a lone lavender sailboat in its window—and then a pet shop that seemed to glow with aquariums. I should get a puppy, Weibens had said. The killjoy. I wanted a puppy, but then *he* had to go and suggest it. Maybe I'll get an iguana or a ferret and name it after him. I strolled into the pet shop.

I have never understood the attraction of tropical fish. They are always small and monotonous. When they occur in schools, you have compounded monotony. My theory is that the green aquarium lights and aerator bubbles hypnotize them. The ones in front of me, however, darted away in standing waves. And the Siamese fighting fish in the tank next door charged me like flaming pennants. And next in line the forty or so parakeets behind bars churned around in a pastel blizzard, unable to find a perch far enough away. Up and down they went, until they began to drop like leaves to the bottom of the cage.

"Sir"—at my elbow—"please don't do that to the budgies."

I scowled at a slender salesclerk. "Do what?"

"They're very nervous," he said very nervously. "You can't wave your arms around or make threatening gestures."

"You're out of your . . . bird."

"Even if you just touch the cage—"

"I didn't touch the cage."

The birds kept dropping like ticker tape at a parade.

"Sir . . . sir!"

I turned the corner into the puppy section along the rear wall to get away from him, but in a matter of moments the yapping started.

". . . you're doing it again," said Dr. Doolittle at my elbow.

"Doing what?"

"I don't know; I was trying to calm the birds you upset, and now the puppies are all whimpering. This is a *pet* store."

"A pet store. Damn, I thought it was Busch Gardens. Then I'm not going to get to see rogue elephants?" I raised my hand before he could say "sir" again, and ambled out of the panic.

Waterfall Man Attacks Pet Store.

Rainbow Foods was much better. All the animals there are dead.

I had to squeeze the Probe between a garbage bin and a retaining wall when I got back to the apartment, and then, to avoid the barking dog, I walked the length of the complex past where I had parked before. Coming around the side of the building, the first thing I saw was the snowman. Only now he was broken open like a plaster cast and scattered on the ground. Extremely cold snow will shatter like that, but there was something odd about the pieces. The inner surfaces were sculpted too.

I turned to set one armload of groceries on the step so I could fish out my keys, but someone pushed the door open from the inside, saving me the trouble. I caught it with my foot. "Thanks," I mumbled, straightening too late to make eye contact. Up the floating hall steps I padded, this time setting the groceries down on the welcome mat to dig for my keys. I opened the apartment door, dragged the sacks into the empty living room, kicked the door shut. The lock clicked behind me—I absolutely heard that. I hoisted two plastic sacks to the drainboard in the kitchen, leaving the other two on the floor. Out came the new yogurt—exactly ten cups—and the lettuce, apples, orange juice, margarine. Then I opened the refrigerator.

For just a second the gaudy birdcage was reprised for me, flashing yellow, green, blue, and the fish tanks, riotous with tropical flecks and crimson fins; but then again, it was more like Rainbow Foods, where everything was dead. Colors fluoresced and oozed from a half dozen molds. Spores twinkled. "Ripe" cannot describe the stench. Ammonia, yeast, the butyric-acid smell of rancid butter—my eyes watered and the tissues in my sinuses and throat tingled. This was more than instant rot. It was virulent. I flung the refrigerator door shut so hard that it seemed the putrefaction knocked back in a rush to escape. Gagging, I bolted to the sink and turned the water on full.

You can take only so many invasions before you go on

the offensive. The fact of the matter is that my apartment is being controlled, my mail taken, my phone calls erased, my bills paid, and my food tampered with. Someone in the commerce of all this has to know something. The phone numbers for the utilities were still on the back of a pizza ad where I had written them. A service rep named Helen caught the full brunt of my tantrum.

"I *know* the bill was paid," I bullied like a bus coming down a mountain. "I'm asking you how the money got there."

"How? By check."

"Signed by who?"

"I don't have that information, sir."

"But you know it was a check."

"It could have been a money order."

"Your accounting department could tell me, right?"

"Billing doesn't make copies of checks, sir. You'll have to call your bank."

"It's not *my* check!"

Long pause. "Would you like to speak with a supervisor, sir?"

I backed out of the conversation. But she had mentioned the bank, and I grabbed my checkbook, dialed the phone, sat through the false brightness of voice menus: "Your account balance is . . . two thousand, six hundred and six dollars, and ninety-five cents. For the last twenty transactions—"

Not according to the register in my hand. Not even close. Six hundred and six dollars and ninety-five cents was staring me in the face. Someone had deposited two thousand dollars. And then a precise but polite voice behind me said:

"Never look a gift horse in the mouth, Mr. Carmichael."

He looked like a cross between Marcel Marceau in mime makeup and the late Sir John Gielgud. Very white. Bloodless, in fact. His great, sad eyes pooled the light as he sat there in my living room recliner watching me. One of his eyebrows was split by a waxy scar, hinting at the death or corruption of his fine, aged features. He was dressed in a pin-striped business suit, dated but dapper. His large, doughy hands were gnarled at the knuckles, his nails blunt and bluish. And he was wearing a wedding band of very dull gold.

My mind was spinning like a CD-ROM trying to find the right track. I wasn't sure whether this sudden appearance was an extension of what I should resist or the answer to all the questions that were accumulating.

"Who the hell are you?" I demanded, starting out of the swivel chair next to the phone without drawing my feet close enough, so that I ended up dropping back. "How did you get in here?"

"I'm afraid I've made a very bad habit of invading your privacy. It was done in a good cause, however. Your cause, Mr. Carmichael."

His voice had a mellow inertness to it, as if it had been recorded in a studio with deadening acoustics.

"Taking my mail, erasing my phone messages, and that . . . that travesty in the refrigerator? You think those are good causes?"

"The situation in your refrigerator is beyond my control. You'll have to get used to things like that. It happened because you handled everything. But for the rest of it, I paid your bills, including your medical, and made sure you were insulated against threats."

"Threats?"

His thin, expressive lips moued thoughtfully. "It's a hostile world out there, Mr. Carmichael."

"The deer in the road? The bus?"

"A deer is a creature of instinct. Instincts are also beyond my control. But if your ordeal with the bus is still haunting you, perhaps you should examine that."

"I always get a little peeved when someone tries to run me off the road."

"You have nothing to fear from the bus, Mr. Carmichael. It was a mistake, an act of desperation. They aren't rational, you know. And they're terrified. You're their hope. You have no idea how profound your situation is."

"What situation?"

"I'll tell you that whenever you're ready."

"I couldn't be more ready."

"Are you?"

"Just blurt it out. What do you want from me?"

"I want you to know the alternatives."

"This is bullshit."

"When you understand the first alternative, you'll accept the second."

"Okay. Okay. Deal me a card. What's the first?"

He smiled, twirled his hands, ending like the red glove in the street with his palms up—except he wasn't pleading. "The first is welcome back to your life, Mr. Carmichael, such as it is."

"Hit me with it, Jackson. What's the second?"

"Do you understand how it's going to be? You have your life back, even though it's not exclusively yours."

"'Scuse me? That's it?"

"I'm afraid this is premature. You haven't tried to live in the open yet—"

"Are you threatening me?"

"Quite the contrary. If you can't see that I'm trying to help you survive—"

"Get out of here! You're trespassing. In fact you're breaking and entering. I'm going to change the locks, so don't try to come back."

I stood all the way up this time, tried to look menacing, but he just sat there, dark eyes glistening. There was something potent about him that made me hesitate, and as soon as I realized this, he also rose up—medium height—as gracefully as a cat.

"As you wish, Mr. Carmichael. But try to think of me as an ally. Because you have an enemy, and it's not who you think it is. I'll be close by."

He glided smoothly toward the door, and I bumped after him, wanting to demand a dozen more answers, yet enraged that he had gotten into my apartment.

"Who is my enemy?" I blustered.

He turned at the door, not quite making eye contact but exposing his deferential smile. "I'll tell you, because the sooner you accept it, the sooner you'll know what you are. The thing you're attracted to won't have you. Your enemy . . . is nature." Then he was gone.

I watched from the window as he walked into the street below and, without looking up, raised his left hand in a subdued wave. From that distance, I was struck by the fact that the air seemed faintly violet around him. The farther he got, the more pronounced that became. When he passed the snowman, I felt an absurd suspicion that he might actually have something to do with its oddly ruptured condition. That's how lunatic I've become. The sentinel snowman, spying on me; bursting into a new incarnation—the very white Mr. Freeze—as soon as I left my apartment. But that's what occurred to me. I wish I had let him stay a little longer. He might have said something that made sense.

12

"Daddy, there's something in the closet. I heard it. So did Danny."

Danny would never admit he heard anything, but his eyes would plead with mine as urgently as Jessica's, and I would go to the closet and mangle the darkness and utter an incantation that was wholly satisfying to two children who loved me and believed in the power of fathers. That's what I thought about when I drew myself up in bed this morning, afraid to look around the corner into the kitchen. Because it was happening again—the ammonia smell, the yeast, the butyric acid. Hello, yesterday. I still haven't come to terms with that absurdity. It was much easier to believe it was a sick joke, which is what I did believe until that mummer-faced wretch told me it was because I had handled everything. And now the stench filled the apartment. Like Mr. Freeze said: It can't be controlled. Duct tape isn't what it used to be.

But when I got up the courage to leave the bedroom, it wasn't coming from the refrigerator. It was the stuff I had brought in and left on the drainboard after I slammed the refrigerator door.

The head of lettuce looked like a hideous decapitation. A brown, pulpy mash glistened where its severed stem had been, and the leaves were sloughing off in layers like gangrene. The apples were just russet, weeping lumps that could have been stillborn fetuses, and the margarine had bubbled out of the carton in a yellow froth. But the yogurt took the prize, because of course you can't beat "cultural" diversity, and the stuff that was spangled all over the counter was practically fluorescing. I could see spores rising while I stood there — though the heat register on the kitchen wall sometimes makes the air shimmer like that.

Easy to overreact when you think you're under siege from the groceries that ate Chicago. But it was just . . . accelerated rot. I put on rubber gloves and cleaned it up, using half a roll of paper towels and two garbage bags. Ditto the fridge. Because by then I was slightly fascinated by my power over food. The stuff just falls apart in my presence. Genetic self-destruct.

"You have an enemy. . . ."

This has nothing to do with Mr. Freeze and everything to do with me. I'm not being poisoned; I am the poison. If food could get cancer, this is what it would look like.

"Welcome back to your life, Mr. Carmichael, such as it is. . . ."

Okay. I can handle this. If I have to scarf down canned food for a while until I get these crazies out of the picture, I can do that. A zillion years ago, before exercise cured me, I was diagnosed with hypoglycemia and lived on raw hot dogs and tuna for six months. So, a little deprivation won't hurt. I can probably sneak up on really fast fast food, and God knows how I love drinking nothing but water.

This is really all about attitude, a head game, my . . . mental state. Whoever my true enemies are, since when haven't I been all about self-denial and mental toughness? At least, that's who I am since my rebirth after the divorce. And now that I'm free of that damn hospital, I am in full control again. Nothing is going to psyche me out. Especially not a few special effects. Mirrors and food so far. I can win this.

In order to avoid the bathroom mirror, I brush my teeth in the kitchen sink now and shave by touch: right hand pulling the razor, left feeling for bristle. No problem. Probably lost less than a quart of blood this morning, and I feel smooth as a baby's bottom—if you include diaper rash. I know I look okay because I caught a few glimpses of myself in the rearview mirror on my way to work, which because of its small size and the context of surrounding activity seems less mesmerizing than the still pool of glass in the bathroom. No major nicks. Not counting the red gash still on my forehead. That wound doesn't seem to be healing. As if the point where I first touched my reflection in the mirror left a brand. My false coat of arms. Not really me but a bar sinister on my illegitimate image.

I got to The Ski Shop by ten thirty. The Ski Shop. Whatever the season, it's still The Ski Shop. Somehow Sam sells and repairs bikes and in-line skates during the summer without changing or embellishing the name. For my first day, he put me to work hot-waxing back orders in the storage room.

I like the smell of glider wax. It's one of the few indoor smells I still do like. You hold the wax up to the little travel iron over the skis, kind of like raising a pepper mill over a salad, and you dribble glider tip to tail. Sam does this in one zigzag sweep, and the droplets line up as evenly as stitches on a Pierre Cardin suit. Mine tend to cluster like a line of Dead Heads outside a Grateful Dead ticket office. You iron the drops into a uniform film and then scrape it all down with a metal edge. The idea is to fill the micropores in the hi-tech ski bottom, but the wax shavings just keep fluttering up like scarves out of a magician's sleeve. You end up with a pair of skinny plastic boards capable of suspending the human form over ice and snow. Your weight stays on the cambered part of the ski, and you are literally held aloft in the glide phase.

This afternoon I worked on a pair of classic skis, meant for striding in twin tracks, and then a pair of top-of-the-line skate skis, which allow free strides. I prefer to skate, and I lingered over the latter, giving them some final strokes with a nylon brush to make sure the base wax was seated.

Sam came back then, watched for a few moments, and asked if I had been out that morning.

"We got an inch of powder last night," he said, dark eyes aglow. "I ran the groomer on the south side of the mountain before dawn. What is waiting for you out there, Bowie, is eleven K of groomed and inviolate trails."

"What I've got out there is no boards."

He gestured toward the rig and the Fischer RCS racing skis I'd been working on. "Those are yours," he said. "Pick out some graphite from the pole rack."

I looked disbelievingly at the skis with their Salomon racing bindings. "I can't let you do this, Sam."

"Do what? I'll get more work out of you if you're healthy, and I'm not gonna sell out my stock anyway." He watched as I ran my fingertips down the base. "It's just a pair of skis, Bowie. Let someone give you something before you choke on that independence of yours."

"Now that I think of it, I do have some skis," I said, as if I hadn't heard him. "My old junk Combis are still in the car. But I'm not really ready to go out yet."

"Okay, if you think Combis will keep you happy. The Fischers are yours, though, when you want them."

He thinks I'm too proud to accept anything, but that's not it. I called him for a ride from Mayo, didn't I? I let him buy me dinner. The real reason I didn't want to accept the Fischers is because even though I'm dying to get back on skis, I'm still a little nervous about it. Every time my imagination whisks me onto a pristine trail I end up at the waterfall. There be dragons. So I waxed and scraped and put on bindings until midafternoon. Sam knew perfectly well that the smell of wax and epoxy, the bright, wet colors of the skis, and the touch of cork and fiberglass would eventually be more persuasion than I needed. When the floor draft of someone clumping in from the trails and opening the door out front reached me, I made up my mind: I belong to the ice and snow. *At the end of the day* . . . I promised myself.

Just after two, Sam tossed me a Slim Jim beef stick laminated in plastic from behind the counter, and I picked out the ripest banana from the bunch he offered. While we snacked and drank bottled water, he showed me how to key the cash register and went over pricing and sales tax. My helping meant he wouldn't have to leave one customer to ring up a sale for another, and at slow times he could go out on the trails to groom or ski while I minded the store.

At four o'clock, when I finished the backlog, I ambled up front, knifed my hands into my pockets, and announced that I was going for a little run on the south trails while it was still light. "Take the Fischers," Sam goaded me in a gangland undertone. And I did.

My last ski had been doom and gloom, but the return was pure diamonds. A million icy prisms tossed sunlight from tree to tree, and everything I love came back to me.

You can never really remember a winter's seduction. Like a stiff drink, it always surprises you.

The south trails are slow to trickle down the mountain, and therefore forgiving. The waterfall is on the north side. And this mountain I keep referring to isn't a mountain at all. Or if it is, no one has bothered to name it. It's just a series of steep, irregular steps, heavily wooded in places, that hems in a creek and a road on the north side. The creek eases down, cataract to pool, like a child pausing at each step on a staircase, until it lets go in a final rush to the waterfall. That's where it really gets rugged and wild.

I turned south, gliding wide through the turns, brushing snowy boughs in the narrows. The snow was responsive, taking the edge of the Fischers like a brake when I wanted, compressing into clean slicks when I wanted that, holding the stabs of my poles without grabbing them. Everything was smoothly capped, and except for the ribbed track of Sam's grooming rig hauled behind a snowmobile, and the hatchwork strides left by the few skiers who had been out, it could have been an airbrushed fantasy. Except that at the bottom it started to snow.

And the snow was on fire.

I saw gray flakes at first. Then embered ones. Then flaming motes in tortured arcs. I threw my arm up to squint at the mystery that was pelting me as I stood in a depression. Then I took off my glove to confirm what my eyes were telling me. Ashes. Volcanolike, they were spewing over me from behind a ridge to my left. The one I caught in my right hand smeared black on my palm.

If it was a campfire, what were they burning? I could hear flames spanking low beneath the wind as I started forward, and I saw orange tracers reflecting up and down tree trunks like a bar graph above the ridgeline. It smelled . . . sweet. Cloyingly sweet. Like a luau, like a pork roast. Amazing how I can still be caught off guard, because it wasn't until I picked up the acrid whiff of burning rubber that I knew beyond any need to confirm what was waiting over the ridge.

The skis and poles were out of sync as I staggered into a running gait to get away. I tried not to think about what was fueling the flames, tried not to feel the powdery ash on my cheeks. Because luaus smelled like that, and pork roasts, and burning buses full of dying human beings.

Believe me, I'm fighting this. Funeral pyres don't move around in time and space. Unless two streams of reality—cosmic and earthbound—are flowing through me at the same time, it couldn't have been there. That's what I'm trying to believe as I write this out. Easier now than on the trail, where the pungent smell of burning tires was unmistakable, and a horrifying ululation was inseparable from the wind. I did the right thing. I didn't look over that ridge.

13

And I didn't tell Sam. I know he would set me straight—*it was secondhand smoke, Bowie, left over from the fire in your imagination*—but I need to conclude that all on my own. And, besides, when I got back to the shop Sam threw me another jolt.

He fished down into the scrap barrel and delicately raised a tangle of black crescents. "Glad you're not sick to your stomach. You ate one of these beauties a while ago."

I could feel his searching eyes as I skinned off my turtleneck sweater. "It's my latest trick," I said. "I make fruit feel old. In fact, any food. You should see my refrigerator."

"What are you talking about? The bananas spoiled, that's all."

"No. Everything I handle gets supermoldy, superquick."

He blinked. Thought. "How do you eat?"

"Nothing seems to happen once I've downed it. But if I just touch it—zap. Two hours later, a feast of mold."

He dropped the tangle of black crescents back in the barrel and tensed his lips as though to whistle. I clambered into the green fiberglass shower stall at the other end of the storage room.

"Wish I knew where my life is going, Sam," I hollered out, turning on the water while I tried to decide what I could tell him. "It's like I've been a big, stupid outsider . . . and suddenly I'm discovering the wavelengths of all this cross-chatter that's going on . . . not words . . . it's smells and markers, patterns, body language, looks, colors . . . the rhythms of sounds . . . and the wind . . . the wind is like a conduit channeling everything at me . . . when I was out there on the trails just now, it was like coming back to an old neighborhood . . . major dramatic . . . who died, who lived, who left foolish tracks the night before, who's the alpha male . . . you see it every day, so you know what I'm talking about, Sam . . . since my accident, it's like that everywhere . . . I'm not talking woodsy . . . this is how I read people now . . . something terrifying to human beings is out there, and it won't let me go."

"You know, a certain amount of what you're experiencing now may be because you've been in low gear for two months," he said when I was out of the stall and drying off. "It's like a long sleep and you wake up sharp and impressionable."

"It doesn't feel like I'm awake. It feels like I've entered a big, dark room crackling with stupendous information I can't sort out. Someone has taken the blinders off me, and now I can see that I'm on a high wire and there's no net. I'm not even sure whether I'll fall up or down."

"Sometimes traumas leave people with heightened perceptions."

"Yeah, golfers who get hit by lightning. My ex gave my clubs away before she was my ex, Sam."

He hiked himself onto the edge of the workbench. "Did you consider what I said about a good therapist?"

My heart fell. "Whatever happened to those metaphysical worms you were talking about?" I asked dully.

"Still a possibility. I'm just saying you could get help accessing what you don't consciously remember."

"Why don't you help me? If you really believe all this is just a way I create to deal with repressed memories, then connect the dots for me."

"I could mess you up, Bowie."

"The wonk I was seeing at Mayo didn't have any scruples. Or any clues, for that matter."

"You told him what you told me?"

I laughed out loud. "Tell me what I could be blocking, Sam. Guilt because a lot of people died? What did I have to do with the bus? I didn't cause it. I don't feel guilty about it."

"If you didn't trust that shrink, you should've tried someone else."

I decided to lay it on Sam. If he didn't believe me, I'd just find a rocking chair and blow spit bubbles till hell froze over. "Oh, I've got a regular support network, didn't I tell you?"

"Good."

"Not good, Sam. How come someone's taking care of me? How come my bills are all paid and there's two thousand dollars in my bank account that I never put there?"

"You're kidding."

"I don't usually misplace two grand, Sam. Plus the checkbook doesn't list it, and the deposit date was mid-December. You remember where I was in mid-December, don't you?"

"Okay. That's a genuine mystery. You'll have to find out who it was."

"Oh, I know who it was." For the first time he looked something other than imperturbable. "He showed up," I went on. "Not at my door, but inside my apartment. Don't ask me how he gets in. He just does. I was sitting right there, and I would have heard the door open. He knew about the rotten food—said he had no control over that. *That*. Like he controls everything else."

"What did he want?"

"He said it's a hostile world and that I should think of him as an ally. He said that my enemy isn't who I think it is."

"Who do you think it is?"

"A bunch of dead people. But my uninvited visitor says my enemy is nature. I threw him out." Sam stared through me, lost in reflection, and I added: "It's okay to tell me I'm nuts, Sam. Tell me I'm nuts."

He shrugged, shook his head. "Something's happening. It may not be as bizarre as you think, but . . ." He kicked the barrel where the bananas lay. "I bought those fresh yesterday, a little on the green side."

I brushed the gash on my forehead. "See this? It's where I touched one of them, and it won't heal."

"Looks healed to me."

"What are you talking about?"

He searched where I was pointing, and I felt a new quaking in my gut. He couldn't see it. Couldn't see the mark. I wanted a mirror. *I didn't want a mirror.* I could feel it—the raised, pulpy flesh—but it wasn't there. Thoroughly rattled, I couldn't deal with it at that moment. Couldn't challenge Sam, out of fear I was challenging myself, my sanity in his eyes.

"Remember the deer, Sam?" I said, almost begging. "Suicidal, you said. It was strange, wasn't it? I mean, it wasn't like most deer accidents, where they get blinded and misjudge an oncoming vehicle. He just confronted us. You saw. And I knew something was wrong beforehand. I could tell as soon as I took the wheel."

"What could he want from you?" he posed absently.

"The deer?"

"Your visitor. Your 'ally.' Do you think he might want the rights to your story about the accident?"

I hadn't considered that. Maybe there is a rational explanation. Odd approach for a journalist—an impossible journalist—but why else would someone undertake my welfare? We left it at that. The loose ends were like the debris in the storage room, left over from outcomes that nevertheless ended satisfactorily. Never mind the bananas and the Red Badge of Outrage on my forehead. Ditto smoke and mirrors.

14

I thought writing the previous chapter would take my mind off what happened after I left Sam's, but it didn't. It's just after midnight, and I am still very upset. So here's the addendum. I left The Ski Shop about five hours ago. When I got to Sheshebans I stopped at a McDonald's drive-through to eat. Two double-quarters with cheese and a diet Coke, no ice. I parked at a strip mall and ate, because I might not have made it all the way back to my apartment twenty minutes away before I had a bag full of mad-cow disease. Despite the sharpening of my other senses, eating is bland and tasteless. Since this coincides pretty much with the onset of my ability to zap foods, I'll accept that the loss of appetite is psychological. I eat when I get weak and my stomach growls.

So I get the food part—*"Do you understand how it's going to be?"*—but, of course, Mr. Freeze wasn't talking about minor dietary adjustments. And a tough son of a bitch like me probably has a better chance against lions and tigers and bears than what the bastard *was* talking about. Because it isn't just sensory overloads and the sputtering of reality that are attacking me in mirrors and dreams and moments of introspection. It's isolation. You can batter away at the outside of my ramparts, but if the key in the lock on the inside is turning, it's going to be a short siege.

Funny, a loner like me bitching about isolation. Sometimes I'm really stupid about that. Like in the pet store the other night. I didn't get it. I'm still not sure I get it. But here I was tonight going back to the apartment alone and thinking that television and the Internet weren't going to cut it. I wanted something warm and breathing in the room with me, conversation unnecessary. And the strip mall where I wolfed the McDonald's had a pet store. So the postponed impulse from yesterday flickered back to life, and I left the car and crunched through the snow to the small store with the big sign: HOW MUCH IS THAT DOGGIE IN THE WINDOW?

No fish.

No birds.

Puppy cages along one wall. The owner was filling water dishes, and a broom was out. It was almost eight p.m., and I stepped inside having already made up my mind.

"I was just going to lock the door," the man said.

"I want to buy a puppy." I gestured toward the first cage. "That one there." Pathetic. It could have been the Russian two-headed dog, for all I knew, because the cages were sideways to me.

The owner stood back, a sallow man with a boyish shock of hair over his high brow. "Don't you want to see him first?"

"Sure. He's"—I read the card on the side of the cage—"a boxer, right? I like boxers."

The pup was eager enough behind the wire. A little brown, doughy fellow with too much skin. He tottered out, wagging his stubby tail, and the man turned him toward me. But the pup seemed barely able to see through eyes lost in the wrinkles of his brow, and he followed his nose back to the man's hands. Again he was turned toward where I was crouching and tapping my fingers on the tiled floor. A couple of drunken sailor steps toward me, and he lifted his head, sniffing cautiously. His tail slowed a beat. Then he shivered. Then he backpedaled and voided his bladder. He made a noise not quite a whine, not quite a growl.

"He's shy," said the man. "You have to give them time to get used to you."

I duckwalked a step and reached out, and now the pup trembled violently and began to whimper.

The owner cupped a hand under the pup's bottom and lifted him. "Here, here, that's no way to act. It's late. Did we wake you?"

Gingerly he extended the animal, but as I reached to scratch the furrowed brow, the whimpering sharpened. Then, with not much strength but with definite malice aforethought, the little guy nipped.

"Maybe you'd like to see another one," the man said.

"Sure." I rubbed the milk-teeth prints on my knuckle. "How about that black one there?"

Three steps closer to the cages brought deep-throated growls and bulging white crescents from snappy faces. The man looked astonished. "They smell something," he said. "Do you work with wild animals, by any chance?"

I crunched back to the car, breathing hotly. So now I get it about being an anathema to birds, fish, and puppies. It took a while to register (*"You have an enemy . . . nature"*), but now it's sinking in. And the dog howling down the street. That one, too. God knows what I'm radiating that they pick up so readily. Maybe it's the antiseptic smell of Mayo; maybe it's smoke from the woods. I'd rather be hated by people.

My hurt filled the car with no place to go but the gas pedal. I was back at the apartment in under five minutes, and the first thing I saw was the rebuilt snowman. Same spot, same finger-tunnel eyes. I slid hard into the curb and pulled out one of the new ski poles from the back. Then I trudged directly up to Frosty, a.k.a. Mr. Freeze, and ran him through with the carbide tip. I jerked a chunk out of him with the retracting basket. Not satisfied, I let fly a haymaker that decapitated him. The streetlight lent a faintly orange hue to the separation, suggestive of blood, but again it wasn't enough, and I kicked and stomped until the snowman was snow rubble. I think I just committed a murder. Either that or some kid is going to hate the world come tomorrow morning. What's gotten into me?

Screw you, Doc Weibens. Writing doesn't help. This is the last chapter I'm going to do.

My knuckles hurt.

January 13, first light

I sat up all night in front of the computer. I watched my hard drive defrag itself, little blue box by little blue box, percentage point by percentage point, first grabbing up green clusters and moving them, then turning them red, then turning them blue. My life needs sorting out, and this is as close as I can come to it. Like doing a jigsaw puzzle; like arranging a sock drawer. I knew the defragging would get done perfectly, completely, millions of bits of information sorted out and put in their proper order. It was very healing while it was going on. Too bad it lasted only seven hours.

When all the rows of little blue boxes were in sequence, a dialogue box came on and asked me if I wanted to close the disk defragmenter. And that's when I crashed. Me. Personally.

Because *nothing* has been sorted out in my life. It is all just fragments torn up in the act of dying two months ago, and thrown back together in a resurrected life, not fitting together, not communicating, incomplete. I am Frankenstein's monster, Lazarus walking, a hybrid of some kind. Even puppies hate me. Reasoning may be one of the most successful strategies for short-term existence here on this planet, but it makes you dull to the ruling passions and postscripts beyond. Depend on your brains and you lose your most primitive sensitivity. But not me. Mine is coming back.

I know I wrote that I was done writing last night. That it was the last chapter. But if I don't do something, I'll lose it completely. Writing is like opening a valve on a pressure tank that's about to blow. I have to write. Or scream. Or run. Or ski. Or beat up snowmen. So I'm writing already again. But I'm giving up chapters. This is going to be a journal. Chapters are a choice of pauses in a drama. There are no pauses in my drama.

January 13, 8:59 A.M.

A man rang my doorbell for three or four minutes until I buzzed him up. I heard the disembodied voice calling up through the intercom telling me he was an insurance investigator, and at the top of the stairs he turned out to be a very young gum chewer, dressed like he was going on a field trip with his senior class.

"It's eight thirty in the morning," I said.

"I saw your light on." His voice sounded as canned as it had through the intercom. He never unwrapped the tartan scarf he wore, and he didn't carry a briefcase, didn't hand me a card.

"This is about my accident at the waterfall?"

"That's right."

I shrugged, led him inside.

My blinds were closed and the brightness outside barely raised the room level to gloom. I could have changed that, but I let it make a statement that he was a bloody liar about seeing my light. Except for the computer screen, there wasn't any light. He moved stiffly, for one so young, and took a seat without it being offered.

"My HMO is supposed to cover hospitalization for thirty days," I said. "I think the rest of it was paid by someone else. In fact, maybe you can tell me who."

"I'm not from your HMO."

There was something odd about his gum chewing. In the gloom I could see his jaw working away, but I couldn't hear him. I could hear his socks rubbing against his shoe leather; why couldn't I hear him chewing gum? I could smell the dampness on his jacket; I should have smelled mint or wintergreen or cinnamon or Juicy Fruit. Whatever he wanted, he was putting on an act.

"You're here about the bus."

"You were the only witness," he affirmed.

"I was busy dying in a waterfall. The bus didn't happen until after I was trapped. I didn't see it."

"Oh." Not a jot of surprise in that "oh." "Then how do you know it happened *after*ward?"

So we were both bloody liars.

"I know it happened. I didn't see it," I repeated.

"Then you heard it?"

"If this is about a lawsuit, you might as well know now I won't testify. You can subpoena me, but I won't be a big help on the stand."

"This doesn't have to be that formal, Mr. Carmichael. If you'd just be as forthcoming as possible, I could leave, and you'd never hear from me again. People go to jail for refusing to cooperate."

The word "jail" has an unreasonably profound effect on me these days. "You want to put that in writing?" I said about his not coming back.

"I promise you, if you tell me everything—*everything*—I won't have to come back."

"I don't think you'd understand if I told you everything."

"Oh, yes. I'd understand."

I was sitting in the computer chair, clenching my left fist as if it held a pair of dice. What did I have to lose?

"All right," I said, flinging my fingers open. "I heard the crash. I saw it, even though I couldn't have looked right at it. Remember, I had water pouring over me. It may have parted like a curtain now and then, or even refracted the light from the bus, but how much can someone really see and hear who is all but dead inside an icy roar? I'll still say I saw it and heard it. How's that for unassailable testimony?"

"I believe you, Mr. Carmichael."

"You mean you believe I had a hallucination."

"No. I believe exactly what you said. So tell me—specifically—what *did* you see?"

He knew. Even Sam hadn't been this receptive. He knew and was prompting me. As flimsy as this sounds, at that moment I knew it for a fact. It was for my own edification that he had come, so that I would understand and accept what had begun on November tenth. Was this Mr. Freeze's man Friday or was he freelancing? I wanted to be calculating, to trade information, but as with Sam, as soon as I started to tell him about the accident, it all came spilling out in a hoarse, shaky voice:

"I heard the bus whining down the grade. It was trying to slow . . . to stop. And it didn't. I saw it rocking and sliding . . . and it hit two trees . . . two trees at the same time . . . and it burst into flame. The people inside were tossing all over and screaming, grabbing, holding on and . . . burning."

"What then?"

I looked at him uncomprehendingly. "They were dead. Nineteen of them anyway."

"Anything else?"

"You mean the bear? I never saw the bear. The bus hit something—that's probably why it was rocking and spinning."

He leaned forward. "Did you see them come out?"

"No! It was just . . . flames. Globs of color."

"What about after they were dead?"

"Man, you are a morbid son of a bitch."

"What about after?" he repeated.

"You didn't come here stone-cold, did you? You talked to someone at Mayo, or . . . someone else?"

"I told you, if you were totally candid, you'd never see me again, Mr. Carmichael."

"Yeah? Well, I saw a hole in the air." He never blinked. "And it was so damn glad to see me, I thought I'd been saved. But I wasn't. Not by it. So, if you understand so much, explain that to me." He just kept coaxing me with his baby-soft eyes, and I couldn't stand the silence. "And then it blocked my view of the bus," I added.

"Blocked? You don't mean blocked. It was a hole."

"All right, it put a hole between me and the bus." My mind clawed for every frame of film in my memory, and for just a moment I saw that the hole was a hole because it bent light. Light moved out of the way for something unnervingly vast. It didn't stop with the bus; it went on and on. And all of us—the nineteen and myself—who were suddenly dispossessed of ourselves, were poised where the light bent.

"It put a hole between you and the bus . . ." he encouraged.

"A hole. A tunnel. A connection."

"And . . . ?"

"That's all I remember."

"Is it?"

"I said it was."

"Stay focused, Mr. Carmichael."

"I think we're done here."

"What is a tunnel for, Mr. Carmichael?"

"For leaving. Get the hell out of here."

He sighed. Chewed his imaginary gum. He was sitting in the same chair Mr. Freeze had chosen, and he rose up like he knew the drill for getting tossed out of places. At least that part fit my concept of an insurance investigator.

I watched the window, as I had when Mr. Freeze gave me his little farewell wave, but my "insurance investigator" never came out at all. And after a couple of minutes of watching alertly at the window, I burst out of the apartment and dashed down the floating steps. No one there. What's that poem about meeting a man on the stair who wasn't there, and then he isn't there again today, and the speaker of the poem says my, how he wished he'd go away? I opened up the entry door, and he wasn't in sight on the street. Mind games. He waited until he heard me leave my apartment and then he slipped out while I was coming down. That was the momentary explanation I seized on. Too bad there was fresh snow on the stoop. Because I don't have a theory as to why there were no footprints.

January 14, 2:07 A.M.

He was another journalist. So says Sam.

Standing in The Ski Shop around noon yesterday, I was half persuaded. Sam speculates that "Baby Face" pumped one of my neighbors about me, then went into one of their apartments for more information or to pay someone off while I was looking for him outside. It didn't occur to me until later that there still should have been footprints from his arrival. To get around that, you have to suppose that he was in the foyer where the call system is before the snow fell, or—and this is a little disturbing—he *is* one of my neighbors.

Sam says he smells a book in all this and that the journalists don't want to pay me for the rights.

It started snowing up a literal storm a couple of hours later in the Sheshebans area. Nobody was driving in, and Sam decided to ski the south trails for as long as he could before it got too deep. He left me hot-waxing skis and listening to jazz over the radio. Real jazz, like King Oliver and Kid Ory—icons in my shrine. I was never a great musician, but if I hadn't been a failed writer, I would have been a failed trumpet player. Which is why it is completely unexplainable that I switched radio stations. But that's what I did, even leaving the dial on something unfathomably political. I did it without thinking. I did it because the music was annoying me.

When you work with your hands, thoughts flow around a theme. I had been kicking around Sam's suspicion about journalists, but now I was intrigued by my sudden antipathy toward music. So the first thing I went for back in my apartment tonight was the old Bach trumpet. It felt good in my hands—a piece of metal with familiar contours and heft. I tried the finger action, like saying "hello," and gave the valves a few flicks to loosen the lube, and brought the horn to my lips and blew. I played a phrase, I think almost as if I had never been away, but it left me unmoved. How could I have lost my feel for music? Rending. This is more than between the ears. I remember how to play, but what I hear is memorized noise. Like coming from the dentist's office and trying to savor dessert before the Novocain wears off.

I pulled the mouthpiece and cleaned everything as if I had just played a set. I rubbed the Bach with a cloth for a long time and nestled it into the liner of the case. I've gotten a lot of pleasure out of that thing. Sometimes, when I was losing my kids, it was the last stop sign before self-destruct. Tonight I put it away probably for the last time.

So another avenue cut off. Make that two, because when I booted up the computer there was no shortcut to my address book on the desktop. No program, in fact. My address book left town without leaving a forwarding address. Poof! The social-life police have been in here again. But the joke is on Mr. Freeze or Goldilocks or whoever it was, because I haven't used my address book since Pre-cambrian times.

Just to see what else was missing, I opened CompuServe, and to my surprise the modem came out with, "You have mail!" But it was from Mailer-Daemon. Good old MD. Just what the doctor ordered — a bounced e-mail. Because that's what you get when you send something to an invalid address, Mailer-Daemon's return-to-sender with a geeky explanation:

USER UNKNOWN . . . THE FOLLOWING
ADDRESSES HAD PERMANENT FATAL ERRORS . . .

I've never heard of e-mail being returned to the wrong computer before. It should have gone back like a nickel on a string to the computer it was originally sent from. How could that be mine? The member name on the address that it bounced from was "JAbberjocky." But there's no way I can check it out at that end, since the address is no longer in service. Weird. Not to mention the strange, strange message:

Charlotte—
I'm coming back. The terrarium.

Definitely not an e-mail I sent. Then again, the main thing that happened at The Ski Shop today — the thing I've been building up to write about — could have something to do with it. Could. I've got to figure this out.

It started after Sam hit the trails, and after I switched the radio mindlessly from King Oliver to political commentary about the 2000 elections. The dancelike extensions of scraping skis lulled me against the stultifying drone of lame-duck Clinton issuing pardons like the Holy

Father, and Bush Junior resurrecting his father's cabinet, and Hillary trailing silverware out of the White House, and Gore remembering boyhood lessons that never happened. I dribbled wax along a ski, and the smells rose in currents of paraffin and methane and something that just smells hot and dry. Repetitive work is like a dream. You review the past, reorder the present, rehearse the future. *"What is a tunnel for, Mr. Carmichael?* Sam thought I was repressing something about the bus. *"What is a tunnel for . . . ?"*

The sweet smell of melting wax began to transmogrify into something intimate, until I realized with a jolt that it was the sickly odor of burning flesh. I tossed the wax aside, set the torch down, took my time retrieving the scraper. But the tissue-thin curls of wax that lifted off the ski with the first strokes reconnected and completed the memory: I remembered the stains rising out of the burning bus. At the time, it had seemed just part of the shifting fire and smoke, that nightmare palette coming out of a crucible death, but now it returned so vividly that I was shocked. Distinct stains refracting fire moved in line with the hole in the air. *"What is a tunnel . . ."* It is one thing to imagine dispossession, another to believe you have actually seen soul transfer. The physical evidence was right there all the time. I closed my eyes and the radio blared and the silent storm roared, and in my deaf and deafening universe, I recognized that an obsession had come home to roost.

I don't know how long I stood there. In fact, I'm beginning to suspect that I went somewhere, did something. For certain, yesterday—starting at around two thirty—I lost more than two hours. I remember staring at the windows like they were silent films, unreeling with streaks and pops as snow came down, each snowflake thin and translucent, trying to lie about those stains in the air. Here's the obvious choice: Either I went away and came back, or I stood there for the entire two hours. Because that's where I was at just before five when a blast of cold air washed over me from the open door.

Sam came in, pulling off his gloves. He looked around as if to detect who I might be speaking to, poised as I was in the middle of the floor.

"I was just singing," I said.

With *All Things Considered* for accompaniment blaring from the radio, it seemed unlikely, but Sam was too excited to question it.

"You have to catch this, Bowie. The trails are rocket ice swirling with white sawdust. Grab your skies before it gets impassable. I'll close up the shop."

It was a convenient time-out. I needed time to think. Time to forget. Time to decide what I wanted Sam to know. There still isn't an ounce of trust in me, and I wish I could blame that on the accident, but all my flaws can't be attributed to a baptismal death in a waterfall. I was drowning long before November tenth.

Still, it was a mistake to leave the shop on skis. It was almost dark. The woods were closing ranks, massing with shadows on either side of the white trail. I used to love this time of day—the twilight changing of the guard. Down go the creatures of the day to their burrows and hollows; out come nefarious hunters on wings or retracted claws. Now I feel like I'm in the loop.

Sam's return tracks smoothed away under my snowplow as gravity drew me into the first series of drops. Up and down I went, attacking whenever the trail squandered momentum, gliding when it dropped into purple gloom and, at last, twenty minutes later, into the noir realm of hunters and prey at the bottom of the run.

Despite a failing sky, the cold air braced and quickened my vision. There are narrows where you have to switch from skating to stride, and there are uncertain sweeps where ice hides under snow. Sam's tracks were already blown over, except that now and then I caught a rut. The fact that they were covered at all was odd. Normally you hear the wind rushing like a freight train above you, and you might occasionally be pelted with twigs or a cornice of snow that lifts off a branch, but rarely does it blow up a winding trail like that.

Rocket ice and white sawdust, Sam called it. When it swirls like that, you'll swear the momentary shapes that form and vanish are more than just snow. A bear rears up, a wolf, a snow queen in flowing veils. The first time I saw such wonders was with my sister when we were twelve or so, standing in a winter field on some farm—an uncle's, I think—while the wind broomed up one colossus after another: djinns and giants, witches and angels, a writhing dragon and a towering castle of light. I was excited, but Laura thought I was trying to scare her.

"Did you see that?"
"What? It's just the wind."
"No, no, it was a white knight on a white horse!"
"Shut up, Bow."
"It was clear as a bell."
"Shut up. Everyone knows you're crazy."

This evening I remembered that conversation—clear as a bell. Maybe she was right. Hallucinations are inevitable in my life. The whole waterfall thing is preprogrammed in my head. Maybe I died on November tenth and joined my snow phantoms, and everything that's happened since is the hallucination. Maybe I died tonight. Or maybe these bizarre things are real, and they happen to me only because I'm susceptible. Don Quixote Bowie. Ready the net, Weibens.

"Laura?" I called at the bottom of the south trails, just to hear my voice.

The wind shrieked, and whatever the state of my imagination at that moment, I was certain I wasn't alone. Something was bounding silently through breaks and tunnels in the underbrush, keeping pace. Dense silhouettes hemmed and overhung my little white highway, and I began to step-stride and double-pole until I was in a full sprint, totally spooked. It was coming again—the nerve-shattering gateway—and I had all but invited it this time. No mirror, no floating, no rapture with speed; I was peeping through the hole in the sky like it was a knothole in a ballpark fence. And the terrible thing—the really terrible thing—was that a part of me—a very small but undeniable part of me—*liked* what was coming.

Pulse rising, muscles heating up, air burning through me like rocket fuel—I trained for this. I've been trained through a million years of flight and mortal combat that has come down to a test of strength and endurance on skis. But last night was the real thing. Except that what was stirring the underbrush alongside me wasn't a competing evolution. Men sense that: the identity of the enemy. I sensed what it wasn't. It wasn't natural.

I could hear it snapping twigs in the brittle cold, and breaking away snowy mantles, and once, a branch whistled along its flank. So it traveled on limbs. It had weight and form. But nothing natural in central Minnesota stalks man.

I kept to the center of the trail, certain it was the perverse stag crashing next to me. If you've ever encountered a buck during the rut, hissing and holding its ground, you know the difference between Bambi and a full-grown animal driven by a single purpose. This one wouldn't need a mating season. I was convinced he would suddenly appear in front of me, rack lowered, cloven hooves stamping, and I would have no place to go.

But it wasn't a deer that knocked me to the trail. No explanation makes sense. An animal would have to be maddened, or feel threatened, and even then it would take me down from the legs instead of hitting me on the back of the head and neck. If something dropped or fell out of a tree, how big would it have to be in order to stun me? There was a broken branch lying not far away, I learned later. I suppose it could have snapped off and caught my skull just behind the center of gravity, and then the momentum of my skis could explain how I got several yards away. But that's not very convincing either.

What I remember is the faint hum growing to a roar. I knew it was coming toward me, knew I was lying down on the trail, but my mind was detached from my body. A long way away my fingers and toes signaled cruel pinches, but inside my head I was warm and unconcerned. It was the vibration that finally got through. All that snow to tamp it down, and yet I registered the tingle in my bones and the fizz in my blood. That's because I was *under* the snow. I opened my eyes and felt the displacement on my lids. It must have been a light coating, because now the headlamp on the groomer penetrated, dim but brightening. And the smell of the machine, rank and unctuous. If the ribbed tracks missed me, the tightly knit harrow teeth on the drag behind them would not. They would rake through my flesh as easily as through snow. I went to five alarms. I tried to roll. But now, in the very act of breaking through the light powder that shrouded me, I discovered why I could not roll free. My crossed skis caught the trail and locked.

Sam says he never saw that. He thinks he just found me lying on my side, curled up like I was taking a nap. He came along on the snowmobile, having had second thoughts about recommending I go out in the gathering storm. And the reason he swerved at the last second and missed me was because another skier or—and he's not sure about this—maybe a snowshoer was coming out of the woods.

Right.

I didn't hear this explanation until we were back in the cabin; but Sam stayed on the snowmobile while I retrieved my poles, and I would have noticed another person's tracks, if there had been another person. And there was no car excepting ours in the parking lot. I didn't argue with him. Sam would have pointed out that trail users come in all the time from adjacent lake areas.

"Lucky you didn't get frostbite," he said to me when we were slurping soup heated in his microwave.

"You're talking to Waterfall Man," I said. "I'm way beyond frostbite."

When Sam smiles, his lips don't change, but the muscles in his jaw lengthen. "My mother used to say we are reborn with each sunrise," he said. "She thought everything that was an asset was cumulative. The liabilities are part of yesterday. Stay positive, Bowie."

"Well, I'm positive if it wasn't for your quick reflexes, I'd have the dead-at-sunset part down pat, anyway."

"It's going to get better."

"Think so? I want you to give me a straight-up, one-sentence, best guess about what's going on with me, Sam. No fluff, okay?"

He looked me straight in the eyes and said softly: "You think you're possessed by someone who died on that bus."

Four hours earlier, two of which remain completely lost to my memory, I had again confronted the nagging conclusion that I am time-sharing my body, and emphatically rejected it. But from the moment Sam heard my incomplete story on the trip home from the Mayo Clinic six nights ago, it has been perfectly obvious to him.

"You don't think I might have really died, and then . . . then when they brought my body back, my soul didn't come with it? That in some way a new soul came into me—hard-wired by my brain, my memories, and all that—but not the same soul?"

"If man has a soul apart from his brain, then I think you're still running on original equipment."

"I wish I could believe that. Metaphysical, Sam. Remember? You said when my memories come back, maybe it will open up a can of metaphysical worms."

"Have they come back?"

"No."

"You may be lost, but I see the same Bowie I've always seen. You said a minute ago that maybe your soul didn't come back with your body. You said that maybe a new soul had replaced it. Replaced it? Are you sure that's the right term? You're still here. Don't you mean 'joined' it?"

And that's the gist of what we said to each other a few hours ago. He thinks I'm schizophrenic, I guess. I didn't tell him about the fugues and how someone is trying to isolate me, or how the slightest retreat from hard reality—a mirror, a dream, a blurring of vision—can trigger a dismantling of all my reference points, or that I believe this will be the death of my soul or, if that's not possible, at least its relinquishing of my body. That would have fit glove-tight with his inference. Because I think he's right—I'm a multiple now. Only it's not a clinical split into two or more personalities. It's two or more souls warring for my mind and my body, and one of them came back to my apartment this afternoon and deleted my address book and my e-mail. And it sent that message: *Charlotte—I'm coming back. The terrarium.* That's what happened to those two hours. How's that for a hypothesis?

January 14, 7:10 P.M.

When I awoke this morning to a dawn as gray as the dream I had just left, I knew I didn't want to face the Sunday crowd at The Ski Shop. All my senses were and are pathologically acute. It's like I'm tuned to the wrong station, picking up subtle distortions and faint whirring sounds from the next room. Things drift into anomalies. Dry things start to glisten; anchored things levitate slightly and I have to concentrate to make them behave. I can see them as they are, but I also see them losing their physical properties. Shades of acid drops I have known.

Like the color. I can't shake the conviction that I actually saw a new color. This has escaped from one of my dreams. But, dammit, daylight is my time. When my eyes open, the nineteen pairs of eyes in a bus on the dark side should close. Those are the rules: We meet halfway, in dreams, in moments of diminished concentration, in things that fool the eye—like mirrors.

I still have free will, and they need my cooperation. If they force me, they run the risk of ruining their vessel of return. So they keep on encroaching, hoping I'll accept one or more of them as part of my consciousness, or need them to find my way back, or that somehow I'll lower the resistance that blocks them from becoming part of me.

What happens if one of them does get through? Is it like a single sperm, launching a new life and shutting me off to the rest? I think they've been coming at me one at a time so far. How else could I see coherent visions? But now one of them has another cute trick.

It happened late this morning, when I put in my right contact and the saline solution stung more than usual. I batted my lashes like a roaring twenties flapper, but the burn worsened. *Reversed,* I thought, and took the lens out. Letting tears dilute the saline in my right eye for a moment, I fished the left lens onto my fingertip to gauge the curvature and started to dock it over the left eye. But this time the sting caused me to pull my finger back before the transfer was complete. Which was a good thing, because while my right eye felt like I'd clamped a seashell over it, the left was seeing only rainbows.

Only. Ten seconds later both eyes were screaming.

My squint into the bathroom mirror caught shadows rushing forward behind my reflection. Grabbing a hand towel, I stumbled to the kitchen to splash water in my face. For several minutes I hung in the sink, flooding one eye, twisting to flood the other. I soaked the towel in cold water and held it against my eyes. Nothing worked except keeping them both closed. And that was the insidious idea, wasn't it? To make me keep my eyes closed. Lying on the floor of the living room, my heart pounding and a compress over my right eye, I fought the onset.

Someone had sabotaged my contact lens solution with something that dilates. Just another attempt to beat me down psychologically until I'm a rudderless ghost ship waiting to be boarded by one of them. But they couldn't do it at Mayo, and I wasn't going to just surrender like some paralyzed host waiting for the maggots to feed. I still had abstractions. I still had words. *I'm on the living room floor, the floor, the floor . . . nice beige carpet. Grape-juice stain under the couch. They can't flood me with hallucinations while I'm squinting at a grape-juice stain. But, oh, it smarts! Have to close the left eye, too. Just for a few seconds. I can always bring the houselights up. . . .*

Against the burning distortion I closed my uncovered eye, and for a few moments nothing happened. The burning may even have helped distract me from inner turmoil. But then the great firewall of sanity began to crumble, and that breathtaking gulf I dread yawned through.

Curtain up!

I blinked furiously at the ceiling with my partially functioning left eye, but it was like firing the shutter of a Nikon at the sun. One quick glimpse before the blur, and the hot, salty tears drove their needles home. I remembered the layers of dreaming in the bathtub, and how easily I was deceived into thinking I had returned to reality, as if for every person there is a dream they can't escape. I squeezed my eyelids shut again.

Have to let them get on with the gulf . . . soon as it gets terrifying, I'll stop it.

But it didn't get terrifying. The ragged curtain dissolved in a vast spiral of sand, winding, winding. It crested and dove onto a long, flat plain, and when it was just twinkling dust, I saw a dead city.

I can force my left eye open anytime. . . .

Just a city. Dead. Worn and uniformly gray and buried to the shoulders of mute skyscrapers that rose forlornly above a finely sifted white ash. The white ash fanned out from oblong vents on the exposed faces of a central obelisk. Judging by the height and the probable limits of its base, the obelisk's foundation must have been hundreds of feet into the ash. There were weathered runes above the vent on one of the sides angled away from me, unreadable at that distance.

But the dominant feature of all that survived in the city was so expansive that it came upon me only by degrees as my eyes swept the horizon. A decapitated colossus ringed the outer limits. Its vast wings, which must have been almost entirely buried, were spread like ramparts. Enough of these stood above the surface to show the membraned construction arcing into finials at intervals of hundreds of yards. The resemblance to a bat's ligatures was unmistakable.

But there was less of Gotham City and more of M. C. Escher's architectural impossibilities in the narrow staircases that rose from the ash to stupendous heights, even above the skyscrapers. I did not understand them. There were no platforms, no loose ends to show where some titanic structure had collapsed, leaving its ascents dangling in space. In fact, by any plausible engineering, the steps should not have been able to remain there at all. But they were stark and framed against the oily agglomerate that took the place of a sky.

... still here, I am still here.... Fingers flexing lightly on the carpet of my apartment. *To see or not to see; that is the question. Should I make the painful attempt to open my eyes now? Not yet ...*

So where was the light coming from? I looked for suns in the slowly bubbling sky over the dead city, but it was just steel-wool gray—scratchy like that—as if to fly in that sky would tear birds to shreds. And the gray stone and fine white ash were inert. There were no shadows anywhere. Light was simply present.

The view changed, but not because I moved. I couldn't move. The city moved. It enveloped me. I could smell its heat and the kind of rot you get only from desert tombs or museums. Mummy rot. Back in the apartment, my left eyelid flickered.

This is a test.

Never mind that the eyelid was drying and flaking away, exposing my eyeball and the red, raw orbital tissue. That was just a trick to make me think it was already open. Because how could I watch that happen to me unless it was an illusion?

I am in control.

Deeper into the city now. Clearly the inner linings of the oblong vents on the obelisk were agitated. And there was something kinetic in their color, like metal that has cooled just below molten. The fine white ash was still coming out, as it must have for numberless ages, imperceptibly building the causeways that fanned through the city. I did not want to stay near the vents. And as if this aversion endowed me with instant choice, I was suddenly moving freely, walking, then running. But I couldn't escape the atmosphere itself, and the particulates in the air crawled over my skin—"burrowed" might be a better word. I was opposite the facing of the obelisk with the weathered writing now, close enough to see that the runes were actually letters in the Arabic alphabet that read:

CREMATORIUM

And the fine white ash continued to rain down as the business of its ghastly bowels unfolded.

That's my limit for grotesquerie, thank you. I recognize the man behind the curtain beckoning me offstage.

It was me, lying on a beige carpet. Time to pull the trigger. Time to open the baby blues. And if I didn't do it right away, it was only because the history of this dead place was so utterly fascinating—as if the inhabitants of the city were feeding themselves to a mass killing machine. It wasn't like I tried to open my left eye and couldn't. (*That's ridiculous! I can open it anytime.*) I hadn't actually been threatened yet. There was nothing personal in the annihilation fantasy. Not a thing.

And that was the ushering misjudgment, the little complicity that put me there in the vision—really there—full senses five.

Something more than five senses, a pressoreceptive reflex, sharpened inside my body. The hot smell parched my lungs, and the dust caked around my heart, impeding my blood just when demand was critical. I slowed to a walk, then a stagger. Ahead of me loomed the embracing wings of the decapitated colossus.

Time to open . . .

It didn't look like a colossus anymore. It looked like the Great Wall of China, stretching for miles in either direction, crescents peaking uniformly in huge, burnished finials. The membrane could have been brazed, except that iridescence shimmered corrosively in its folds. It hung like a bronze drape, disappearing into immeasurable depths of ash or substructures or something grimmer than I wanted to know.

Open your eyes, Bowie!

I opened my eyes. I tried to open my eyes. A formerly voluntary response, now unresponsive. I beat my fists on a beige carpet, but what I felt against my knuckles was the brass membrane of that thing that ringed the city. And my knocking made it start to hum. Like a perfect bell that catches the slightest breeze, it rushed my insignificant reverberations away as evenly as ripples in a pond. But the flaws I introduced into the silence of ages leaped from section to section of the great rampart and back again, wave crashing into wave.

I resonated to the core with it. The macabre carillon was wiping out my senses. I knew that my identity was fracturing, that if this was literal, there would be no more me, but something irresistible was reassuring me it would be all right. What was this place? The world has no memory of such a city, but it lies at the coordinates of an arid infinity and a hopeless eternity for anyone who thinks they are an entity. There are no individuals in the universe.

OPEN YOUR EYES!

I tried. Couldn't. Nothing was feeding my senses. No pressure against my back, no air in my lungs, no ambient temperature against my skin. Communications were down but consciousness remained. The only thing I could do was invent my own reality. Time for improv.

White and textured . . . white and textured . . .

I willed this from memory, and the abstraction of my living room ceiling slipped in and out of its geometry before locking into a rectangle. Much better than an abrasive sky. I went for the beige next—went for the carpet that no longer existed at the tips of my fingers.

Warm friction . . . warm friction . . .

Then the compress on my eye.

Moist, cool . . .

But each pale memory I summoned canceled the last. They wouldn't come together.

A cold rage conceded the fact of my being in a mundane room in a mundane world but placed me again in the shadow of that decapitated winged colossus. If my individuality was restored, so was the tyranny of my senses. The city was awakening to the thunder I had instigated. Shrieks and groans echoed through the vents of the great obelisk. I saw arms and faces breaking through the surface of the ash. And even the narrow staircases that leaned impossibly into the lightless sky swayed—except that they weren't steps . . . they were segments, the kind of organic appendages that grow on arthropods. A real scene-stealer was lying under the fine white ash. I could hardly wait. In fact, I wasn't going to have to wait. Because the architecture of the city was draining away with the ash, and I was sinking into the whole shattering maelstrom.

It was the appendages that riveted my attention. I did not like the configuration that was emerging: a bony mantle that could have been a brow ridge with twin hollows beneath it. To my horror, I had found the missing head of the colossus.

Or rather, it had found me. Because it seemed to be moving. The scale of it diminished me, and the resemblance to something avian was dispelled as distinctly reptilian features emerged. Like sand rushing to fill the void in the bottom of an hourglass, the ash suddenly vanished into the maw of serrated jaws that were opening to welcome my fall.

There would be no act of imagination to rescue me this time. This was a rush that would storm all self-awareness. And as if that overpowering free fall weren't enough, the cold katabatic wind of the universe ganged up behind me for a final push.

And that is when the phone in my apartment rang.

It rang and rang and rang. I heard it. I felt it. With each repetition my pulse cadenced stronger. I began to feel the carpet and the compress. Then my left eyelid nudged open and a blessed burning splinter of textured white pierced through. The answering machine announced its regrets in my voice: "Sorry I'm not here at the moment. . . ."

But, oh, I was, I was.

My eyes are almost back to normal now. I've been sitting here all day, settling my nerves, thinking, staring out the window. The snowman is out there, staring at me, looking exactly like it did before. Like a Frankenstein's monster or a golem that comes together in parts. Victor Frankenstein's mistake was burned. A golem was given life with a magical formula written down and placed in its mouth, and it was deanimated by removing the paper. What will it take to undo my nemesis? I'm tempted to run him over with the car, or make him into snowballs and hurl them up the street. I should knock him down and then watch until the father-son or whoever built him comes to resurrect him. Then I can just feel stupid and ashamed, instead of haunted and desperate.

The seal on the free sample bottle of Neo-Synephrine that I never used has been broken in the medicine cabinet. I called Pearle Vision Center, and the optometrist told me that it could cause blindness if it got in my eyes. So that's what he/she/it used to spike my contact lens fluid.

Whoever triggered the answering machine didn't leave a message. In all probability they saved my life, if not my soul. I can't get it out of my head that it might have been Danny or Jessica. Not that that's likely. Of course it's not *likely. But it's Sunday,* I thought. *They're probably home.*

This afternoon, when I began to feel grounded again, I tried to call. If Dolores had answered, I would have hung up, because whenever we talk we turn into subhumans with opposable tongues. But I just felt this tremendous imperative singing in my head, like the kids were trying to get hold of me, and I figured there was a pretty good chance one of them would answer on a Sunday. Nobody answered. The phone number is no longer in service.

She can't do that. Dolores cannot move and not tell

me. So say the courts. I don't think she's even allowed to change her phone number without telling me. They're supposed to be living south of the Twin Cities in Burnsville. The fact that I haven't heard from them after all this publicity must mean something bad. What if she's told them I'm dead or suffered brain damage? Or maybe they *have* been trying to get hold of me: *Daddy, Mommy made us move....*

I looked for them the only place I could—the Internet—and it didn't take long to find a new address. Their theater group has a roster page on its Web site. But I read all the cast notes and the production dates and the details of rehearsals and travel and sweatshirt orders and photos, and I realized how disconnected I am from their lives. How can I just call in and be reinstated into the mystery of a family? And if I do make contact, how can I hang up the phone again? I can't say hello because I can't say good-bye. So I didn't call, but I wrote down the phone number and put it in my wallet. As if I could forget.

I wish I'd gone to Sheshebans. Even the Sunday skiers with their pets and their whiny kids would have been better than sitting here alone, enabling the isolation. Old habits are clashing with new needs in my life. I'm living out of cans and bottles now. Dishwashing is down to a fork and a spoon.

So, I was still sitting in front of the computer late this afternoon, just me, myself and I, when it dawned on me that I could find out about the bus. Lots of articles about a fiery bus crash with so many deaths. When I typed in, *Minnesota +nineteen dead,* the search engine brought up over eight thousand sites with information about the accident. It was a chartered bus coming back from an outing at Mille Lacs. There was a newlywed couple among the casualties, and a kid who was recovering from

Hodgkin's lymphoma, and four sisters visiting from Sweden, and a man who had survived an earthquake in Latin America last year. They were all part of the same church outing. Timothy Lutheran. The pastor was also on the trip; also one of the dead. The three who survived were sitting in the back on the side away from the driver. One is a lawyer who is filing a class-action suit against the bus company and the church. Another said the bus driver was yelling at them to hang on after he hit the brakes and they began to slide.

I didn't expect to feel the way I do about all this. It's overwhelming. So many lives, so much detail. This proves Weibens is wrong about my carrying guilt around because of the bus. The reason the personalization of the crash hit me so hard was because I'd never even thought about it before.

I was blinking back tears by the time I pulled up the picture. It isn't a very good shot, but it is in color, and it shows them standing alongside the yellow bus at Mille Lacs. You can't tell a lot from their faces. There are the Swedish girls, I think, holding on to American souvenirs and wearing Minnesota Gopher knit caps; and the balding man in the black overcoat next to the uniformed driver is probably Timothy Lutheran's late Pastor Evans. There are half a dozen boys, and two of them look frail enough to be the lymphoma patient. I guess the newlyweds are the beaming couple cheek-to-cheek in the back row. I can't match any of the others to the stories, except one. And that's not really because of the story. It's because of a detail that I've seen before. A red tartan scarf. Baby Face had one just like it.

January 15

Whatever was, is, and shall be, is my enemy. If it has cells, if it needs light or air or water, it loses control when I'm near. I am profoundly wrong for this world. I will never be able to hide in a crowd.

That's why I have to cut off all communication. I need a safe place away from the city, away from nature too—at least populated nature. Something I can control. Something that's pure ice and snow. There are such places. I can fish and hunt. If I go somewhere with too much fauna and flora, they might be dangerous to me. And I don't think I can grow anything that won't corrupt. Where will I be safe? Stone is safe. Ice is safe. Dead things—wood, dried grasses, animal skins—and man-made composites are safe.

How could God do this to me? Jesus Christ, I pray to you. If you are there, intercede. God of hosts, like hell! I'm a host, and who is the god for me? A hole in the air? That's my god. The god of nothingness.

January 15, 9:09 P.M.

I didn't write that, I didn't write that, I didn't write that. The entire previous entry—I did not write that. I've been up in Sheshebans all day; how could I write it? The whole time I was up there is continuous in my memory: Sam and the shop, hot-waxing, each of us getting in a long run on skis. When could I have left? I'm going to have to start checking the odometer on my car.

I should be more upset by the fact that my apartment has been trashed, but it's what's happening inside my head that's the real threat. As if I really wrote that—and I admit it sounds like me—making up my mind to leave everything and go into exile, where they can pick me off.

The tone of the violence in my trashed apartment is a thing apart. The medicine they gave me at Mayo was in the basket. My CDs are scattered around, some of them thrown away. Same with my books. And a Bible is open on the dinette table with page after page torn out.

I guess they were looking for one in particular—page rage. Because it's hanging there on the wall, spiked with the ice pick from the kitchen drawer. And there are a bunch of arrows drawn in red Magic Marker over the wallboard pointing at three of the verses. Ecclesiastes 3:19–21:

19 For what happens to the sons of men also happens to animals: as one dies, so dies the other. Surely, they all have one breath; man has no advantage over animals, for all is vanity.
20 All go to one place: all are from the dust, and all return to dust.
21 Who knows the spirit of the sons of men, which goes upward, and the spirit of the animal, which descends?

On the wall above the page, printed in gothic letters, were the words: *THE LIES OF SOLOMON*.

To the left of it, above an empty rectangle drawn the same size of the page, was written: *The Book of Bowie*.

What is that supposed to mean?

I've been missing something all along here. Something with religious or theological significance. It goes beyond what I had supposed: that things like my nightmares of candles in a church, or my hallucinogenic visits from the minister in Mayo Clinic, were just subconscious associations I made with the fact that the bus was on a church outing. But this outburst on my wall is disturbingly real and specific and intense. Suddenly I've got both feet in the cosmos instead of just one. I don't like this.

The worst thing about the apartment damage is that Jessica's and Danny's theater pictures from the end tables are all smashed. Jessica was staring up at me out of the basket, still looking surprised, wearing her rainbow purple from the play—the color of suffering.

I lifted out the frames and picked away the broken glass. Danny is biting his lip as he sits in the wagon. His shirt is torn—the picture is torn where it shows his shirt.

My fingers are on fire from brushing away splinters of glass, but I couldn't fix the photos.

I put them in the filing cabinet. I wrapped them in toilet paper and then towels and nested them carefully in the bottom and locked it. Then I flushed the filing cabinet key down the toilet. I won't be able to get to my precious pictures anymore, but neither will anything that takes control of my body.

I'm open to anything now: stakes through the heart, voodoo, exorcisms. I'm going to take it to them. These bastards have to be dug up and dealt with.

January 16, late

Just an average day of corpse hunting. Three for nineteen. No stakes, no voodoo, no exorcisms.

I was down to seven names for Baby Face off the Internet when I started out for TLC—Timothy Lutheran Church—in East Tristan this morning. And the first thing I realized when I got to town was that my pilgrimage to their grave sites was not unique. The clerk at the Conoco station rattled off directions like a tour guide. I guess with nineteen suddenly dead in one church, the congregation has seen it all, from the media to ghouls.

Timothy Lutheran has a redbrick façade and aluminum siding. Out front, the marquee glass is cracked, and there was frost built up inside this morning. This is Tuesday, and the door was locked. The parking lot was plowed around a lone car sitting under a smooth carapace of snow that could have been there all winter. I think it may have belonged to Pastor Evans. I parked next to it and walked the block north to the churchyard.

No crypts, no mausoleums, just a lot of evergreens

around the perimeter, and a lot of tombstones in the first two-thirds of what is roughly an acre of land. They picked a bad site. The subsoil is obviously moving, because the older tombstones are cracked and uneven. You get the impression that some of the dead aren't resting in peace.

I can vouch for that.

I went in through the iron gate and trudged along foot-deep snow where it wound around headstones. It wasn't wide enough for a hearse. I don't know what they do for funerals. They must have had a tough time carrying coffins all the way back to the available plots in November. Nine new markers are clustered there, so they dug at least that many graves through the frost. I imagine the Swedish sisters were flown home, and of course the charter bus driver probably wasn't from the church, and some others may have been returned to family plots elsewhere or been cremated—which, given the way they perished, is redundant.

The nine new markers were hemmed in by granite crosses and stone angels, as if the older dead have grown taller. I was aware of these peripherally as I moved down the row. Halfway through reading the inscriptions, I felt the animation. One of the looming presences had changed. I spun around, and there was the black overcoat and homburg exactly like the one on the Internet. The man wearing them didn't have to remove his hat for me to know he was balding.

"Pastor Evans—yes," he said, smiling faintly at my shock. "You must have seen that picture and read the article from the *East Tristan Weekly*. A football team is the maximum number of names their stringer can keep straight. Unfortunately, the bus was about eight over his limit. So you can't expect an accurate obituary." He held out his hands and turned them, as if I were doubting Thomas confronting a risen Christ.

I was looking for someone, I mumbled, and, trying to correct the impression that my social intercourse took place in a cemetery, I foundered into sentence fragments about the red scarf.

"You're looking for Alex. That's his headstone right there." He pointed.

Alex Franke
1970–2000

"Thirty years old," I murmured in surprise.

"Twenty-nine. His last name is pronounced Frank-ee."

I stared at the tombstone, pretending reverence.

"You need not feel awkward coming here," Pastor Evans said. "I'm sure they appreciate visitors. It must be horribly dull being dead. Of course, they would choose life if they could be in your shoes." He waved at the graves. "These stones are like highway markers, meant to be read, meant to guide the footsteps of whoever passes by. I want to thank you for coming. You should always feel safe and welcome here. On behalf of the nine"—he gestured pacifically—"I thank you and invite you back. It's a good place to come when you feel assailed."

"I don't feel assailed."

"No?"

"No."

He was accustomed to reading people's anxiety, that was all. My mere being there spoke of some distress. I thanked him and said good-bye. He watched me all the way back to the gate.

It was simple to check the phone book and drive to the blue Cape Cod where Franke had lived, but it was hard to get out of the car and walk to the porch. What if I was wrong about seeing him in my apartment? Did I really want to lay this on some grieving family that had never laid eyes on me? And what was I going to say, "Hi, I'm an insurance investigator"? Telling the truth was out of the question. My finger was on the doorbell before it occurred to me that Franke might not have had a family, that the house had been sold or rented or—

"Yes?"

She held the door almost shyly, so that it shielded part of her face, but the part I saw could have been Alex Franke's sister. There were the same clear eyes and delicate skin. But the left hand that pressed against the panel still wore a wedding ring, and in answer to my first question she confirmed that she was Alex's widow. I muttered who I was, and she immediately opened the door for me to enter. I followed her to a living room, already captivated by her frail neck and broad shoulders.

"It's really nice of you to come, Mr. Carmichael. Reverend Kendall led a prayer for you the Sunday after the accident, and then we heard you came out of your coma—"

"Reverend Kendall? I thought your minister's name was Evans."

"Please . . . sit down. Pastor Evans was killed in the accident."

Her clear gaze never wavered.

She made small talk about how Reverend Kendall had stepped in on an interim basis and how the search committee was interviewing new candidates for minister, but my emotions were whirling around that pleasant man wearing a black coat and homburg in the churchyard. No question anymore. None at all. I am not insane. I may be dead, or partially dead, but I am not insane. The universe is insane.

Whatever qualms I had about manipulating her went cold, then. When you can't tell the living from the dead, deception is merely trendy.

"Stop me if I'm out of line, but it occurs to me that maybe the families of the victims need some closure that I can provide," I said.

"You're not out of line, Mr. Carmichael—"

"Michael."

She smiled. "Rebecca."

"I know there were three survivors, and I'm sure they must have told you something, but they can't know much about what was happening with the others—"

"You . . . actually saw?"

I don't need to detail what I said next. My mouth opened and it was like flies came pouring out: "I doubt if anyone suffered . . . those who got out, got out and lived . . . the others were unconscious . . . couldn't have survived the crash . . . I saw figures . . . no one was moving . . . the fire was terrible, but I think it was all over before then."

She nodded slowly, with a horrible kind of dignity, and all the while my gaze skittered around the room until a photo easel on the coffee table arrested it. For just a moment I saw the man in the frame without registering the fact that Baby Face was staring back at me. I saw only a sailor, dark blue neckerchief lying smartly across his shoulders. This was the Alex Franke I was burying, and I could almost feel his rage.

"If I can do anything . . ." I offered. Do? Maybe she could use a little séance. I cleared my throat dryly. "Is that him in the picture?"

She knew which one without turning around. "Yes. His navy photo."

I wanted to probe, bombard her with questions, search her house the way her husband had searched mine. But what I said was, "Really, if there's anything I can do, I've got a little money—"

I reached out and covered her cold fingers. She pursed her lips. Even sympathy had become unbearable to her. She pulled her hand away and babbled about the support group of surviving family members and how they had kept close for a while but now were struggling privately to come to terms. They had sometimes met at the church with Reverend Kendall, and they still talked on the phone, but it was becoming painful to see one another. She mentioned half a dozen names that barely penetrated my hearing. And then she said: "Maybe it's a good thing we're letting go of each other. Maybe Charlotte is right. We have to move on as individuals."

"Charlotte?"

"Charlotte Arnasen. One of the widows. Her husband, Jerry, was on the bus. She threw everything out, or gave it away, and now she's sold her house and moved to Mankato."

"And her e-mail, that would be . . . JAbberjocky?"

"You know her?"

Only a cynic would have made such a wild guess, but it was correct. JAbberjocky. JA. Jerry Arnasen. God knows what details of his life are encrypted in that e-mail address. I don't want to know, don't want to care about him, but that's why the e-mail to Charlotte bounced. Because she had thrown everything out, including his e-mail account. *Permanent fatal error,* Mailer-Daemon had said about his address. Am I supposed to believe *he* sent the e-mail from my computer? *Daemon* mail, for a fact.

"No, not personally," I said about knowing her. "I'd rather not explain, if you don't mind. I think I should go now."

She smoothed my abruptness by offering her hand as we stood, and we went through the name exchange again, only this time it was "Bowie" and "Beckie." I squeezed her cold fingers and avoided eye contact until I was on the porch steps.

"Don't hesitate to ask for anything," I repeated.

Of course, she has no idea how to contact me. Which is good. Because why would she want to contact me?

I drove straight back to the church and parked next to the snow-covered car. I plodded north to the cemetery, through the iron gate, looking carefully at the plots this time. The dead were in an uproar at my return. I will infer this from the blowing and churning that suddenly erupted. There are five other headstones polished like the nine in the last row. Three of them list 2000 as a terminal date. Two of these are situated in family plots. The third is almost in the middle of the churchyard on a knoll that looks like it has been set aside. And there in gray granite is the inscription:

Jacob Martin Evans
Beloved Shepherd

"Evans?" I shouted, and the word left my mouth in a steamy shred, like something grave-spun. I kept turning, shouting. I was shivering, or trembling. I shouted for him to show himself.

"Assailed?" I yelled. "You said to come here when I felt assailed—well, I feel assailed!"

I ranted and raved, but he didn't show. I looked for his

tracks, separate from mine, but the swirling snow had already beveled everything together.

I kicked his tombstone. He wasn't using it. *"... they would choose life if they could be in your shoes,"* he had said about the dead. *"Choose life ... beats death,"* the Cheshire-cat minister who woke me every night from the sedatives at Mayo had said. His face had kept sliding off, and I never got to see his features. Until today.

I went back to the parking lot and, to vent my frustration, pawed the words "not dead" in the dune of snow that covered the car. For all I knew, it wasn't his car, but I needed a target for retaliation. There were no tracks, no breaches around that white shroud, and yet I suddenly had an inspiration that there was someone or some*thing* inside. This is where he had gone. This was his secret unholy of unholies.

Clawing through the crust to find the driver's-door handle, I tugged. The ice had sealed it—something had sealed it—but it gave an inch. The added resistance thrilled me with impending discovery. He was actually inside. He was holding the door shut. I swiped at the glass, but the snow crust was like Styrofoam against my bloodied fingers. I grabbed the door handle and braced my foot on the rear side panel. With snaps and clattering the ice let go.

"Evans!" I cried fiercely, throwing wide the door.

Empty. A crucifix dangling from the mirror.

"If you're not dead, I'm not dead!" I shouted, and entombed the thought with a slam.

But I couldn't shake the feeling that he had been there until the very last fraction of a second, that a mortal force—or a withering vestige of it—had been hanging desperately on to the car door handle from inside. No sulfurous smell, no floating miasma, just a hair-raising, flesh-crawling conviction that he was vanishing at the exact moment that I was breaking into his lair. The last thing I remember is the sermon title gloating from the church marquee as I drove away: DEEP CALLS TO DEEP.

Wednesday morning, January 17th

Things I didn't write last night.

From my online dictionary: *Terrarium (noun). An enclosure, usually earthen, containing selected living things.*

From Jerry Arnasen: *I'm coming back. The terrarium.*

Like he's going to rise up from the earth. I should have looked for his name at the cemetery.

It hit me this morning that I know more people in cemeteries than I do who are walking the planet. My mother, my father, a slew of bad companions, and now a busload of departees who got in line behind me at the waterfall when it looked like I was checking out for good. I always said I would live forever, but if I'm going to do that, I've got to broaden my social circle to include more people above room temperature. Like Beckie Franke.

When I left East Tristan I drove to the shop and worked all afternoon in the back. Skiers came and went, but I couldn't bring myself to interact with customers. When things died down around six, the door lock snapped up front and the store lights went out. I turned off the workbench bulb and felt my way into the shop and sank down on the pine bench where skiers try on boots.

Sam sat hunched over the cash register, watching the

snowfall in the quarter-moon's light through the window. For a while we shared the magic of flakes as big as communion wafers coming down in silence, and then he said:

"Some Algonquian tribes believe that snowflakes are secret words whispered by Noshi, the father of all, to heal the earth."

A few million whispered snowflakes healed the earth outside the window, and I told him what had happened at the cemetery and about confirming that Alex Franke was the baby-faced man who had visited me. I told him a lot of stuff, matter-of-factly, knowing he wouldn't challenge it. I even told him about the fugues. Confessing to Sam is never difficult, but the darkness took away my last inhibitions.

"I'm wrung out," I said. "I don't want to meet dead people. I wish I could understand, but I can't, and now I just want to accept it and figure out what I have to do. I want my life back the way it was before. Either that, or . . . get on with it, you know? If something irreversible happened to me when my core temperature dropped to fifty-five degrees, okay, take me the rest of the way."

"You're talking bullshit, Bowie."

"Everyone dies; it can't be all bad."

"According to you, Alex Franke doesn't think it's so good."

"Okay, I'm talking bullshit. I don't want to die. But something in me is compromised, and Alex Franke or someone is taking advantage of it. I've got a busload of suspects, and I'm tired of being an open door. Whatever is going on, I'm not in on the secret, so I'm not in on the deal."

"I don't think Alex Franke is the problem."

"No?"

"If he is, then why doesn't your invader do what Alex

Franke would do? Instead of going to see his wife in East Tristan, he makes you go to your apartment and throw your kids' pictures away. You dump medicine and delete address books. And what does Franke have to do with rotting food?"

Not a damn thing.

"I can't reason it out anymore, Sam. If you can exorcise my demon, psychologically or otherwise, for God's sake, help me."

He leaned back, moonlight sliding off his features onto his shoulders and hands. "The first thing to do is to make up your mind you want to win this battle. You say you're not in on the secret, so you're not in on the deal; but you are in on the deal, and if you want to have control of it, you'll have to know the secret."

"Do I hear an assumption that this is really happening to me?"

"Really happening doesn't mean it's not coming out of some psychological chaos inside you. This secret may wind up being between you and you. Or not. It sure as hell started with something external. In any case, Alex Franke is a flimsy explanation. It's the first one you grabbed."

"What do you mean?" I asked, apprehension tingling.

"Why does it have to be one or the other—Alex, just because he came to see you, or this Jerry you think was in your mind when the e-mail was sent, or the minister? There were nineteen killed on that bus, weren't there? Maybe it's not *one* of them. Maybe it's all of them."

Oh, that's what I needed to hear. Thanks a hell of a lot, Sam.

Wednesday evening

It's dark out, and the wind is roaring around the cabin like a Windigo trying to find its way in. A Windigo—that's Indian palaver for a giant that can move like a wind high in the trees. Sam stood in the middle of the store this evening with his arms upraised like he was embracing the roar and told me about it. He says a Windigo brings cannibalistic madness. For all his scientific knowledge, he deals out wild cards like that now and then. I don't know what he believes.

Just when I think he's become infuriatingly rigid in his interpretation of everything, he comes in with an armload of mumbo-jumbo articles and books and says it's worth a look. That's what he did before he went home tonight. To tell the truth, most of what he left is total crap. What does strike me in all this material, though, is the enduring belief in metempsychosis—the transmigration of souls—through the ages.

I thought it was pretty much a Hindu thing, but pick a culture or a religion and there's a spin on transmigration. Plato and the Greeks? Check. Jewish orthodoxy? Check. African, Oceanic, Aboriginal, South American—yo. Even the occult branches of Christianity, like the Gnostics and the Manichaeans. But not Christianity itself.

That's the only one that doesn't believe in it. If I had described what happened to me in any culture but a Christian one, transmigration would have been a given. Sam says it's a conceit of man that he's immortal, and that I can find historical support for any bias I bring to the table. But I don't have a bias. I have an experience.

I don't think I truly believed in the existence of a soul before November tenth. So, transmigration was not right there, planted in my subconscious. And even if I was in denial and grasping for a way to keep on surviving in that waterfall, I didn't recognize transmigration in what I was seeing. The poor bastards in the bus might have been in denial. They're the ones who were grasping for survival. I didn't hitchhike back with them.

And I guess that means they are trying to be reincarnated in me. But even if reincarnation is the way of all souls, there is something else going on here. True, the fact that my body technically died, then came back to life, must have presented a unique circumstance. Nevertheless, multiple souls in any single vessel can't be the norm. Especially a vessel that already has a soul. Was it the suddenness of the violent deaths on the bus and a frenzy of denial that pushed them into my bizarre round-trip from extinction in the waterfall? Hard to believe that something as profound as reincarnation could be so arbitrary. There must be another control here. I sense it. Some undeclared process or purpose or player . . .

"Maybe the soul can function independently, like a rescue disk for a computer," I said before Sam left for the night. "Maybe mine booted my body back to life."

He laughed.

We got heavy into metaphysics then. I've got the edge on him in education, but he's well-read and smarter than me. I accused him of narrowness, of not having the balls to approach knowledge with intuition. He accused me of defaulting into wish fulfillment.

Impasse.

I like some of the phrases I've read in this stuff he left. *An ocean of divinity . . . the primal stream.* The images are what are so telling, like a common dream, a genetic memory that comes from a bedrock of spiritual essence, to mix the metaphor. So, how come I'm an anathema? Maybe I've got that part wrong. Sam has me half-convinced. The rotting food could be just some purely biological effect. There are people who set off store alarms and metal detectors. And what about those survivors of lightning strikes Sam alludes to, who ever after cause radio interference? I rot food. Bummer. Thank God for airtight bottles and fast-serve windows. As for killer puppies, what does that mean? They smell something on me, that's all. Have to watch where I step. Then, too, I got clunked by a tree branch. Happens when you're in the woods and it's windy. And Bambi's dad has photosensitive eyes every time he stands in front of an onrushing Probe GT with its headlights on. When you're spooked, it all comes together in a conspiracy.

I feel saner than I've felt in a long while. Thank you, Sam, for these kooky books. They have restored my perspective and sanctioned me as a member of the human race. Run-ins with the dead or not, I am among the living. I do believe I'm going to go skiing yet tonight. Why not? And when I'm done, I'm going to read some more, and then I think I'll just sack out here in the store for the night. Sam has a cot set up in the storage room.

Dawn

Thank God, it's finally getting light out. I keep looking under my chair and up to the rafters, but if any of those horrors are still here, they probably won't come out in the light. I'm wearing two pair of socks, so that I won't feel any of that ghastly living slime on my flesh again. But I think I'm going to take them both off so that I will, because if the hideous horde comes back, I want to know it before it overwhelms me. A breath of air on my ankle is going to send me through the roof.

Last night, I kept to the south trails under the waning moon. My skis chattered and hissed on the phantom blue crust but dug in when I pressed them out. It was just the right balance of speed and control, and the old cockiness was back. It was probably less than an hour before I was back in the shop, heating a can of tomato soup. Tomato soup is my nostrum, associated with healing, because my mother always made it when I was sick. There were days I stole from school just for the ambience of tomato soup. And after the soup I ate last night came the sleep of exhaustion. Sleep welcomed me like an old whore, and I fell into her arms without a qualm.

The cot in the back room is too short, and the scallops where the canvas opens for the wooden legs let cold air under the comforter. For all that, I must have been dead to the world, because I awoke naked on a thin flannel blanket, having kicked it aside, apparently, when the horror began. I vaguely remember brushing something that raced across my right eyelid. But around two a.m. a sensation that started out as dull as a bandage suddenly became an ice pick in the ankle.

I slid upright so fast that the canvas burned my thigh. Something nearly weightless dropped on my neck and ran into my hair; another feathery assassin found the back of my knee. My heart began kicking in my throat, connected somehow to the afterghost of red drifting in my field of vision, as if I had just seen my blood explode.

I reeled onto my feet and made the discovery that has kept me unnerved ever since. The floor was no longer smooth and solid to my bare soles. It was textured and slimy. Not just a spot on the boards—the *whole* floor. Fragile things popped under my weight as I staggered and danced. I went down before I could find the pull cord hanging from the light, and a ghastly wave of febrile legs broke over me.

If the floor had been a hot griddle, I still could not have made it back to my feet. So I rolled like a fallen animal in its death throes. I crushed as many of my tormentors as I could. The fire of fangs and pincers went selectively cold, but each sickening inch of contact was moist and curdy, and what survived in the hollows of my neck and the small of my back dug in deeper.

More were coming. My left knee banged into the workbench hard enough to knock hooks off the pegboard, but even that crippling pain couldn't distract me from what felt like a gossamer net dropping down. I had to get up or be smothered. Bracing on all fours, I struggled upright and did not repeat the mistake of lifting my feet to walk. I swiped down my body, I flailed at flying things—though possibly I was batting the knotted end of the pull cord as well—and I shuffled a few inches at a time.

For some reason—inadequate blood supply or the violent thudding of my heart—I was momentarily deaf, but suddenly that sense kicked back in with extreme acuteness. I heard the snap and click of tiny entities raining against the walls, and, strange as it seems, it took away some of the insanity of what was happening. Because it had to be a single species triggered by a seasonal anomaly from a nest in the logs, I rationalized, a one-of-a-kind swarm of flies or small beetles. It was not an eruption of everything natural in my vicinity, as if I were so *un*natural that all primitive things were affected. Relief from that fear flashed through my mind even at that moment. But a contradiction flew into my face, something big with razzing wings and multiple legs that hooked or glued themselves opportunistically to my lips and burrowed for my mouth. I spat and swiped and shook the remnants off my hand in the darkness, and that's how I found the light string....

If I could take back what I saw when the light came on, I would. It was not, as I had lamely hoped, a single swarm that had awakened prematurely from an unexpectedly warm hollow in the cabin walls. It was an apocalypse of insects and spiders that will continue to pour out of every crevice I turn my back to for a long time. A Roman circus of centipedes and jet-black metallic things and things with virulent stripes were all moving across the floor, walls, and ceiling. They thickened the air. I raked obscene vermin out of my hair. I stamped and swatted. But they were in my ears, my nose. Moaning in mortal terror, I thrashed my way into the shower stall.

There was pitifully little water pressure, and I didn't wait for the icy burst to clear the lines for the hot water to come. Loosely cupping the nozzle, I made an awkward pirouette while deflecting spray down my body at yellow smears and pulsing spider parts. I dug and clawed and pinched, trying to get the agile survivors, but each time I thought I crushed the last one, another broke in a frenzy up the inside of my thigh or into my ear canal.

The water turned warm, then hot. It felt good to be scalded. I kept my arms raised and let the searing spray drum on every part of me it could reach. It seemed like only a few seconds before the water turned cold again, then icy. But my skin was slightly anesthetized by then, and my mind too, I guess, because I couldn't stop the obsessive cleansing. "Scorched earth . . . scorched earth," I metered aloud in my terrified delirium, and I marched in place as I rotated like a carcass on a spit. ". . . scorched earth . . . scorched earth." It wasn't until a deep core chill began to creep out of my memory of the waterfall that I turned off the shower.

But now, as the water gurgled away through the drain, a mad hum from outside the tiny cubicle took its place. Huge shadows played against the translucent stall door. Dismayed, I opened it a crack.

The shadows were being thrown by insects flying or crawling around the lightbulb. There were so many of them that I could smell the burning of the ones that dropped like stones. It came as a relief to see that they were killing each other. Segmented things pinwheeled across the floor in broken arcs. Tumbleweed motes of three and four spiders gyrated in mortal combat. So it wasn't just me they wanted to attack.

The explanation that they were all awakened from overwintering at the same time is loaded with contradictions. This wasn't a single species arising at its appointed hour to mass around a sidewalk crack. It wasn't the appointed hour for anything. Spiders and insects at the same time? I don't know much about vermin, but six legs and eight legs don't hold their conventions on the same dates. The only thing they all had in common was that I incited them.

I left the shower stall by using two pieces of cardboard for rafts, pressing them down one at a time on an array of combatants. Ignoring the insects that dropped on me, I worked my way across the floor to the workbench, where there was a can of Black Flag. The can was so old it was rusted, but I misted the storage area and now everything is dead. I hope they are dead, because if I suck up any more Black Flag, they'll have to add my name to the kill list on the label.

My body is a mass of bumps and welts. The wave of burning that woke me up is turning into a dull ache, and the scalding shower has left me with bright patches on my chest, thighs, and cheeks. I feel like I have arthritis. Little rivulets of blood are running out of my sleeves, but the sensation of having clothes on seems to spread the pain around so that it doesn't localize. I've combed my hair till my scalp is raw and bleeding, and I keep gagging. The feeling that some of the horde are still alive inside me is way past imagination.

So, I'm at the computer now. Even though I was pretty sure nothing was crawling around out here, I waited for daylight before I came up front. And I'm not going to try to clean up that slaughter of creepers until Sam sees it. I want him to tell me that *this* just came out of the psychological chaos inside me.

I don't know how an outré knowledge gets into the dreams and nightmares of mankind, but there are figures along the way of history that show it does. Goya, Lovecraft, Hitler, to name a few. It may be that certain individuals are just channeled close to it in their consciousness. Others may come to it accidentally, like I did, through a horrific instant of contact or some glimpse of a howling abyss. But how come none of them make dogs whine and turn bananas black? The Hitlers even attract followers. I attract frontal assaults. Frontal and rear and both flanks, under and over. Last night was Armageddon. I want a hug. I want to meet Barney the Dinosaur or Leo Buscaglia. I want the same "welcome back" reception Lazarus got.

I think the reason I'm an anathema is because I did more than just glimpse another dimension last November. I brought some of it back with me. The abyss awakens its own sensory paths, exclusive of external stimuli, and you feel its vast, unstable loneliness and wildness as if it were mushrooming out of your gut, exploding and scattering your atoms throughout . . . whatever. The cosmos. Do-dah.

It's a mistake to dwell on this. But how can I put distance between me and infinity? That's the problem. This outer glimpse that was forced on me is now in my blood, in every brain cell that fires an impulse. It has scorched its way through me, and I can't repair the fracturing vision it left behind. Can't. Must. If I'm going to survive, I must. Live a lie, live a lie. Say a thing seven times and it becomes true. Do a thing seven times and it becomes real. Okay, then. This is all bullshit. All melodrama.

Last night it started with that triumphant feeling I got reading about the transmigration of souls. It just felt so good not being a total freak anymore. You can't imagine how good it feels to find out your "delusion" is shared. I didn't know squat about metempsychosis when I started skiing down that mountain on November tenth, so how likely is it that I invented something that just happens to coincide with the spiritual enlightenment of mankind down through the ages?

January 19th, 10:55 P.M.

Friday. I've lost a day, but this time it isn't to a fugue. All I remember after writing about the creepy crawlies at The Ski Shop is that I felt sick and stepped outside to get a couple breaths of cold air. The next thing I knew there was a white ceiling above me, and I was an octopus with plastic tentacles and an IV. I was in Rush-Timmons Diagnostics and Emergency. Big name, small facility. That was about noon yesterday, I'm told. Something that bit me at the spider jamboree must have been in the big leagues. Of course, I inhaled enough Black Flag to bump my head on the moon. By the time my brains caught up to the scene at Rush-Timmons, fully cognizant and able to hold a conversation, I was stabilized and out of danger.

An intern questioned me, and then a doctor showed up who was easily tall enough to slam-dunk a basketball, which he could have palmed. Leaning over me to check my pupils, he asked if I owned any exotic pets. I guess that was just his conversation starter, because when I said no, he gave me the clinical version of what had happened to me, using terms like "anaphylactic shock" and "urticaria."

"I got bit by a lot of spiders," I said.

"Yes, but do you know what kind they were?"

"Itsy-bitsy, gargantuan, and all kinds in between."

He straightened up, eclipsing the far wall and half the ceiling. "Well, we haven't figured out the venom. The toxicologist says he doesn't think it was a brown recluse or a black widow. Where were you?"

"It's sort of a log cabin. Probably a Noah's ark for anything smaller than a rat."

"Were you asleep?"

"Yeah."

"Did you see them when you woke up?"

"Yeah."

"And you think there was more than one kind?"

"We can be clear on that, Doc."

"But you can't tell me what kind?"

"I wasn't doing scientific research. I was doing an Irish jig."

He looked frustrated. "I've never seen anything like this. Without pinning down a type of spider, there's no telling what caused your reaction, or if your system was merely overwhelmed by the numbers. Odd behavior for spiders, though."

Menagerie Uses Waterfall Man for Target Practice.

I don't believe the Rush-Timmons people knew I was the survivor of the core-temp anomaly they must have read about. I was afraid it might complicate my situation, if they did, so I didn't inform them. Just like with Mayo, I wanted to get out of there, but despite my insistence that I was recovered, they kept me overnight. When the doctor returned this morning he advised me to wash my bedding and hire an exterminator. Then he signed the release. The nurse asked me if I had a driver, and I said it would be the same person who brought me in.

She checked the chart. "There's no name or number of a person who brought you in."

I asked to use the phone.

Sam was relieved to hear my voice, a fact whose significance escaped me until he said: "Where the hell have you been?"

That put a chill in the air. Sam—who must have seen the spiders, seen my car, seen my skis—hadn't found me lying unconscious in the snow, as I had supposed. Who then? The sane explanations began shearing away like granite slabs off a cliff. The Ski Shop was too far from the beaten path for me to have been seen by a passerby. And no customer would have gotten there before Sam did—or if they had, they would have told him what they had found.

"I went up and down all the trails yesterday, and I called the police in the afternoon," Sam said. "Where are you?"

"In a place called Rush-Timmons, and I don't know how I got here, but they're releasing me."

"I know where Rush-Timmons is. Pick you up in ten minutes."

When I handed the phone back to the frowning nurse, I leaned into her face.

"Excuse me, but who brought me in?"

Her eyes took on deference and she shook her head. It was the receptionist next to her who answered.

"A young man," she said. "He wouldn't come to the desk and register you. I saw the attendants arguing with him."

"What did he look like?"

"I couldn't see him very well. He had a scarf around his face."

"Red plaid . . ."

She thought. "Yeah. Red plaid."

One of the two attendants at the door remembered that

my Good Samaritan had driven an old junker. "Kind of dull gold—like old copper," he described it. The other thought there was something odd about his hands, that maybe he had been missing a finger.

I stood outside, not really feeling the cold but feeling very much as if I were being buried in a slow, methodical snowstorm. It is still snowing. Each bizarre thing that has happened to me is like a single snowflake, not particularly noticeable until it's followed by another and another.

Sam came in his old Toyota. We covered half a mile before he said, "Well, you must be in better shape than you look, seeing as how they let you out the front door."

"I think they were expecting a hearse to pick me up."

"You do leave interesting clues, Mr. Carmichael. I saw that you slept on the cot, and of course there was your car, and there was enough insecticide floating in the air to leave a rainbow around the light, so I assume you know all about the million-bug march in the back room."

I drew my fingers down my face as if to paw away that resurgent image.

Sam noted the effect on me with a glance. "*That's* why you were in Rush-Timmons?"

"That's why."

He assessed the bites on my hands and face. "Man, oh, man, if it wasn't for bad luck, you wouldn't have any luck at all."

"Luck—good or bad—had nothing to do with it."

"Well, what else would it be? Bowie, this can't be related to the other stuff, if that's what you're thinking."

My laugh sounded harsh in the tightness of the car. I looked out the passenger window. "You know what really scares me? If I'm looney tunes, then there isn't any place I can stand and fight."

"You aren't looney tunes."

Sam says it, but he won't endorse the possibility that what's happening is absolutely beyond-the-pale, prima facie evidence of heaven or hell or other dimensions or cosmic will or spiritual upheaval or the distinct and alien nature of an afterlife. So that means he still thinks it's all coming out of me.

There was a skier waiting to buy a trail pass when we got to the store. I recognized him from past winters; he recognized me. I avoided his eyes, knowing what was coming. "Hey, aren't you the one who got trapped in that waterfall?" This kind of thing has happened before. I say I'm not, and they go on about the accident and how you would expect brain damage at the very least from that. "Well, I'm glad it wasn't you," this one said. "Here I've been thinking all these weeks, 'I know that guy.' I don't care what they say about bringing him back like that; the poor bastard can't possibly be okay after being dead so long. Glad it wasn't you."

I entered the storage room braced for spider carnage, but, of course, Sam had swept it clear. He had also lugged in another stack of cheery books. I don't know why, but I just laughed when I saw that. The world has crashed, and Sam is still supplying me with dreary clues to explain it. Somehow that seems like hope.

So instead of gathering up my coat and car keys, as I had intended, I picked up *Death and Superstition* from the workbench and started to read about how souls were once thought to have left the body as small flames. Seventeenth-century contemporaries saw souls in terms of light sources they understood—candles, lanterns, dispossessed flames, fungal phosphorescence. Corpse lights and corpse candles usually appeared in churchyards, but sometimes in death chambers; and often their persistence presaged future death. The souls rising from the burning bus had been stains, I thought, and yet there was a kind of inversion there, like a photographic negative in a B movie, where light becomes shadow. I had seen things with my mind rather than my eyes. The world around me was a gloomy ether, filled with neural lightning whose crepitations fragmented my senses. Light and shadow were one, a demonic synthesis or corruption of . . . what?

I tossed the book aside, and to nail my suspicions about who had driven me to the hospital, I drove to East Tristan. There was the Conoco, and a few blocks later the redbrick Timothy Lutheran. DEEP CALLS TO DEEP was no longer on the marquee. ECCLESIASTES 3:19–21 was. The Lies of Solomon. So sayeth the red Gothic letters on my wall. Enough to send my guts south again. Like I had just stepped beyond personal destiny to something incalculably important to the order of the universe.

My heart tripped when the parking lot came into full view. There were two vans and a white Escort parked next to the side entrance of the church, but the other car—the one that had been buried all winter and whose door I had yanked open—was missing its carapace of snow. It was an old copper-colored LTD, rusted around the wheel wells, and I could make out the tracks where the tires had backed out over the adjacent fringe of snow that the snowplow hadn't reached.

In the best tradition of Sam the rationalist, I admitted to myself that it could be coincidence. I mulled it over until reasonable details fell into place. Someone had gotten around to clearing the snow off the windshield and seeing if the engine still ran. They had driven it to charge up the battery, that was all. And after I was done with the reasoning, I parked twenty feet away and walked around the LTD at a little distance, as if it were emitting dangerous radiation. Because in my gut I knew that this was the dull-gold junker that had driven me to Rush-Timmons.

I can't tell you why the thought that I have been in a car with one of them when I was unconscious leaves me white and drained. What's the big deal, after all I've been through? But when their presences loom, I see shadows striding across the galaxy, and my blood roars like it's going to reach escape velocity. I don't want lost souls close to me. Not when I'm dreaming, or mesmerized, or under drugs in a hospital, or blind, or unconscious. So I had to find out about that car, and there were the two vans and the Escort belonging to people in the church who might know.

The side entrance opened on a landing between two flights of stairs. The short one led up to a carpeted foyer; the long one went down to a tiled floor. From the one that went down came the familiar thud and clang of folding tables being set up. I remember one-acts, recitals, and fish-fry fund-raisers where I made that clanging. The anthem of the good father. But it would be women down there at this time of day, I thought. Dutiful mothers, bored matrons, lonely widows—especially lonely widows.

It was a good guess. So I shouldn't have been surprised when Rebecca Franke's clear gaze met mine before I was halfway down the steps. But I didn't notice much about the other two after that. Beckie pursed her lips just the way she had on Tuesday, when I had offered to help. A little tension in her features to stem a stab of emotion, and already I'm familiar with it. I feel distressed at being associated with her husband the way I am, as if he is already appearing in a light in my eyes she will recognize. Beckie Franke is someone who will mourn a long time. I could envy Alex Franke that. If only he were unalterably dead.

I wanted to ask about the car in the parking lot, but she would have known it had something to do with the bus, and I couldn't bring myself to manipulate her again. So I mumbled a pretext about checking out the rummage sale they were setting up, fooling no one. Beckie's eyes followed me around the boxes of books, plastic garbage bags filled with old clothes, toys, kitchenware, and worn-out furniture. The other two women threw doubting glances but deferred to Beckie, having gleaned that there was a relationship between us.

I ambled up and down between the tables, trying to think of a graceful exit. It annoyed me that Beckie—smiling faintly—seemed to grasp my dilemma. And then I saw the large clear plastic globe sitting on a stand, half-filled with potting soil in which was planted some kind of delicate ivy, and my eyes came boldly up to hers. Hadn't she told me about Charlotte Arnasen, who had given everything away, canceled her husband's e-mail address, sold her house, and moved to Mankato? And here in the church where she had no doubt disposed of some of that property was a terrarium.

"This wouldn't be Charlotte Arnasen's, would it?" I asked deliberately, hovering above the globe.

"As a matter of fact, it is," she said. "How did you know?"

I stared at the thing on the stand, trying to grasp what it might mean to the ominous e-mail: *I'm coming back. The terrarium.* What organic horror had taken root in the rich soil?

"Sir," one of the ladies called as I lifted the top hemisphere of the plastic globe. "We're not op—"

She stopped as I plunged my hand inside and began to grope through the black earth.

No one moved toward me. Crazy men walk into offices and church basements and do crazy things. Women just back off. They weren't going to stop me, and I was going to find whatever obscenity might be lurking in the dirt, even if I had to dump it on the floor.

Doc Weibens had watched me reach into the soil of a hibiscus pot and grab the whole damn universe. I had a presentiment that whatever was in the terrarium was going to attack my hand, that twin lines of serrated teeth were going to gnash my fingers into meaty pulp. Still, I probed the moist dirt while lime-green ivy wound around my wrist as effectively as shackles. Maybe the object of my quest was small, I thought. Maybe it was something virulent that would spread poison without revealing itself. I scooped the stuff to one side, and suddenly a gelatinous thing undulated away from my touch. It was almost a relief to know I had been right. Pinching a corner, I dragged up a thick glassine bag.

If anyone was surprised, they didn't show it. Of course, they were focused on a crazy man and calculating avenues of escape. I looked at Beckie.

"Maybe you want to give this back to Charlotte."

She was close enough to see that beneath the smears and caked soil there was a considerable amount of white powder in the glassine bag. It was Jerry Arnasen's secret stash of drugs—a quantity sufficient to figure him for a dealer with a heavy investment. Probably not so secret to his wife, or he wouldn't have tried to e-mail her about it. *I'm coming back.* He thought he was going to resume his life. Chilling.

I dropped the bag back in the terrarium. Nothing else I said was going to matter now, and I just turned back up the steps. *Have a good life, Beckie Franke,* I thought; *you gave more than you got.*

I crossed the parking lot and was just opening my car

door when she came through the side entrance. We stood like that, twenty feet apart, me in a windbreaker, she rubbing her arms against the chill, now holding the dirt-streaked bag. She took a few indecisive steps. Her voice was tight when she spoke, but that could have been the cold.

"Why did you come here?"

It would have been easy to tell her I was looking for the terrarium. Kinder than inviting her into a world much darker than her grief. But the simple truth is, I wanted her to like me. Me. And she didn't know me yet.

"My car is warm, if you want to get in," I said.

She must have seen the insect bites on my face, must have wondered why I looked so haggard, but she went immediately around to the passenger side, and I slid into the driver's seat, thinking she was as desperate as I was.

"I don't have any more lies about Alex," I said. "What I told you the other day, I had no business saying. The truth is, everyone went down with the ship. Alive and burning."

Attaboy, Bowie. Slick. What the hell was I doing? But I knew what I was doing. I was wiping the slate clean so I could start a relationship. If she broke down or slapped my face and stalked off, so be it. There really wasn't any other direction to move in.

Despite the heat still ebbing from the engine into the front seat, our breath smoked, and I was afraid to turn the key and run the defrost for fear it might look like I intended to drive off. Her side of the windshield steamed up first. The tremble in her voice was pathetic.

"You saw Alex alive in the bus? You saw all of them?"

"Believe me, I know exactly what all nineteen were going through." Oh, I'm a regular bluebird of happiness.

"And you came here to tell me that?"

"I didn't know you were in the church. If I had, I wouldn't have gone in."

"You came for this . . . this bag? It's cocaine or heroin or something, isn't it?"

"Looks like it. Enough to qualify for major room and board at the state's expense. Your friend was in the big leagues. But I didn't know the bag was in there either."

She thought for a second, started to restate her question.

"I don't want to tell you how I knew about the terrarium," I said.

"What did you want then?"

I gestured at the fogged glass on her side of the car. "There's an LTD out there. I wanted to know if it belongs to Pastor Evans."

"It belonged to him. No one has the courage to suggest hauling it away. Someone said something about waiting till spring and getting a new battery. As long as it sits there, some of the congregation feel like he's still among us."

"They've got that right." It's tough to just sit on good news like that.

She looked across at me.

"It doesn't need a new battery," I said. "It's been driven. Who's got the keys?"

She shook her head absently. The car was as insignificant to her as the thousands of dollars' worth of powder she was holding limply in her hand. Her thoughts remained on the connection I had given her to Alex. Maybe what had happened to her husband those last few seconds in the holocaust bus wasn't an issue for her. Maybe just my being there at the end brought him closer to her, so she thought I was doing her a favor after all.

"If it wasn't all about closure last Tuesday, why did

you come then?" she said. "It wasn't to lie to me about how Alex died."

"No."

"Well?" She waited. "You're not going to give me any 'You're better off not knowing' crap, are you?"

"The hell I'm not."

I could hear the shakiness in her breathing. Then she said: "I think you want to tell me. You need to tell me. You need to tell someone."

Tell a widow you spoke to her dead husband, and that you send surrogate e-mails for the dead, and that you spoke to the spirit of her spiritual adviser in the cemetery where her hubby is buried? Give me a break. "You should leave now," I said.

She considered it. I'll give her credit for that much common sense over her frightening willingness to pursue such a macabre subject. She put her hand on the door handle, but that was as much of a move as she made. I'd like to think that what happened next shows there is a connection between us, or at least an intuitive grasp on her part of my pitiful need, because she just sat there until the silence made me look at her, and then she said with perfect composure: "Tell me."

I wanted to dump on her. She was right about that. Not just the cameos with Alex Franke and Pastor Evans but the whole grim odyssey. I'm lonely, disenfranchised, a pariah to my family, under siege, maybe losing my marbles, maybe even dead—I keep thinking of that Bruce Willis–Haley Joel Osment flick—so how noble am I supposed to be?

I took advantage of her. I sputtered it all in something less than fifteen minutes, more than I told Sam, because she is a woman, and when I was done, I just laid my head on the wheel and waited. I was drowning in a flood of self-pity, and her next words were going to pull me ashore or push me under.

"Sometimes I see him, too," she said in such a detached tone that I knew my personal drama had hardly registered. "Maybe not the way you did, but I blink and he's there for a second, or I pick up his voice in a crowd. I feel his eyes following me." She touched the back of my neck. "I believe you."

Just like that. It was tempting to write her off as emotional and susceptible, but between the two of us sitting misty-eyed in the front seat of my car, I was easily the more emotional and susceptible at that moment. And the fact that she could touch me on the neck in a motherly way meant she knew it.

After a time she said, "Do you think you might see him again?"

"I'll let you know."

A sharp and unhealthy hunger sparked in her. Alex coming back. It didn't matter how he came back, or in what morbid condition; she could only envision him as he was the day he left for Mille Lacs with the doomed contingent from Timothy Lutheran. Suddenly she was anxious to help.

"You said you came to find out about Alex. What do you want to know?"

"When I went to your house Tuesday I just wanted to confirm that he was the person I saw."

"The picture."

"Yeah, the picture."

"That was all?"

"I was fishing. Maybe I thought I'd recognize something that might—you know—confirm one way or another."

"That Alex came back with you from your accident."

"There are enough studies of near-death experiences to explain it psychologically, but—"

"You should have told me what you wanted."

"You would've tossed me out."

"No, I would have shown you his things and let you see what he was like. I still will. Follow me home, and I'll show you everything."

"I don't think it matters now."

"Of course it matters. I mean, you can't tell. What's to lose?"

Just sanity. Just reality. She read my unenthusiastic body language.

"I can tell you this much: You're not like Alex at all."

I sat in the car savoring the hope in those words while she went back inside the church and came out again with her coat. Then I followed her white Escort to the house. She made coffee, and we talked without saying much, leaving our thumbnail histories begging. Then she took me through her rooms. She hasn't thrown out a whole lot, I don't think; probably won't for a long time. A man's clothes are still in the closet, tools in the basement, sports gear—tennis racket, golf clubs, fishing equipment—on the back wall of the garage. No ski stuff. Alex never skied, she told me. She's right. I'm not like Alex Franke. He was just along for the ride to Mille Lacs that day, she said, one of the obligatory adult sponsors. She would have gone herself, if she hadn't had the flu. They were a group. Originally it was Lutheran Youth Explorers, but when the chaperones began outnumbering the kids, someone dubbed them Ageless Adventurers, and that pretty well described the mix. They even had patches for their jackets and sweatshirts. "And scarves," she added. "They bought the scarves just before the trip. Nice red plaid scarves."

Nearly two dozen of them. Imagine that.

I never moved a muscle, but she saw that this information had an effect on me. I've never seen a woman who picks up feelings so unerringly. Damned dangerous. I'm getting too much of what I want from her—what I missed with Dolores.

"I've got to go now," I said.

She looked profoundly disappointed. At the door she asked, "What am I going to do with that stuff in the bag?"

"The happy powder? Give it to the police, if you want your friend arrested. Throw it down the toilet if you don't."

I looked at the photo on the Internet again when I got home, and two of the sisters from Sweden have scarves tucked into their collars. Some other people look kind of bulky in the shoulders. So that complicates things. Night has sealed me in like a lock on my door, and nineteen former people who don't accept the fact that they died all have keys.

January 20

Sleep should be a time-out. I should be allowed to sleep. But they are all here, hiding on the edges of my soul, waiting for my mind to dim a little and let them in.

Last night, a few minutes after I turned off the light, I heard breathing. At first I thought it was the heat coming on, but it was breathing. I know what breathing sounds like, dammit, and it wasn't mine. When I was sure it wasn't the heat or a draft, I turned on the light. There was nothing there, of course, so I turned the light off and it started up again. I wanted to find it, fight it, strangle it. I shouted at it in the dark. I said crazy things.

When I was done throwing a fit and the tiny apartment was ringing with my voice, I sat very still. Passion seems to make them retreat. My will is the key. When I am resolute and angry, my defenses are at their strongest. That's why they want to sap my determination and fill me with doubts about everything. That's why they try to isolate me. I snapped the lamp on again, took a quick hard look around, snapped it off.

Five seconds passed. Not even. The sharp exhalation was as if something had been holding its breath. I jerked my head off the pillow just enough to listen. Faint respiration came to me, shallow and short, like it really wanted to hide. Somehow the impression settled on me that it was female, that an element of cunning less physical and more psychological was present in the room. The strain on my neck was killing me, but I stayed rigid until I was sure I knew where the breathing was coming from. It was near the window.

"I see you," I said with phony bravado, and it stopped, but only for a beat. The cadence came back fuller then, abandoning caution.

If a voice, celestial or demonic, had spoken to me, I probably would have been afraid, but it was just breathing. My mind's eye tried to give it substance. One moment it was a malevolent gargoyle crouched on leathery legs at the edge of my dresser; the next it was a pale blue flame, a corpse light, trying to penetrate the veil between us with an urgent message I needed to hear.

I was exhausted and depressed and I could have cried out in frustration. So many unrelenting hauntings. Why couldn't they keep regular hours? Hauntings and intimidations nine to five, closed weekends and holidays. Oh, Jessica, come banish your father's nightmares! Go to the closet and utter the magical incantation and mangle the darkness.

What I needed more than burying my head under the pillow and ignoring it was to *know,* to end the terrible suspense of *not knowing*. So I had to get up and find this thing that was imitating human breathing. And I had to do this in the dark, because it wouldn't be there in the light. But it was like jumping down a hole. Like reaching into a flowerpot and being sucked into another universe.

What happened next is straight out of Poe's "The Tell-Tale Heart." You wouldn't *believe* how stealthy I was. Migrating to the edge of the mattress too slowly to make a sound, extending my right foot little by little until it hung out from the bed. My left foot followed from under the covers, so gradually and with such awkward pressure on my hip as I pivoted that both my feet grew ice-cold before I was ready to swing upright. But I didn't have to swing upright, because my weight was sliding me off the edge of the mattress inch by inch, and I just let it happen until the side of my right foot touched the carpet. And all the time I was doing this—ten or twelve minutes, easy—the breathing continued. It even softened and lengthened with pathological calm, as if it had detected and adjusted to my plan.

Impulses fired in the back of my mind, warning me that I was courting fate, that the entity in the darkness was actually waiting for my lunatic rush, but the very act of stealth emboldened me. Even if it could see my every motion, I felt like a snake moving so slowly that it was below the threshold of alarm. My mouth, which had been dry with terror, was salivating like a hunter's. I was going to shout when I sprang—shout with as much ferocity as I could muster. Confronting my enemy seemed suddenly extremely simple. Letting my weight shift onto my feet, I catapulted blindly across the room, uttering one great cry and spreading my arms to capture whatever was there.

I don't know which of the textures my clutching fingers contacted first. It could have been the filmy thing that wrapped itself around my wrist, or the fleshy surface that yielded, or the hard one that didn't. It happened almost simultaneously. Sitting here now I can accept that it was probably the sheers on the window, followed by the edge of the stuffed chair, followed by the wood sash. In any case, I was whirled from one object to another. Nausea replaced recklessness as quickly as if I were punched in the stomach. And I'm at a loss to explain whatever else was going on, because—incredibly—I couldn't find my way back to bed.

I groped and staggered to the point of exhaustion, and

wound up hugging the floor, praying for gravity to stop the spinning. A deep loam smell enveloped me, and I tasted my own vomit, which rose hot in my throat and went back down cold. I squeezed my eyes tightly shut and clung to the floor while the apartment seemed to lift off its foundations. When everything was still again, I crawled around a room that was miles too large, looking for my bed. I think I searched most of the night.

Two months ago I would have believed the rational explanation: that I hit the wall and the rest was a Chinese fire drill in my head. I think, now, that I grabbed onto something . . . kinetic? . . . that I contacted something half-formed on the border of physical reality—metaphysically kinetic—and that I helped it do what it wanted to do. The breathing returned toward dawn, soft and even, and it led me back to bed. I don't know what happened exactly for those minutes or hours in between, but I may be recalling the tangible aspects of another fugue. You tell me. Because when I got up this morning, clearheaded and alone, this is what was on my computer:

> I know what you're thinking, and that's how I can find ways to rush into your mind. Your thoughts are a bridge I can cross. I have no empathy, no sympathy, no compassion for you. The sooner you give up your sense of self, the better. That will stop the pain. It's as easy as accepting what you know happened that day. Let me stay. Let me be the first. If you are going to stop me, you will have to rescind the truth every time it starts to emerge, because that is my moment. You will have to guard the lie of your existence. But you can't do that forever, can you?

Afternoon, still the 20th

I'm typing this on Sam's computer.

Customers in and out today, and each time the shop emptied we were back at it. Me waving the printout from the hard drive in my apartment, Sam listening patiently, then posing objections and explanations. Easy for Sam to sit there and tell me I didn't embrace the energy of a soul and dance with it all night. Easy for him to pick holes in the note from my uninvited guest.

"How do you know it's a second soul?" he said. "Or if it is, that it isn't just an invention of your mind? Even you admit it was probably your body that went to the computer and typed it."

And that's where he dug in. I argued weakly that it was beyond science and he shouldn't expect me to give him an explanation that science could test and accept. He pointed to the pile of books and articles about metempsychosis and mankind's lore of the soul, all of which he had brought me, and asked if that showed he was closed-minded. "'. . . as easy as accepting what you know happened that day,'" I quoted from the note. Hadn't he himself been telling me that I already knew what had happened that day and was repressing something? Good thing I was, huh? Obviously, it was the transmigration. If

I hadn't repressed it, who would I be? At the very least I would be a spiritual hybrid of two people. At worst it would be nineteen plus me—if I even survived the usurpation. Instead of that, I'm holding them off. Their souls may all be inside me, but they are not sharing control. So, in a sense, the explanation is both psychological and metaphysical.

My psychological state is apparently the only thing preserving me as a solo act: Michael Bowden Carmichael, still alive if not well in Minnesota. I must be a very willful son of a bitch. And another part of that stubborn mind-set that's helping me survive is that I just don't get it. If I did, it might be harder to reject them. How can the souls be inside me and at the same time call up physical manifestations of themselves? I saw Alex, didn't I? I saw Pastor Evans. Shades of *Night of the Living Dead*. I can't accept that. Zombies, familiars. What do the Irish call them—fetches? "I *don't* believe in ghosts, I *don't* believe in ghosts...." Not when they can call up their external apparitions from inside my head.

Maybe sheer psychological intransigence is what brought me back to consciousness in the first place in a body and a brain that remained essentially undamaged at 55.1 degrees. If that's what repression is all about, put it right up there with immunology for self-protection. What a delicate paradox I'm in. If I accept what's evolving inside me, I hasten the reality. The truth becomes the truth when I believe it. So I have to slowly open the box without letting "Jack" spring out at me. I have to know without accepting.

"Don't you see what's happened, Sam?" I said. "I'm the record holder. The lowest core-temp survivor ever. And that must have lowered something else—a physical or spiritual barrier, whatever . . . and then came the coincidence of other deaths nearby. . . . I mean, it was some kind of opportunity. We were all dead, and here was this perfectly good body—don't you get it?"

He got it. He wasn't buying it.

"You're making an awful lot out of 'Let me be the first,'" he said.

I blinked at the paper in my hand. "It's right here. What else can it mean? You're the one who told me that everyone on the bus could be possessing me . . . or trying to."

"Exactly."

"Exactly? Come again. Why are we suddenly agreeing?"

"I gave you the idea. You took it home. And now it shows up in this note."

"Ah. Your suggestion and my overwrought imagination."

"Don't you think that's a possibility? My jury is still out, Bowie. When the evidence is incontrovertible, I'll believe it. I got it from both sides when I was growing up—my Ojibwa mother's lore and my father's Lutheran hellfire. If there is a soul, I've heard most of the details. It just seems a whole lot more likely to me at this point that you're subconsciously building scenarios that work out some issues inside you."

"Tell it to the spiders."

"The world is a *cirque noire* and Mother Nature is a great ringmaster. Something drove the spiders and insects together, probably. Earthquakes do that. Other things could too."

"Lawdy." I shook my head. He let me calm down for a moment, but when someone pulled into the parking lot, he looked at me again and decided to sum it up.

"If there are natural phenomena, then there must be

unnatural phenomena, Bowie. I firmly believe that. I'd love to know about the real universe where parallel lines meet and physics breaks down. Is it replaced by some grander form of logic, or is it something passion-driven and magical? Show me a clock that measures space, and a telescope that sees time, and I'll know we've finally escaped our limitations and put the puzzle together. The things that work for our little lives are just aberrations of a more stable set of truths, and only egocentric fools don't suspect that there's something more. So maybe what happened to you is a glimpse of it. I'd like to find out. But I won't do that by leaps of blind conviction."

Sam always leaves me feeling dumb. I think I'm pretty well-read, but he comes to knowledge through an unfathomable blend of common sense and intuition. Egocentric, he said. *Sense of self,* the note said. I should have pointed that out.

January 21st, 10:15 A.M.

Still here. At least the mirror says so. Same body, thinner face. Gash on my forehead gone. Spider bites mostly healed. But the eyes that are supposed to be the windows of the soul are stonewalling me. I can't detect what I feel inside. Of course, I didn't have time to give it much of a look. There was a line of faces behind me in the glass. . . .

Victorians used to build mirrored rooms called psychomanteums to summon spirits. That was in one of the books Sam brought me. A mirror is supposed to be a portal for the soul. Maybe I should turn mine to the wall. People used to do that in a room where someone had just died in order to keep the soul from becoming confused when it escaped the body. That was in the books too.

The fact that I'm not dead is getting to be the biggest mystery. Surviving the spider venom, the stag in the road, the bus, and Sam's snowmobile may not be particularly remarkable, but yesterday was. Yesterday deepens my doubts by miles and miles.

It was just after four when Sam returned from skiing, and a few minutes later I was stepping into the bindings of my old junk Combis, knowing that I wouldn't be going any place suitable for the Fischer RCS skis he gave me. The Saturday skiers would be on the groomed loops, and

I cut away on a narrow wrinkle of grungy snow that snowshoers had packed tight. This led east to where the lakes are.

The cold felt good. I unzipped my collar and let the icy gusts slap me around. I took all the longest routes, and after about forty-five minutes left the trail altogether and came out on a ridge right at the treetops of the largest lake.

The picture-postcard view was seductive. An intricate etching of branches superimposed itself over the whiteness of the lake and its gray islands. One colossal cluster of branches was so delicate that it seemed to be craquelure on a blue-gray masterpiece of haze and far horizon. Enchanting. Nature framed in three dimensions puts the viewer in the painting. But this was only the foreground. Sliding sideways, I came off the ridge, between boulders, and onto the windswept ice of the lake.

Lakes are a different kind of skiing. When there aren't any snowmobile tracks, and the surface is a frozen meringue like it was yesterday, you just lock your knees and double-pole. The sun fought through the haze, a fist of cold fire low on the horizon that drove a shadow off each carved dune. I roared along like a bobsled, smashing crest after crest.

Exposed as I was so far out in the open, I knew the danger of the wind. I was okay, though. My fingers around the pole grips were toasty from clenching and unclenching, and the two polypropylene layers under my ski suit were still wicking away most of the sweat from my body.

A good three-quarters of a mile from two ice-fishing shanties to the north and a few houses hunkered down on the south shore, I reached the approximate center of the lake and stopped to revel in the openness. Sidestepping in increments as tight as the minutes on a clock, I boxed the compass. The sun had turned as green and luminous as foxfire through a mist, and a snow squall was kicking up a few degrees away. I was now into the painting as far as I could go. I watched the squall come on.

It mesmerized me: first, the snow peeling off the ice—a diminutive rush, like a flurry of children starting up a soccer game—then driving toward me as if I were a goalie, then soaring past like penalty shots, until the soft barrage blurred into white walls. If the boulders back on shore were the basin of the waterfall, this was the white tunnel connected to the bus.

I turned my back and instead of a steady hand on my face, the wind buffeted my shoulders. Skeins of snow bound my legs, lifting me. All very pleasant—being cradled like that, belonging to a relentless river of life where each snowflake was like a bleached white soul, cold and pure. Comforting to lose my identity, to merge without definition or individuality, every mote diffusing. This was equilibrium, I thought; this was the universe in perfect harmony.

. . . the sooner you give up your sense of self . . .

I twisted around. Did I say comforting? Boring is what I meant. Comforting to know I wasn't homogenized like that. No universal perfect harmony for me.

And then as I faced into the gusts, my heart stumbled. Four figures were coming toward me. I had thought the fatal thought—that it was comforting to lose my identity, to merge—and the minions of Mephistopheles were coming for my soul. But it was only maverick winds, of course, spinning robes and forming gestures out of snow. Then again, they were huge angels, rising from the ice with feminine grace and beating their wings. They were tall and bulky, and they swayed hypnotically rather than ran, as if to belie some urgent purpose.

Remarkable how long the wind held them together like that. Hard to believe they weren't real beings. If my sister, Laura, were there, and we were cataloging wind chimeras again, what would she have seen? Definitely sisters. And that's what I began to see. Four sisters, trailing scarves in their wake.

My fingers were starting to feel pinched, and the sweat that hadn't wicked away encased my torso in cold armor. The squall, graying now, stung my cheeks. With a little rush of adrenaline, I realized I had stood in one place too long. The far shore had receded in shades of muslin gray that might have been more snow. If I didn't get moving again, I could be in trouble so far from shelter. Suddenly the diaphanous quartet swaying toward me collapsed back into the ice.

What happened next keeps replaying like the downbeat of a song. Maybe it's because I imagined the four sisters continuing to dance in the gloomy depths of the lake. Maybe I was looking for the cause that ended their dance. But there was a thump directly beneath my left ski. One thump. When you are on ice, it is always creaking, snapping, settling. This was different. A thump.

The second thump was to the right of me. Then two more just ahead. The acoustics, even considering that I was standing in the wind on a lake, sounded unnatural. This wasn't a seep pushing through a pocket of trapped air. This was something *banging*.

I leaned hard on the poles and kicked into a full sprint. My windbreaker rattled stiffly, making it sound like I was running in a sack race, but each yard I put between myself and the thumps in the ice brought back a measure of composure. I turned south toward the houses. That was the nearest shore, and once in the lee of trees I could work my way back to the trails. The trouble was that the wind was blowing into me and I was slowing. My ski edges clattered and my pole tips pinged off the lake surface. Very thick ice. Which explained why the next thump sounded so muffled.

The visceral premonition of earth-gone-to-hell rose in my blood like a tide. Time for mayday; time for save-your-ass flight. More thuds now to the left. Answers from the right. Willful thuds. I dug harder with the poles, trying to carve edges, but the skis slipped. I went to a knee and immediately felt the drumbeat through the ice. An electric shock couldn't have brought me to my feet quicker. I locked my knees and began to double-pole. But the wind had a say in that, too, and I barely inched along.

You always know when the cracking stays deep on the underside of pack ice. Surface cracking is like a windowpane snapping. Deep is dull. The next one sounded like a pistol shot. Then everything started to let go. Ice sections groaned, sheets grated, air pockets popped, and each few seconds there was that sharp snap that could mean only that the splitting was coming to the surface. I squinted hard for black water, but the wind was freezing my lashes shut. It started not to matter. Because the insane reverberation and the roar and the hiss and the thundering were all coming together.

I don't know how far I got. I remember the first slushy sounds, and then the splashes of the carbide tips chunking through puddles. Open water yawned beyond the dark gray patches close at hand. I skied almost as a reflex. I skied until I fell into icy shock, and rose up elbow deep, and then slowly sank into black water.

The lake was warmer than the air, but not as warm as the trapped air escaping from my clothes. The wind had unexplainably stopped dead, and this seemed to stifle the oxygen in my brain. Below the surface, things were brushing against my legs. I began to seize up. Mercifully, numbness and disorientation spared me further details.

I really didn't suffer that much, if you want to know. I think I was like a thief who is secretly relieved to be finally caught. My ill-gotten gain was time. I had only technically escaped death in the waterfall two months earlier. Now that loophole was about to close. I could stop struggling.

In this state of surrender, it took me a few moments to realize that my skis were actually resting on the lake bottom. Small reprieve. There was nothing firm enough that I could pull myself out on, and for as far as I could see—less than fifty yards—there was no shore. I was chest deep and freezing.

The green sun was gone, having set or sunk in the haze, and I began thinking this wasn't a bad place to die. A death chamber soft and gray. No mirror to turn to the wall. I could just let my air out and sink. I even rejected the thought that the mammalian reflex that had saved me in the waterfall might save me again in this icy water. *Waterfall Man Does It Again!* No, thank you. I thought about the impact of my death on Jessica and Danny. They probably wouldn't care that much. It had turned out to be a good thing after all—this separation, this painful phasing-out we had all been forced to do. When everything was said and done, it was a good thing.

And that was when the haze in front of me wavered.

The tenuous mist whorled like a fingerprint of displaced air. Something was coming low on the water, straight toward me. I caught a white flash and ripples to my left—denizens fleeing the chaos beneath the surface, or maybe the fling of a Swedish dancer's fingers, or (hallelujah) the advancing stroke of an oar.

Through the haze he came, the silhouette of his head and shoulders dead-on for rescue. I cried out from relief alone as the prow of the craft loomed into my face and glided silently alongside. The lake was suddenly eerily still.

"Hang on," his voice grated, and the moist air seemed to dampen all its human timbre.

Exactly how I got on board is a blur in my memory. I remember my benefactor's rigid hands prying me from the poles and the skis as I lay half across the gunwale. He countered my lopsided drag with his feet braced on the bottom of the craft to tamp the rocking, and a blanket dropped around my shoulders before my legs were even under me. I centered myself on the second cross-seat as he sculled a half circle and pulled for shore so smoothly that the mist seemed to move instead of the boat.

How he had rowed straight to me never crossed my mind last night, but now it seems impossible. The explanations are absurd: night-vision goggles? fish sonar? divine guidance by four snow angels who were once sisters from Sweden? And even though rowing unerringly toward shore is less miraculous than finding a single object in the haze, he did that too, with no obvious means of navigation. None of these mysteries occurred to me in the boat when I was shivering violently. And besides, I had another reason to feel uneasy.

At first I thought the wrap around his face was the tattered collar of a coat. But the air thinned intermittently, and the space where his face should have been pulsed a dull, oxblood red. Sitting there, staring straight at him, that drifting color became the focal point. Umber, ruby, umber again. Oh, yes . . . it had to be a scarf. A red scarf.

And each time he leaned toward me to set the stroke, he hesitated . . . as if tempting me to snatch it off. I was clutching the blanket around me, and the ache in my body told me that hypothermia wouldn't need much help, so I wasn't about to answer the challenge. But if my hands were unavailable, my eyes were riveted on his.

He must have known by the pawing on the wooden hull that we were close to shore, that the water had turned to slurry again, because he never looked around, but took three hard pulls on the oars to drive us onto the snow-crusted beach. Then he swung from the bow seat over the gunwale and tugged the rowboat up another yard.

"Can you make it up the beach?" he asked in the same dull grate.

Water leached from the soaked linings of my boots, and I had lost my ski gloves. I followed him with my head tucked down, lurching stiffly in the packed grooves apparently left by the boat being dragged down from behind a two-story house that sat on a slight rise. There were no lights on inside the house, but I saw a car in the drive. It was a large car. An old car. I never actually made out the vehicle logo, and the shape was indefinite under fresh snow, but I was sure.

It was an LTD.

Cynicism and fear are easier on the nerves than shock. I accepted the worst. The car, the man. Too exhausted and frozen to balk, I slogged into the passenger seat as he glided behind the wheel. The crucifix that had dangled from the mirror the day I wrenched the door open in Timothy Lutheran's parking lot was gone, but a shredded cord still hung above the dash, as if the object it had suspended had been torn away impulsively. He started the engine and heat poured immediately from the vents. Why was the engine already warm? He flicked the headlights on. Backing out, we turned toward the highway.

"Is that your house?" I managed through chattering teeth. "Was that your boat?"

He nodded.

"You must have been watching me out there, right?"

"I was watching."

The scarf muted his words, and in any case, I couldn't place Pastor Evans's voice well enough to identify it, or Alex Franke's.

"You saw what happened on the lake, then?"

"I saw."

"How do you explain that?"

"It's not safe this time of year."

My jaw clenched with cold as I tried to form a succinct statement. "It's January. When is it safe?"

His eyes turned and rested full on me for a moment. "You shouldn't go out on lakes. They're always dangerous. Skiing is dangerous. Being in the woods is dangerous. It's safer just to stay indoors."

"Who the hell are you?"

"I saved your life."

"So that it can be your life?"

There was a long silence, and then he recited, "You're from The Ski Shop, aren't you?"

In another minute we had turned onto the cutoff, and then we were at the shop. His hands were tucked into the shadows around the bottom of the wheel, and I thought there might be a finger missing. Suddenly I reached out and whisked the scarf away.

What would I have done if it had been Evans? But it wasn't Evans. It was a stranger. I can sit here now and reflect that a red plaid scarf is just about the most common kind. There are probably tens of thousands in Minnesota.

I've checked the Internet picture of the bus victims for my rescuer, and I've got the images down to two possibilities. Neither one is clear enough to be a positive match. This is important. Because if someone from the bus is trying to protect me, who—or what—is trying to kill me?

January 21, 7:50 P.M.

The house on the lake looks desolate in clear daylight. No footprints around the doors, mailbox frozen shut, drapes drawn. The rowboat is flipped over on blocks with the oars under it. Except for the LTD, whose tracks stop six feet short of the garage, nothing has gone in or out of the drive since the last snowfall.

Call me my own worst enemy, but nothing is going to force me off the lakes and out of the woods. If anarchy is the face nature is going to show me, I'll just have to make up the rules of survival as I go along. But I can do that. To surrender freedom is the same as being kept at Mayo. And anyway, this morning there was a good chance that my skis were on the ice or floating in open water. I crunched through the snow down to the beach.

The lake was a solid sheet of white too painfully bright to contemplate, and the farther out I squinted, the more my eyes teared up. I lobbed a heavy stone ten yards from shore and it stuck like a shot put. A smaller stone sailed over fifty yards and was lost in the glare with still no splash. I shuffled onto the ice.

Discovery: Ice is another of those things that destabilizes reality. Like mirrors, like dreams, like steamy baths or breathing in the dark or doctored saline solution—put this one on the list. Ice. Another way to lose control. You walk lighter on ice—another alienation from terra firma.

Yesterday my life was saved by my enemy. Today it's getting through to me that that means I have two enemies. One wants to save my body but kill or compromise my soul. The other wants to kill my body and—who knows?—maybe that will save my soul. Yesterday it was the enemy who wants to kill my body. Call it *nature*. I hate to admit that Mr. Freeze (refer to him pointedly as M. F.) was right about that, if a little disingenuous in calling himself my ally. *You have an enemy, and it's not who you think it is.* But today—standing on that chessboard of ice—I think it was my soul that was under direct attack.

If I keep my perspective, I'll keep my independence. Going out on the ice was my choice—mine—and I tried not to see a conspiracy in the sudden gusting of the wind, pushing me along from behind. Even though the snow dunes were like standing waves aimed in the other direction, it could have been a normal shift in the wind that made them spew crests backward. I kept my head down, watching my feet. When I glanced back at the beach a minute or so later, I saw only glare. At that point the first stone I had thrown was behind me, but the smaller one came up sooner than I expected in an ominous patch of gray.

Far enough, I thought. *Point proven about my freedom to go where I please, and to hell with the skis.*

And just then the shadow of a cloud raced across the surface, wiping out the glare over the southern half of the lake, revealing a lumpy corridor that ran out from the beach.

Yesterday in the wind and the haze it had seemed like the whole lake was erupting, but now I could see it was only a swath, twenty yards wide, zigzagging as I must have in my desperation. And something else. In the dimmed whiteness farther out: the unmistakable figure of a snowman.

There were probably a dozen like it around the lake. Kids played out there. There would be snow forts and shoveled ice rinks, dog tracks and broken bits of red and blue plastic sleds. But I had to know. Had to see if I'd recognize the damn snowman—like they don't all look alike—because there was something come-hither about that forlorn pillar on the ice.

The shadow of the cloud passed, and I was squinting again. Trudging, squinting, trudging. At fifty feet I began to suspect... at twenty feet I stopped. The head, clearly defined by a purple knit cap, sat on the ground. My knit cap. The one I had lost on the ice yesterday. My ski pole was stuck through the snowman's face. The grip of the other pole was embedded where the left arm would be, its carbide tip resting in the ice. And old Frosty was sitting on top of my skis, as if he had been skiing when disaster overtook him.

I don't like symbols. Symbols undermine reality. Juju, voodoo, a totem pole—add a decapitated snowman. Defiance withered in my breast. Too many headless things in my life. Fears linking up with dreams, trying to convince me that my mind is separate and apart. I scurried back to the beach chilled and subjugated, not even retrieving the junk Combis.

While Sam was out grooming this morning he found an owl frozen to death on the trail. He said he saw it sitting in a tree in broad daylight on his first pass at the bottom of the south trail, and he thought then that it might be frozen to the branch. When he finished packing snow, he made another pass to put down texture, and the owl had blown over dead. I think he was just making the point to me that everything bizarre isn't unnatural.

Dead owls may be a natural phenomenon, but the Greeks believed the death of one of them heralds madness. Symbols. After they undermine reality, you start to trust them.

When I got back home there was a handwritten note with a phone number at the bottom, folded over and dropped in the mailbox.

Sorry I missed you. Please call.
Beckie Franke

She's been on my mind. Now and then you meet a woman that you know any man would cherish, one who doesn't think of herself as a victim. You want to give to someone like that. I guess when you're coming off a divorce, you can be attracted to what a woman isn't.

And I know I leap to conclusions whenever I begin a relationship, but when I phoned and Beckie picked up on the first ring I started thinking dangerously again. The truth is, she's shown no inclination toward me. There is nothing between us.

"I hope you don't mind my tracking you down like this," was the first thing she said.

"Oh, I'm totally furious."

Her laugh is the faintest breath over the phone, and any woman's laugh is like applause to me.

"I have a strict rule against letting appealing women through the door," I said. "Bummer I wasn't here to tell you that over dinner and a bottle of wine."

She returned an ambivalent pause I interpret as not quite rejection. But then she said, "You know why I came today."

"You want to know if I've seen Alex again."

"Have you?"

"No."

She made a neutral sound. "I didn't really think you had. You would have come and told me if you had, right?"

"Right."

"But then again, you might not know . . . I mean, if you're right about his trying to be in your mind, then . . . then you wouldn't necessarily realize—"

"He's not in my mind."

"No, of course not."

"I'm doing it again."

"What?"

"Lying to you."

"Then he is in your mind?"

"I don't know. Maybe. Sometimes." She waited. I had to deliver something. "Did he have any musical ability?"

"Musical ability? Not unless you count drumming his fingers. He was seriously into Tiny Tim when we got married. Is that important?"

"Just a loose end."

"You suddenly have a musical talent, and you thought it might be Alex," she guessed.

"Turn it around. I've lost one. The day the music died, you know? Probably just the stress since the accident."

"Really."

An alarming "really." Too willing to believe that her dead husband's tin ear was having an effect on me.

In a way, I'm relieved that she isn't interested in me personally. We got in another exchange or two, and I knew she was leading up to us getting together, but she's afraid I'll take it the wrong way. And she's right; I will. Even though I know she just wants to detect Alex in me.

Oh, I could take this downtown, play it to the hilt, get a lot closer to her as a surrogate Alex. If I wanted. But I wouldn't do that. I don't think. And if I did—if I do—what's to keep me from blaming it on Alex being inside me? It could happen. Me becoming his vessel to reunite with his wife. That would be the test, wouldn't it? If I resist her, I'll know I'm still me. Bummer.

That's what I was thinking when the phone connection began to break up. It didn't sound like she was on a cell, and even if she was, there was a TV going in the background, so she wasn't in a car or something moving out of range. But the line went dead. I jammed the phone down, picked it up after a second. No dial tone. It was my line.

I tried to drive to a phone booth, but, unbelievably, the car wouldn't start.

Two A.M.

The fact that I'm writing everything down proves that I'm sane. One person wrote this. One only. I just went back through to make sure the perspective is mine alone. If there is insanity in what I've recorded, it's not mine. It's theirs.

So I've got to get it all down on paper as quickly as possible, so that it's as fresh and honest as possible. If I try to quilt it into the great American novel I always wanted to write, I'll be tampering with the evidence. Knowing exactly what happened to me may become the silver thread that leads me out of exile and back into the rational world. And, God knows, a few hours ago I went miles deeper into exile. I want out of Unholy Fest. Tonight I was in the wrong church, the wrong pew, and—sweet Jesus, come get me—in the presence of the wrong god.

Sunday, ten thirty P.M., I was still working on the car: reading the manual, replacing fuses, demystifying the little multitester I bought at Target to figure out if the car battery was okay, changing one of the fuel filters, and tapping on the starter. When I gave up in frustration and grabbed the flashlight off the battery I noticed the loosened terminal nut. One turn with the wrench and the car was fixed.

It was too late to contact Beckie, but I had worked all evening with that goal in mind, and now I couldn't just gather up every tool I owned and slink back upstairs to the apartment. I drove to Sheshebans, drove past her house to see if maybe the porch light was on and she was holding a séance with a WELCOME, BOWIE sign out front held up by a floating trumpet. There were blue flickers from her living room. I pictured her lying on the couch in pink pajamas while Letterman deadpanned her to sleep. It was after eleven by this time, and I couldn't muster the gall to go knock.

I haven't tooled past a female's doorstep in the middle of the night since I was a lovesick teenager driving a Plymouth Barracuda rusted up to the door panels. And now that the car I drive is no longer rusted, Bowie Carmichael is. I'm wizened with Freud's, "Love is the overestimation of the sexual object," and Einstein's "Marriage is an unsuccessful attempt to make something lasting out of an incident," so I ought to know better. Maybe it isn't Beckie Franke I'm after. Maybe I'm just trying to recapture a more optimistic time in my life. And if that's what I was doing three hours ago, I should never have turned down a side street in search of TLC.

Timothy Lutheran Church was having a candlelight service of some kind. The reds and yellows in the stained-glass windows blazed warmly, and the martellato belch of the organ's deepest chords carried through into the brittle air. I pulled to the curb next to a fire hydrant, edged a few feet ahead, and shut off the engine.

It wasn't my intention to go in, but it was Beckie's church, and the people inside knew her—probably had attended her wedding in this same building—and I didn't want to go back to stark, raving solitude just yet. I sat in the car, listening to the strident hymn. It ended on an aberrant note. Moments later I heard snatches of a congregational chant metered against phantom pauses—a reading and responsory. The people in the pews would have their heads bowed, their eyes closed. I could just slip into the back, I thought impulsively. And that's how I found myself where I never expected to be just before midnight: inside the sanctuary of Timothy Lutheran Church.

If I thought it was going to be cozy in there, I was mistaken. Someone must have forgotten to turn the thermostat up for the service. Sitting alone in the last pew, I could see my breath. I couldn't see anyone else's, but there weren't that many people scattered around, and I had deliberately positioned myself as far away from anyone as possible. The candles flanking the altar were as huge and garish as crimson pylons, and the minister stood between them, his back to us, scarlet robe hanging like a valance over his raised arms.

But the stunning thing was the minister's voice. It detonated in the apse, raining dynamic phrases like shrapnel over the pews. And it wasn't the words themselves—except for a few biblical references, I never got his drift—it was the ritual prowl of their delivery, a liturgical descant.

"Is there shame in Gomorrah; does Sodom hide its face?" he lined out. "When pride resides in Admah, then shall balm return to Gilead. Let the falcon fall, that the sparrow may rise. Let the sun set in the morning...."

"'... and night sees all,'" recited the congregation.

"Let the harvest come in darkness. . . ."

"'. . . and night sees all.'"

"Let the tide reject the moon. . . ."

"'. . . and night sees all.'"

It is impossible to render it accurately, because it went on and on in that flowery style. He was reading from scrolls that lay open on the altar—large-lettered texts that looked like a Septuagint translation right out of Greek—but then he seemed to switch to Latin. And a minute later it was Hebrew. And maybe after that Aramaic. I haven't a clue about Lutherans, but this was practically speaking in tongues.

The figures in front of me sat still as statues. Not a cough or a nod. They could have been in a rhapsody or catatonic. Didn't matter; the red-robed celebrant wasn't going to turn around for a heart attack or the hokeypokey. He was in his own little world of books and ages and comings. Something like:

". . . the Rubicon is upon us. Thus will power find its poles and dominion its divisions. The foot of the rampart and the edge of the abyss will cease to shrink. Ashes to ashes, dust to dust, clay to bone and bone to clay. Let the Final Testament be written."

"'Now and forevermore,'" responded the congregation.

His arms came down at last, but he pulled the scarlet cowl over his head as he turned. I was seized with curiosity. Suspicion in general seized me. *Seized.* The word is stuck in my head because a revision suddenly dawned on me. Those sweeping recitatives the congregation had mouthed, ". . . and night sees all"—or was it—"and night seize all"? A command. A wish. A dark hope.

I'm sure the writing of this makes the truth seem clear from the start to anyone reading, if only because I said that up front about being in the presence of the wrong god. But three hours ago, I still couldn't be sure. In fact, what came next was classic denial, because if my suspicions were right, what was I going to do about it?

There was an ebony communion tray. Wafers and wine. And the penitent closest to the altar rose and went forward. Kneeling, he accepted the wafer from the minister and received a benediction that sounded like:

"Yort said ehty dob."

Then the wine. Another murmur, whose phonetics I never did get.

One by one the figures in the pews rose, went to the altar, knelt, and received the host, the wine, and that inscrutable blessing. I thought I would see their faces coming back up the aisle, but to my utter frustration, each member who received communion filed off through a Gothic arch behind the pulpit. I could have rushed up there and confronted them. I could have torn the cowl off the minister, as I had snatched the scarf from the face of my rescuer at the lake. But believe it or not, I still wasn't sure the service wasn't something normal in the routines of Timothy Lutheran Church.

I'll take the blame for a lot of things, but not for being restrained in that atmosphere. If I go around yanking scarves and cowls off people, pretty soon I'll be back staring Dr. Anthony P. Weibens in the face. I need self-respect. I need to believe I'm making rational choices. And there in the candlelit sanctuary just before midnight I didn't want to be right about my fears, didn't want to touch the worshipers and find them insubstantial or ghoulish. I think they wanted me to lose it, to flip out, to smash the compass and do something really insane.

So I sat there watching the parade file up, file out. Somewhere after six or seven had disappeared through the Gothic arch, I began to count. I wished I had done that before, because if there were nineteen—eighteen plus the minister . . . well, then. Was it six or seven? It didn't matter, though, didn't matter at all, because I was counting now, and even if it was seven, there were only ten left. Seventeen all told.

I almost laughed aloud with relief. I sat forward, draped my arms over the next pew, and clasped my hands. *Thank you, Lord!*

The last of them received the consecration and were swallowed up by the blackened archway behind the pew. Sixteen at most. Seventeen counting the minister. Just an arbitrary number of late-night worshipers, night owls, and swing-shift workers, shy people, curmudgeons who didn't want to interact with the pledge-drive committee or the Bible-study group. You could tell that by where they sat. Loners. Sure, there was one couple sitting together, and the four who I had rashly begun to suspect could be the sisters from Sweden, but they all sat through the mumbo jumbo and took their sacrament, like living people do, and left according to what was apparently the custom of their communion service. Seventeen.

And then I saw a slight movement from behind the glare of one of the candles. The organ pipes rose against the wall in line with that flicker, and even before she stepped out of the shadows, I knew I had overlooked the organist. She had been mentioned in the online article about the crash—the fact that the church had lost its music. But, of course, this organist was her replacement, because even adding her to the total there were still just eighteen. No more than that. So it wasn't *them.*

Sidling out of the shadows, the organist genuflected, took her communion, and faded off through the Gothic arch.

Now it was just that scarlet mantle waiting for me at the altar. The candles conspired to shade whatever hid in the cowl, and suddenly my mouth was going dry and the fleece on the nape of my coat rubbed like steel wool. Such a deep, deep shadow in that hood. Fathomless, almost. Like a hole in the air.

I was transfixed. It was time to leave; I wanted to leave, but I could not. Instead, I began to weigh the consequences. Why not go up there, kneel, stare into that nothingness? Because it just couldn't be what I dreaded, and if I walked out of the sanctuary—if I somehow *could* walk out—I would never know for sure. I would be retreating one more step toward losing a sane world filled with mundane things and little idiosyncratic human rituals that I have every right to share without hysteria. So, I had to go up there. I had to see that it wasn't an empty cowl. I had already seen the back of his head—an amorphous silhouette—while blistering syllables spewed out of his mouth like hot ash.

I think I levitated in a cold sweat down the aisle. And like the scarecrow, spaghetti-kneed before the Wizard of Oz, I didn't kneel so much as I collapsed in graceless deference. My eyes were starting out of my head, probing the deep black space open to me. But nothing, absolutely nothing, limited my gaze.

"Yort said ehty dob," he sighed like a stealthy wind.

My stare broke to the ebony tray, and I saw that there was one wafer, one thimble of wine. Such good planning. One host left. As if they were expecting me. Shaking like a centenarian, I plucked the thing up. But halfway to my lips, I knew I didn't want to do this. Symbols. Such wrong symbols. Everything. Wrong. I flung the host aside and struggled to my feet.

"Who are you?" I said, backing up the aisle.

Slowly he pivoted and blew out the right candle, then the left. The darkness danced with afterghosts. I heard his robe drop to the floor. Something seemed to fill the sanctuary, driving me back. I bumped into one of the candle spikes that marked each row of pews and stopped. Then, as suddenly as the atmosphere had grown oppressive, it relaxed. A distant door closed in the direction of the Gothic arch.

I was alone.

I hoped I was alone. I fumbled backward to the sanctuary doors, and there must be one hell of a long DMZ between the quick and dead, because I swear it was a hundred steps farther than it should have been. When at last I had the cold handle in my fingers, I twisted it open. Across the foyer I dashed and through the outer doors. Triumph and relief and exultation rose in my breast. But just as I was coming off the steps, I heard the piston sigh of rolling, rubber-edged doors.

It was the bus.

The old yellow bus. Engine murmuring, door yawning open. *Going my way? Take the shortcut.*

May God damn their relentlessness. You are not my bus. I am not your way station. Get a life, get a life . . . but not mine.

Of course, my fears would all sound very circumstantial and unfounded in a session with Weibens. The service would be for shut-ins, bused in late one Sunday night for whatever special worship was on the church calendar. A little odd, perhaps, but not unexplainable. They would come and leave by the side door, accessible through the arch behind the pulpit, because that leads to the parking lot where the bus would be waiting. It would be a yellow bus, because even though they are made by Blue Bird most of them *are* yellow. The minister could be seen to have acted perfectly restrained in the face of my outrageous and even blasphemous behavior at the altar. And why shouldn't the driver think I was one of his passengers? As a matter of fact, the minister—now on board and remembering me heading for the other exit—would quite naturally tell him to pull around and pick me up. And if I didn't dash away in comic panic, I would see all this.

Comic panic or not, I got to my car faster than my car can get to sixty on a straightaway, and I nearly clipped the fire hydrant spinning around, and that lined me up with the marquee, which my headlights caught full, and I did get the Probe roaring past sixty by the time I reached the city limits out of Sheshebans.

But all the miles I've put in since haven't calmed me down. On the contrary, numbers now are adding up to my worst fears. Because the driver would be number nineteen, wouldn't he? Not a member of the church, but nevertheless a victim of the accident, waiting in the parking lot. And you can say what you want about reading into things, about rock-'n'-roll 45s played backward to reveal demonic messages, but that's what I heard being read in Timothy Lutheran Church two hours ago. Not Latin or Hebrew or Aramaic or Greek, but scripture read backward. And, sure, sure, you can play around with sounds and make what you want come out of them. But I *don't* want what I got to come out of them. Because it didn't take me long to parse out that little profanity of a communion blessing, *Yort said ehty dob,* and to work it around on paper to *Yortsed eht ydob,* which in mirror-image terms, if not mirror writing, would be: *Destroy the body.*

Oh, yeah. One other quickie in the hasty, hallucinogenic retreat of Michael Bowden Carmichael. When my headlights flashed past that marquee announcing the current service, I will swear it read: THE BOOK OF BOWIE.

January 22

I'm supposed to make history. That's what I get out of it. The Book of Bowie. I should chuck this account I'm writing and get going on something biblical. *Ecclesiastes Revised,* or *How I Found Room in My Soul for Nineteen Orphans.* I don't want to be history.

Nine thirty this morning I rang Beckie's bell. For all I knew, she had a full-time job, but I drove all the way up there, and just as I rolled back down the drive, here she comes in her white Escort with a load of groceries. I helped her with the groceries, and she made me breakfast.

We talked, and it was just a kind of background murmur to sustain what was really going on between us. So it's not surprising that I remember the melody but not the lyrics. Not a sentence comes back to me until she brought me down by mentioning Alex. She had gone out and gotten a video of *Ghost* the night before, and she thought she saw Alex in the convex mirror above a video rack in Blockbuster's. I sat there like a bump on a log until her voice suddenly drained and she said:

"You don't want to talk about this, do you?"

"I don't? Who says? Just because I'm a good listener when you finally get to the important stuff, you think I'm not interested. I await your apology."

She broke out a faint smile, still trying to discern facade from structure in my personality.

"You think it's easy making chitchat with a beautiful woman when what I really want is to discuss her husband?" I said.

"You have no idea how good it is for me when you talk about him, Bowie."

"Why?"

"Because you talk as if he's alive."

My stomach knotted. "I've had trouble with my tenses ever since the Good Sisters of Mercy beat me with *Warriner's Grammar*."

"Don't joke."

"Okay. He's alive. Or if he isn't alive, he's not dead."

"How do you know for sure?"

"You know how I know."

"Tell me again."

"No. It's hard for me. Not good for you either."

"Oh, but it is."

She leaned so close I could see the pulse in her neck. "I'll tell you what happened Saturday morning," I said, and I told her about the note I had found on the computer screen.

Her voice deepened with disappointment. "It doesn't sound like Alex. He would never say it like that, that he has no compassion for you. Even in desperation."

The blatant ignorance of this assertion stripped the veneer off the moment for me. What could she know about desperation—what could any *living* human know? You can't be any more desperate than to be a disembodied soul looking for a host. You might endure pain to your body, your mind might plunge into madness trying to hang on to its identity, but your soul . . . your very soul— that is the absolute last stand, the fundamental outpost before extinction. The will to survive supersedes all else when your spirit is guttering out. My single moment of unrelieved darkness, of feeling chaos unbind my atoms, qualifies me to know. And even though my body is still intact, I'm stalked by entities without forms whose hunger for warm embodiment is terrifying.

"I'm sorry it's painful for you, Bowie," she said, "but it's such a relief for me to sit here talking like this. I'm tired of mourning. I'm tired of talking about Alex like he's dead when I know he's still here."

"Beckie, you wouldn't want him back, if that's what you're thinking. You wouldn't."

"I know that he can't come back . . . physically."

"If you have some fairy-tale notion about communication with the dead, forget it."

"I don't understand how you can say that after what's happened to you."

"It wouldn't be the way you think."

"You spoke to him, and he spoke to you."

I looked at her coldly. She had left me a note, invited me in to breakfast when I came to her door, played the game. She expected something—needed something—that hadn't come out yet. "What is it exactly that you want me to do?"

"Live here."

In spite of my agitation, the worldliness of that arrangement made me laugh out loud.

"If you stay here, then whatever happens, I can be a part of it," she said.

"You mean in case I lose the war for my soul?"

She looked chastened. "It would be safer for you, too, wouldn't it? I mean, you shouldn't be living alone."

"Living here would make it worse for you."

"How? You're the one in danger. Maybe I can protect *you*. Anyway, it's not fair to leave me out of it now."

I shook my head weakly, but I couldn't say "no" aloud, and she seized on my dismay as if it were a reluctant surrender. "Good," she said, and repeated the word as if it were a done deal.

A woman who is definitely attractive to me has asked me to live with her. Why am I not ecstatic? There is something very unholy in this, and I don't mean morally. She knows I've got one leg over the wall, and she wants a hand up to join me. She can't grasp that the universe on the other side contains none of the neat beginnings and endings that insulate living human beings. That's what she's opting for. That's what I don't think she understands.

"How would it work?" I asked slowly.

"How?"

"Would we sit here until Alex raps three times, or would you just follow me around all day?"

She was too elated to take offense. "Your friend— Sam—he's with you during the day, right? Nothing has happened to you except when you're alone. So, after you leave work, you just come straight here."

"If I come here, I won't be alone."

Her eyes were enormous, her gaze steady, her voice perfectly smooth as she said: "I don't think it will matter if I'm here. I don't think it will matter at all. Maybe it's what Alex wants."

January 23, afternoon

I just reread what I wrote yesterday. Where did I get that stuff: *The will to survive supersedes all else when your spirit is guttering out . . .* ? And at the store I said to Sam, "There's more truth in instinct than there is in reason." Sitting here now, I don't even know what the hell that means. These sweeping apocalyptic statements are coming from outside my experience. I am a hairbreadth away from losing majority ownership of me.

When I swung around to my apartment after work to pick up some essentials before going back to Beckie's, there was a notice in the mailbox from the apartment manager saying that the phones were back in service but that someone had cut the line and all residents should keep an eye out for vandals. I read that standing in the foyer, but I was halfway up the steps before the significance hit me. A cut line in the middle of my conversation with Beckie. You put that together with the loose battery cable in my car that kept me from going out to a pay phone, and clearly my new relationship has dangerous opposition. Whatever came out of that yellow bus as it vomited flames isn't to be trusted. I actually picked up the phone to call Beckie and say I changed my mind and wasn't coming, but suddenly my instincts were jangling as if the line were delivering a piece of me across the cosmos instead of across the county. Because they had to be listening. *Snip, snip*.

I guess the interventions contradict Beckie's theory that maybe it's what Alex wants. Or do we have a conflict here between Alex and the other eighteen? He wants back into his old life; the others want back into theirs. Plus they want to keep me isolated so that my resistance to them is less. Same as lowering my temperature in the waterfall, they want to lower the intensity of my relationships. Like it wasn't already weaker than a gnat's orgasm.

It was dark by the time I reached East Tristan. I didn't mention about the phone lines or the loose battery cable to Beckie. She searched my face as if she already knew she would learn more from me that way than by asking questions.

She had gone all-out to make our arrangement feasible, clearing drawers and shelf space for me, setting up a rollaway in what must have been Alex's office-study, fixing a full dinner. She knows about my effect on open food, and she had the whole meal done and kept warm in the oven by the time I got there. I can't remember the last time I've had a salad and dessert.

We talked and drank some good Chablis she and Alex had been saving for their anniversary, but already the full awkwardness was settling in. We are waiting for some kind of cataclysm to happen to me. We have no plans together, no goals, no mutual aspirations. We're strangers linked by a third party I would like to exorcise and she would like to resurrect. It's as artificial and orchestrated as a round of golf over a business deal.

"This isn't going to work," I said. "We've barely met and we're trying to live together."

"We're not *living* together. You're . . . a boarder."

"I don't feel like a boarder."

"Maybe your expectations are a little ahead of the game."

I had every right to challenge that, but I knew exactly what she meant, and she was on the money. "I'm sure you'll let me know if I get out of line."

Her face softened and she added, "We probably have a lot in common."

"I doubt it."

"Of course we do."

"Like what?"

She is unerring about feelings, but when she reasons, it's like she's trying on a slightly melodramatic mask. "You like to ski."

"You ski?"

"I've always wanted to."

I laughed unkindly.

"Really. I have. Would you take me?"

The smile left my face. Dolores was a good skier, but after we were married she never took the time. Beckie had just reawakened my wounded fantasy of a female companion.

"I'll take you, but I wish you wouldn't pretend," I said.

"Listen to me: I'd *love* to ski with you. Okay?"

God, I'm pathetic. My heart was thundering at the prospect of sharing the holy rites of winter with her, but all I could think was, *I've got my own ambulance chaser.* . . .

"Okay," I said.

As the night wore on and conversation slowed, Alex became inevitable. He is our touchstone. "What if you see him again and he's totally changed?" I asked. "What if you don't recognize him?"

"You mean will I be too much in denial to recognize it, too obsessed to accept it, or too desperate to care?"

"Yeah, that's what I meant." She has a way of paraphrasing bullshit so that it goes away before I can step in it.

She stared at the navy photo on the coffee table. "I'll tell you what I'm afraid of. What if spiritual energy just fades away like an ember in a fireplace? The real danger is that Alex won't be here much longer."

Now, there's a happy thought. "I don't think that's going to happen," I said.

She shrugged. " 'The dead know nothing.' "

"Where did I just hear that?"

"Ummm . . . I think it's from Ecclesiastes. What's the matter?"

"Nothing. Hard to put a good book down."

"What are you talking about?"

" 'Who knows the spirit of the sons of men, which goes upward, and the spirit of the animal, which descends?' "

She positively grinned. "God, Bowie, you're hard to figure. I took you for a heathen, and here it turns out you're a Bible scholar."

"Nay. Writer's envy. I'm thinking of adding a book to the Bible, if I can find some blank scrolls. Maybe I'll just write it on my wall. The Book of Bowie."

"Dear me, the Chablis has gotten you drunk."

"What does that verse mean—the one I just quoted?"

"I don't know."

"Reincarnation?"

"I don't know. Maybe an affirmation of the soul's divine nature."

Red Magic Marker across half my wall says it's the Lies of Solomon. "Why did you say that a minute ago?"

I pressed her. "You know, about the dead knowing nothing."

"I guess . . . I heard it in church. One of the sermons was from Ecclesiastes."

"Wait till you hear the next one."

"Come again?"

"Nothing. I think someone's ghostwriting your church marquee."

Theology dead-ended between us, and by default the conversation reverted to Alex.

"He'll be here as long as I'm here," I said. "You understand, don't you, I want him to go away?"

"I know."

"If I can find out how to stop what's happening to me, I will."

She shrugged minimally.

Later I lay on the rollaway in Alex's study, listening to her shower. A woman who showers before bed is a woman confirmed in physical intimacy. Dolores showered in the mornings the last year of our marriage. Maybe I got it wrong when I wrote that being in Beckie's house felt unholy, but not for any moral reason. It is moral. Otherwise, why did I feel inhibited when I wanted to feel sexual? Alex *is* still here.

When she finished her shower, the scent of peach soap wafted down the hall. I heard something clatter lightly in her bedroom that could have been a hairbrush on a dresser, and then she opened a jar of some kind and clapped the cover back on with the speed of a routine. I pictured her massaging cream into her face. It made me sad that she was doing these things to preserve a future for herself but searching for it in the past. For all that past matters, she could turn into a decaying scaffold of the woman she should continue to be for decades to come, shrinking into the neuroses of a widow, shrinking until her eyes grow glassy with stubborn hope and misplaced loyalty. I admire her fidelity, but it seems like such a waste. This valuable person, so capable of giving and receiving, waiting for a lover who will never return in the flesh. Beckie Franke is too young to sacrifice herself on the altar of a memory.

Listen to me, the wolf drawing up Little Red Riding Hood's itinerary. Like I don't have an ulterior motive.

Before I try to explain what happened next, remember the house is old. Its insulation has settled, its seams have widened, and its attic is accessible through the walls. There weren't any spider casings out in the open where I lay, but the drop molding made me apprehensive, because I couldn't see over the lip that ran around the room two inches below the ceiling. Ditto the canopy for the light fixture, which was slightly off center and left a dime-size hole where the wires were jammed in. I had left the light on, and as I began to drift off, my long-ago Jessica howled at me: *"Daddy, you're all growed up; you shouldn't be scared of the dark. . . ."*

But I was.

The imagoes I feared would come pouring out of that hole left by the light fixture had intelligent glints in their multiple eyes. As I let go of consciousness, the hole in the ceiling accompanied me across the border of dreaming, and I saw one of the creatures squeeze through. He sat there in the cusp of light and shadow, febrile antennae dancing, eyes pale and pupilless, and the longer I stared, the more horrified I became to recognize Alex's face in miniature. A verbal segue maybe, because Alex was a kind of imago to Beckie too—an immature concept she couldn't update to the festering and suppurating reality of death. I started out of the dream.

For the next hour I fought the cycle: fatigue versus fear. But each fitful doze ended with the same jarring awakening. If there is such a thing as essence of Bowie that drives ninja spiders out of the woodwork, an hour should have done it. I got up and flipped the wall switch off. *You're absolutely right, Jessica; Daddy's no scaredy-cat.* Nevertheless, Daddy tucked the covers in tightly around his body and snugged the sheet over his head so that just his face was framed against the pillow. Then he drifted into sound sleep.

It was more than two hours, less than three, when the faint evaporation of air currents on my cheeks awoke me, or maybe it was the fetid guano smell that came into the room. A residue of peach soap still lingered, against which the dry acidity of tiny furred bodies was stark. I thought of mice immediately. Which was close to the truth. Because it was bats. *Die Fledermaus.*

It had taken them a while to get the message, but then their dim little Eocene brains reacted violently to whatever I had dredged up out of that bus. They probably flitted through the blackness of the attic in a frenzy, and then worked their way down one channel or another between the studs and between the joists, tangling in insulation, hitting fire-stops and wall registers, their frantic claws extending between the louvers unseen by me.

The unholiness I had pondered just hours before seemed fully expressed now, and to my dismay, I was and am the source. I am the one who is the perversion of the natural order, even to spiders and bats. With all its competing variety, you wouldn't think life would be that discriminating.

I don't want to make more of this than there is. It is highly unlikely that the two trickles of blood on my right hand are from bites. Beckie thinks I should see a doctor, but there is no way I will undergo rabies shots. Bring on the hydrophobia. I will die strangling on my own mucus before I'll see another doctor. And I admit, the frenzy of the bats makes it hard to tell whether they were mostly trying to get away or if it was a rabid attack. I felt membranes brushing my temples as I scrambled for the switch, but that could be because whatever it is that agitates them is messing up their echolocation too.

With the light back on, the advantage was all mine. There was a length of bamboo sitting in a big clay pot—a carving or a cane—that I grabbed and began swinging with my right arm, while wrapping the blanket from the rollaway around my left. The bats hit the air brakes and veered out of the way. I must have looked like a shabby samurai beating the empty air with ritual moves. Between wild strokes they came at me from all sides. I wedged into a corner and had better luck with the blanket. Each time one of them hooked into the fabric, I went at it with the bamboo. The score was one dead, one crippled, four still banking, when Beckie came through the door.

I warned her to stay out, but with a wide-eyed fury that actually intimidated me, she began hurling everything in sight at the creatures. Books, coat hangers, an extension cord she yanked out of the wall and whirled like a bullwhip—amazing. Quicker than you can say *Xena, Warrior Princess,* two more bats lay dead and the other pair had vanished.

"They're gone, they're gone . . ." I said as she continued kicking things over and poking at shelves. "They fled like bats out of hell."

I was standing there in my underwear; she was in silk pajamas. There are times when, no matter how insane the tension, you just have to laugh. Bowie versus bats. Whatever the implications of this latest deviancy, the truth is that I was comforted by Beckie's presence—by any human assistance in this traveling carnival in which I seem to be the number one freakshow. But she was too intent to see the humor in it.

"I heard him," she said, still searching.

"Who?"

"Alex."

At that moment I guess I doubted her more than she had ever doubted me. "I must have shouted," I said. "You must have heard me."

"It was *Alex*." She looked around in vain, and then, with a soft joy that made my skin crawl, she said: "It's the phone."

I peered at the desk, saw that the red message light was blinking on the answering machine. She took two slow steps, reached out, and tapped the play button.

There was a click, a whir, another click, and then: "Bowie . . . wake up!" The time stamp followed. Two twenty A.M. It was two thirty-three now. Thirteen minutes had passed since the message. The ringer was off, but the recorder was set. It wasn't the acuteness of my senses that had awakened me from deep sleep to the crisis in the room; it was the voice. Down the hall, Rebecca Franke had been more easily aroused by someone she had been listening for since November tenth. I didn't have to ask. The look on her face told me for sure as she played it again and again and again. . . .

January 23, late

Alex's computer. Beckie won't touch it, but she says she doesn't mind my using it. That's good, because I think everything I'm writing here in this growing slab of pages is subject to the Committee from the Crypt, whose most recent address is my apartment. If they're gong to censor all my communications and delete files and add notes, I have to assume they'll get to this one way or another. Call it ghostwriting. So I print it out, and I have multiple disks that I keep updating with the copy utility on my apartment PC. I've made it more complicated to destroy, but not impossible. It's probably no safer than the pictures of Jessica and Danny locked in my file. As Pogo used to say, "We have met the enemy, and he is us."

Today I told Sam that I was living with Beckie and gave him the phone number. He was delighted to hear about what he took to be a bona fide gender relationship, though he blanched a little when I mentioned she was Alex Franke's widow. I'm sure he thinks we'll just facilitate each other's delusions. But he's genuinely looking forward to meeting her. If she meant what she said about skiing with me, that could be anytime.

Sam also brought me a bunch of new material. Where does he get all this stuff? If he actually reads it, my admiration for him is duly ratcheted up, because the subject matter is anything but skeptical about the paranormal. These are unapologetic chronicles of serious spiritualism.

Included in the pile is an article on "psychomachy," which is a branch of study that deals with the conflict between body and soul or good and evil. Unbelievable. If I'd read this two months ago, it would have been crapola. Now it just confirms that what's going on inside me has manifested itself to other humans in other ways. Some of it—maybe most of it—is superstition. Forgotten customs that deal with the disposition of spirits. I'm trying to keep in mind that these weren't scientists or sophisticated practitioners of empirical method but uneducated people trying to understand the forces that controlled their lives. A lot of what they believed was based on coincidence or trial and error. When enough time passes, trial and error tends to hit on things that work and to settle on the things that are real. The fallacies fail; the truths get reinforced. Like folk medicine, whatever cures, endures. You can see the logic that came out of fears. What I want to know is what *un*forgotten realities about spirits were those fears based on?

Once upon a time, when loved ones died, people stopped clocks, untied knots, allowed hearth fires to die, and threw open their windows and doors to let spirits depart. They were afraid souls would get tangled with images, which is why mirrors were turned toward walls. They wanted all energy to dissipate. Animals were thought to have special sensitivity to souls, and in certain European quarters animals were barred from the vicinity of a corpse. If one came in contact with the body, it was killed. I'm not going to stretch that to fit, but why do dogs sometimes shiver and whine in the presence of death? Do "lower animals" remain in touch with faculties bred out of rational man? Ask a puppy. Ask a guppy. Ask a spider or an insect or a bat. Ask me.

And then we come to food. I have here a vastly detailed description of Scottish lowland rites to "prevent the corruption of food by unfettered souls." In the houses of the newly dead, perishables were removed to keep them from rotting, as if decay were contagious. In Britannia they held the same belief but turned the strategy around. Butter was left near a cadaver to "sponge up" the festering and then thrown away. Metal is still thought to protect against accelerated decay, because in some districts iron objects are thrust into food to prevent spoilage after someone dies. What can I say? So far, tin cans work for me. I haven't rotted anything in a can. Easily disproved, I guess, but when you know you can make bananas go bananas in two hours, you start to suspect that there are circumstances and there are circumstances.

I took some of the articles back to East Tristan late this afternoon, intending to show them to Beckie, but that got sidetracked because of her accident. She was coming up the drive in her white Escort when the brake pedal went all the way to the floor. Fortunately, she was just easing along because of the ice, and this and the upward slope kept her from a worse collision. That said, she took out two wall studs and a lot of vinyl siding at the back of the garage.

I heard the noise and ran through the breezeway to find her sitting there with her hands on the wheel, like a little girl who had done something bad. "I hit the brakes," she kept saying. And then she was out of the car and I was sizing up the damage, and she was sizing up me.

"Bad?" she asked, as if I had some mechanical expertise that could revise the obvious. I lifted up the headlight and she looked pissed and chagrined at the same time. "I guess it's bad," she said.

"If you want good news, you're at the wrong end of the car."

I got down on the floor to check the brake lines, but I couldn't see, and I couldn't get the hood up on account of the damage. We could both smell brake fluid, though. Naturally, I'm suspicious. I didn't say anything to her about that, but she knew anyway and tried to make light of the whole thing.

"I haven't had an accident since driver's training," she said, spearing Kentucky Fried Chicken onto a plate. "I ran over a fence one week, and the next week, when we were stopped at a light on the same corner, a guy in a sewer project called, 'Here she comes,' down a manhole, and they all came pouring out like rats."

"You know, after last night, maybe we should rethink this," I said.

"Last night was wonderful." She replied with the same feathery delight that set my teeth on edge then. "I have Alex's voice."

"You have Alex's voice speaking to *me*."

"So?"

"So why doesn't he contact you?"

The raw look she gave me said she had wondered about that, too. "You're more accessible to him, because of the way you . . . because of what happened to you, that's all."

"But if he can come into this house, why has he ignored you completely? If he can leave his voice on an answering machine, why doesn't he say something to you?"

"He will."

"I don't want to hurt you, but he may not feel the same

things. He may not feel at all. You shouldn't be blind to that."

"I'm not blind to it." She rocked a little, tapping a thumbnail on her teeth. "So what do you think he wants?"

"We both know what he wants. He wants to live."

"You can't blame him for that. But he must still feel connected to the life we had, don't you think?"

I remembered her disclaimer about Alex's state of being from the night before. *". . . will I be too much in denial to recognize it, too obsessed to accept it, or too desperate to care?"*

"I don't know," I said.

"Doesn't matter. I just want to know that he still exists somewhere, and how it's going to end."

To hear this woman speak that way, to hear myself speak about aberrant things as if we are discussing retirement or a trip to another country, gives me gold-plated goose bumps. I don't know what she means by asking how it's going to end. Does she think there can be a "happily ever after"?

"It doesn't matter who Alex contacts," she concluded. "You said there are other explanations, and there are. If Jerry could e-mail Charlotte from your computer, then feelings are possible. It doesn't matter whether Alex contacts me now or . . . or ever."

"It does matter. This isn't predictable. I wouldn't call Arnasen's e-mail passionate. Who knows what he wanted her to do with the stash? You're making all kinds of assumptions that may not fit everything that's happened."

"Like what?"

"I just don't think you get it. Something doesn't want me to have connections with the rest of the world."

"Sam is part of the rest of the world. Nothing has happened to Sam."

She had a point. "Sam fits into the equation for me to survive," I said. "I have to work somewhere, and he's pretty isolated himself—"

"Why do you have to work? You told me someone has been paying your bills."

"When I was in the hospital, yeah. Look, I don't have all the answers."

She patted the reading material I had shown her and which had intrigued her. "Maybe the people who died on the bus are angels trying to protect you; did you ever think of that?"

You have to talk to dead people and see their faces in order to know they are not angels. You have to smell the desperation of death to know that what I was experiencing wasn't part of a divine plan. You have to feel lake ice being hammered and a centipede jamboree and bats homing in on you and you alone to know that God is a long ways away. I'm not saying that there aren't Michaels and Gabriels floating around, or that people don't make the cut when they die, but the ones on the bus never got that far.

"Maybe Alex is the one in danger," she continued. "You say you believe that some of these customs about protecting the dead are rooted in truth about the passing of souls; why hasn't it occurred to you that he could be lost and in danger?"

I shrugged helplessly, not wanting to deal with her rising emotion.

She spread her hands over the books on the table as if they sanctioned rather than just confirmed the dark things that are happening to us. I'm sorry I ever showed them to her. As much as I'm compelled to deal with the macabre and the preternatural, she does it enthusiastically. Now I worry I'm enabling her descent into something threatening and unpredictable.

"We should be trying to protect Alex," she said. "That makes more sense to me."

"I wouldn't know where to begin."

"You thought these books were important enough to bring here, and now you don't know where to begin?"

"Which ones did you have in mind?" I asked dryly.

"Any of them. All of them."

I understood that this was where I had taken us, and now I had damn well better do something with the overwrought state I had created. I flipped the pages of the nearest book and it opened at a rite known as *Dishaloof*. "We could sprinkle salt and walk out of rooms backward," I conveyed from the text.

She smarted accordingly. "I didn't ask you to bring these in. If you think they're ridiculous, why did you show them to me?"

"Sorry. I have no business being sarcastic. Obviously some of these customs were just meant as emotional releases for the mourners. And anyway, nothing could be more surreal than my life has been lately. I'll do whatever you want. It can't hurt."

"No, it can't hurt. Let's just stick to the ones that sound reasonable."

"Like . . . ?"

"Like . . . I can see why people kept candles burning around the bodies of their loved ones. God is light, isn't He?"

"Light and darkness is a pretty natural fit with good and evil. Any kid afraid of the closet at night knows that."

"You're doing it again."

"Right. Maybe there's something more to it."

"It says they used candles to protect departing souls from evil."

"Candles? Where would we put them?"

For a moment I had a foreboding that she was going to say the unthinkable. That we would make a grim foray to the churchyard at Timothy Lutheran for some sort of graveside ceremony, or worse, she would want to bring something back. But what she said was: "We'll put them around you."

"Me?"

"I know you're thinking that couldn't help Alex," she said, "but if he's in limbo, or still wandering the way you said, then why not? And besides, we need a way to make sure the bats don't come back; and bats don't like fire. I've got boxes and boxes of candles."

So now I'm writing this at Alex's computer, surrounded by about twenty candles. They're blazing away, burning up oxygen, and if I don't die of rabies tonight, I'll probably suffocate in this inferno. She wasn't kidding about boxes and boxes of candles. She must collect them. I remember the guys in college used to get off over girls who liked candles. Phallic Symbolism 101 for all male freshmen. Light a candle, and when it gets hot enough, it spills its essence. Some of these chunks easily weigh five pounds—big square things with medallions stuck on the front, wax figurines, red and blue spirals, a gold tallow castle with wicks on each of its four corner towers, and bowls of white paraffin. Beckie's collection could have given an inferiority complex to the whole men's dorm. For sure it's given me one. This isn't about protecting me from bats. These are landing lights for something incoming. . . .

January 24th, afterglow

No bats. No spiders. No Chicago fire.

But, hey, today she came out here to Sheshebans, and I don't care whether it's because I'm the vessel for her lover or not. We went skiing. This is the personal fantasy script I wrote a long time ago and cast with Dolores and me. So, if Rebecca Franke was pretending, so was I.

The woman I was with today was adventurous and uncomplaining. Not one of those trudge-through-the-snow and are-we-having-fun-yet types. She is not a creature-comfort person, and I admire that. Physical discipline says a lot about a person's capacity to get outside themselves.

Every weekend I ski past little caravans of couch potatoes who look like they've been socked in the gut and who stare at their feet and never see the trillion, trillion diamonds blazing all around them. Their roly-poly kids throw tantrums, and the whole outing is about getting back to the shelter for hot cocoa and doughnuts. I can understand that everyone doesn't want to be an athlete, but people whose senses go dead six feet from their doorsteps belong under bell jars. Beckie's skiing skills are mediocre, but she enjoys the payback from a little effort. When she's exhausted, she laughs instead of whines. The best thing, though, is that she was dazzled by what she saw.

We stopped at every high point in the south trail to take in pristine vistas: thin streams winding through beds of lavender snow; canopies of translucent stuff held aloft, throwing rainbow prisms on the ground; majestic forests, little arching bridges, vast sweeps, sky palettes. An inch or so of powder came down last night, and that made all the shadows fuzzy, because the sun couldn't find a hard edge on a branch to save its *sol.* Ha-ha. (I got snowballed in the back for that pun.) It also meant that the squirrels gave us their high-wire acts, because they don't like to run in soft snow, so they made circus leaps from tree to tree. We gave them gymnastic scores. There are deciduous stands that look like Gothic cathedrals, and—damn— *I actually shared all this with someone.*

She called me a poet. She said I was different when I was out there. No foolin'? *As in Alex Franke?* I wanted to ask. But he doesn't ski. Didn't. So she meant *me, me, me.*

Beckie and I were gone nearly three hours, and when we got back, Sam couldn't stop grinning. It seems like the beginning of a beautiful friendship for the three of us. You just know when people use a certain tone and economy of expression that they've found common ground. Beckie stayed another forty-five minutes, but finally the exhaustion of a sleepless night and a day of hard play caught up to her.

She was so whacked out she went home to take a nap.

And me, shit. Don't ask me why, but I'm gonna call my kids right now. Before I lose the nerve.

I did it, and my luck held. Danny answered.

"'Lo," he said.

"What you up to, scout?"

"Daddy!"

"How's m'boy?"

"Jess!"—mouth turned away from the phone—"It's Dad!"

The extension clicked, and she was there. I couldn't believe it. Both of them bubbling with excitement because I was calling. I asked all the dumb stuff, and got "Fine," "Good," and "Okay" for answers. Then Jessica asked:

"Daddy, why haven't you called?"

"Oh . . . I figured you were busy."

"You could disguise your voice if Mom answers."

"You think that would work?"

"We need a code word," Danny said.

"What for?" Jessica challenged. "That's stupid."

"Is not."

"Is."

"*You're* stupid."

"A code word wouldn't hurt," I said.

"Dad's trying to humor you," Jessica said.

It was still there. The jealousy and resentment. *Who do you love most, Daddy?*

"Your sister is probably right that we won't ever use it, but just in case, how about 'White Room'?"

"That's two words," Jessica said. And then, away from the phone, ". . . no one, Mom."

I could hear Dolores in the background: "What do you mean 'no one'? Who is it?"

"Uh-oh," I said to Danny.

"White Room," he said, and then it was all Dolores on the extension.

"Who is this?"

"Me."

"I can't believe it. You aren't supposed to call, Bowie,

remember? You're supposed to talk to me first. I thought you weren't going to do this to us anymore."

"You didn't pick up the phone."

Sigh of exasperation. "Am I supposed to police every phone call? I'm trying to give them normal lives. Normal children can answer the phone. Can't you go along with that?"

"Normal children have fathers."

"Normal fathers. I don't know why I'm arguing with you. We've been through all this. Don't make me go back to court, okay?"

"I'm normal."

I guess I can't blame her for laughing. She must have read or heard all about my case from her eager circle. But now she defined "normal" for me, and it was like we were married again. She went on like that, and I remembered how I had shrunk in that house as our family grew, driven from room to room by her projects and agendas that didn't include me. My final stand was the basement workshop—that default refuge of countless American fathers. You begin to retreat to the coldest room in order to escape the coldest person, and after a while you bring in a space heater and a radio, and eventually a television for Sunday-afternoon football. If I'd stayed in that basement, we'd probably still be together, but I retreated to the bars across town. When she was done, Dolores hung up.

"White Room . . ." I said in case Danny was still there, but a strident electronic one-note suddenly kicked in, telling me how totally I had lost the connection.

January 25, the real afterglow

I wear my cynicism like epaulettes, so why was I out of uniform when the enemy came? And it *was* the enemy, despite the ambiguity of what happened and despite what Sam will say. As soon as it was clear that Beckie was going to be moral support to keep me from spiraling into despair or worse, they went for her.

You could smell the smoke halfway down the block, but I thought it was someone's fireplace. It wasn't until I got near the porch that I saw the roof edge sieving white smoke like a steaming pot lid about to blow.

I dashed up the steps and grabbed the door handle. It was warm. Without thinking that I might be fanning a fire inside, I yanked it open. No flames, but the thin haze on the lower floor and the walls had the unearthly glow of a dry sauna. From somewhere above, glass broke. I took the staircase three treads at a time, evoking the brittleness of four ascending notes. The second floor felt like balsa wood.

In retrospect, I think the fire was burning in two places. The closed door to Alex's office was seamed red, and the far end of the hall was leaching smoke from the baseboard right above the kitchen. Not that it matters. Arson is a foregone conclusion, and at that moment I was squinting into the searing air, trying to answer Beckie's calls. She must have been trapped in a pocket of air, because her voice was clear while mine just evaporated into a cough with each shout. Pulling my sleeve over my hand, I grabbed her bedroom door handle. It didn't budge.

"Unlock it!" I squeezed out in the roar of encroaching flames.

But it wasn't locked—there was no give at all against the frame—it was jammed. I stooped and found the wedge between the bottom edge and the threshold. It had been driven in from the other side. I kicked at it. Then I rocked back and drove my heel against the latch, again and again and again, until the frame split and the door slid in enough for me to see into the vivid glow.

Her bedroom had a bureau, a cedar chest, and a canopy bed in one corner. A smashed window was drawing billows from the baseboards at a furious rate. The smoke flowed along the walls like yellow foam, immobilizing the air in the center of the room as if it were a gel. There Beckie knelt, her face almost to the floor.

I had my hands under her elbows before she knew I was there, and I'll never forget her eyes as she raised them in that warped air. Around her pupils the arctic ice was tinctured pink, and the shadows made a grave-sprung mask. The flaming bus and its immolating complement of the dying could not have looked more doomed. She was ready for this—terrified, unwilling to die voluntarily, but ready for it.

Her hand felt oddly cool in that blistering heat. I yanked her to her feet and didn't look again. From there it was a graceless race measured by caustic breaths, each less life-sustaining than the last. We squeezed past the wedged door without letting go of each other's hands.

The draw of smoke was blinding now, and my brain was bobbing at the top of my skull. I felt Beckie sag on my arm, and I jerked her up hard, but she sagged again. It was over, I thought.

And at that instant I heard an abrupt thin note close at hand that separated itself from the fire. Beckie heard it too. I knew she heard it, because suddenly the drag lightened and her momentum was independent of mine again. The note had been compelling to both of us, but I don't know why. It wasn't even articulate. More like a protest, a command. I suppose a burning house gives up all kinds of death sighs, surly growls and sudden shrieks as nails wrench out of collapsing timbers. Still, the temptation to believe it was Alex is strong. Eighteen souls may have wanted Beckie removed from my life, but Alex didn't. Not that way. And why did that faint note galvanize her? It jarred me only because at first I thought someone was trying to rescue us. But Beckie let go of my hand and brushed past me as if directed. And a second or so later— again as if directed—she fumbled back for my hand and led me after her.

Of course, she knows her house better than I do. That explains how she got us through the choking smoke to the top of the stairs. The staircase itself was limned orange, and squinting at the gray doorway far below was like gazing down the midway of a carnival. Chasers of crimson, yellow, white outlined the wall. Worms of molten gold inched along the seams. Paint curled into pennants, then snapped into smoke. For all we knew, the steps would melt like cotton candy beneath our feet.

How we made it to the bottom is a mystery. Funhouse faith was demanded, and down we went, stumbling, falling, oblivious to everything but descent. Then, just as we staggered through the doorway, I heard and felt a giant's searing breath at our backs. Whether or not that was the combustion point of wood as the staircase went up in flames became blessedly moot.

The frigid air was like salve on our faces. We fell against the snow shoveled up along the drive, and for a couple of minutes we just wheezed great reedy breaths, trying to get moisture back in our throats. People came—voices, hands. Neighbors had been alerted by a teenager coming home from swimming practice. Someone had called 911. It seemed like only seconds before fire trucks were there. And then they had oxygen on us and we were helped into the back of a rescue vehicle.

I swore I'd die before I went back to another hospital, but there I was. If there was a difference, it's that I was conscious and in control. The tech in the ambulance radioed ahead with his evaluation, so we got some sense of where things stood. There was an exchange about an endotracheal tube and a term that may have meant collapsed lungs—negative for us—and the reassuring, "No evidence of carbonaceous inhalation." By the time we reached ER, we were insisting we were fine. Two nurses and an orderly expressed skepticism.

"You sure you weren't in the house?" one of them asked.

I lied firmly in the affirmative, and Beckie nodded.

"Rescue says you were."

"Rescue wasn't there when it happened."

"There can be complications if you have inhalation injuries," cautioned the nurse. "We can put a tube in your lungs and give you humidified oxygen during an examination. It's not a difficult procedure."

I kept my voice low to suppress a cough. "Don't need it." Beckie just shook her head.

In less than an hour they released us, and as twilight thickened into night, we took a cab back to the house.

Men in rubberized yellow slickers were still ghosting around the perimeter, but the fire was out. In a flashlight beam directed through the soot-lined front doorway, I saw that the staircase—amazingly—remained. We were told the kitchen was a total loss as well as part of the upstairs, but considering the way it had looked when we were getting into the ambulance, I was surprised to find anything besides ashes. Probably the house won't be torn down. The back portion and the upper story will be gutted and reframed. I don't know about smoke and water damage. We are both too upset to absorb all this right now.

The fire marshal wouldn't let us past the front porch, and he didn't want to listen to my babbling about what had caused it. I was pissed and not thinking straight. I blamed arson—as if they could arrest the dead. The marshal already had his own theory.

"You two sell exotic candles or something?" he said. "There must be a hundred pools of wax in there, and some lumps that aren't even completely melted."

So that will be the official explanation. Never mind that I went around the house myself yesterday morning to make sure all the candles were extinguished. It's like that nightmare I had at Mayo where I tried to snuff out candles in a church, and one always stayed lit. The insurance report will list them as the probable cause. Whatever was wedged under Beckie's bedroom door is now part of the rubble that will never be identified. She has no memory of that. She says I must be wrong about it being deliberate—how could she not wake up if someone came into her bedroom?—and that it was probably just her slipper that got jammed under there when she tried to open the door. I argued that the door would have given an inch or so at least, if she had wedged it over a slipper. She said maybe it had. Maybe she had pushed it shut again and the jammed slipper slid with it. You can suppose that it really was candles to blame—a spark that caught somewhere and just smoldered all day until she was back in there alone and asleep—but I know what the deal is. Did I mention that the shop that towed her car after the accident called and said her brake lines had been "leaking" in *two* places?

So we are both in my apartment, and everything is crazy again. I told Beckie she can't risk staying here, that she's got to get away from me, but she insists. We'll have to settle this later.

January 25, late

Beckie still doesn't agree that the fire was set—or at least she says she doesn't to me—but she finally left early this evening. I feel rotten: Grieving widow struggling but coping . . . along comes a stranger, dragging the ghost of her husband . . . then she's burned out of her house . . . then the stranger—no longer a stranger—throws her out of his apartment. I keep thinking about the way her eyes looked when she was kneeling in the fire. Not a lot of self-preservation left in her tank.

To top it off, our last conversation was borderline ugly. I told her she was in danger, that I didn't want to perpetuate that, knowing what I know. She said she didn't think I knew anything, that I was letting the strain I was under make me paranoid. I asked her if sabotaged brakes and arson were paranoid.

"Even if those were deliberate acts, why do you assume it's all about keeping you isolated?" she replied. I was struck by her tone more than her words.

The desperation she denied she would ever feel has sharpened into something close to the obsession she also denied she would ever feel, and that's my fault. I'm the one who clued her in to the fact of Alex's presence, and I should have foreseen what that would mean to her. How can she understand the black and vacant urge to live at all costs? Or—and this bothers me—that Alex really is at war with the other eighteen over whether they should block me from a relationship. If he is, then his situation is even more complicated than mine. On the one hand, they all want me isolated. On the other, he wants to use me now to reach his wife. But even that is two-edged, because if he can't gain control of me, then it could end up being just me in a relationship with his widow. If he loves her, that has to make him hate me. His choice will be between life or love. It can't get any more ambivalent than that.

Beckie is too driven for any of this to matter. Her hope is ghastly. Any part of Alex is all of Alex for her. She seems to think it will be a purely spiritual reconnection, and she isn't saying anything about the ghoulish physical possibilities. Where the hell does she think I'm going to go? All those candles around my head—I still believe it more than crossed her mind that this might ease Alex's journey into *me,* instead of just protecting him on his way to the hereafter.

"You've never been dead and had the option of coming back," I said. "Maybe no one has before. Scruples may pale beyond the pale."

She gave me a self-righteous look. "Alex couldn't return to a world where he had committed murder. He was a Christian, remember? I guess you're not, even if you can quote Ecclesiastes." She gestured at the scripture still spiked to my wall, with its red emblazoned masthead, THE LIES OF SOLOMON, a display that should have disturbed her more than it had when she first saw my apartment.

"Here comes the guilt card."

"Are you? It makes a difference."

"To me 'original sin' is something really creative."

"I didn't think you were."

"No. I'm not. Not if that means blind, giddy faith and swallowing transparently man-made scriptures and all the inhumanities of twenty centuries. But you saw how I am out in the woods, how can you think I don't worship? Maybe I am a Christian. Take the politics out of it, and maybe we believe the same thing."

I don't think she cut me any slack, because she fell back to her first point. "Even if there is a kind of ruthlessness among the dead, you're the one under siege," she said. "Bats, spiders, icy lakes? Now you're trying to extend that to me. I'm not a victim. I don't want to be a victim."

"Who said Alex or any of the other people from the bus caused those things? They protected me. You heard your answering machine. But I wasn't driving the car when the brakes went out; I wasn't in the house when it started burning. You were. Why didn't the cavalry ride in to rescue you? And that time right after you left the note in my mailbox, and I phoned you, and the line went dead—it was cut. The line was cut. Looks to me like the forces that protect me are lethal to you."

She just kept slowly shaking her head. "There are other explanations, Bowie. You're not being fair. You say you have fugues when you don't remember doing things. How do you know *you* didn't start the fire? You're so quick to assign everything to your neat little theory, only it isn't neat. It has a glaring mistake in it if you think Alex has abandoned me."

"People let go of their loved ones slowly. It's natural that you still feel Alex around."

"Oh, so your contacts with the dead are real, and everyone else's aren't. And that's just . . . natural?"

She cried a little then, and clung to me, and I wish to

hell there was something between us. But there isn't. She was Alex's wife before the bus burned. She will be Alex's wife for a long time yet. When I tried to comfort her, she pulled away.

"All right," she said. "I'll get out of here."

"Do you have enough money?"

"I have friends."

"The church?"

"Keep in touch, Bowie. You can do that. I'll call you to tell you where I am."

A couple of the things she said still disturb me. One is the fugue business. Could I have done it—driven to East Tristan, started the fire, and driven back? I never did keep track of the odometer reading, like I intended. Sam went out grooming for a couple hours before dark that afternoon. It would have been just possible for me to leave the shop unattended, except for one thing: I have concrete memories of what I was doing the whole time. But what if whatever causes the fugues is in control of my memory as well as my body at those moments? That's too insidious to consider. The other thing that bothers me is Beckie's attack on my objectivity. She's just the opposite of Sam in that she is more than willing to accept the bizarre events that have happened to me, but like Sam, she believes my psychological condition is suspect.

I guess the next step in paranoia is to believe that both of them are part of the conspiracy against me, but I don't have the faintest twinge of suspicion, so that's a good sign. If you told me those nineteen souls, or whatever is driving them, are using Sam and Beckie to assail my stability, okay. But then, why would Beckie be in danger? No, there must be a split among the nineteen. I'm getting overwhelmed by these possibilities. The doubts are pure hell. But that's part of the strategy against me. Isn't it?

January 26, late afternoon

You will have to guard the lie of your existence. But you can't do that forever, can you?

Delete. Burn, burn, burn. Too late to kill the message that was on my computer screen last Saturday morning after I attacked the breathing thing in the dark. And God knows, the messenger is already dead. But I offed the vile message from my hard drive and burned the printouts—I mean physically burned them on the stove—and now I can't stop remembering the phrases. I could write them in my sleep. Again.

Forever. Whatever intelligence used that word knows "forever" inside and out, and she/he/it/them is absolutely right. I *can't* hang on forever. I will eventually accept whatever consciousness is necessary to allow the change. It will be a moment of extreme weakness and despair, or maybe abject surrender. What the hell do other souls feel like when they are inside you? You? There is no "you." You become them. The other souls. Or a hybrid. Is that how evolution works? Is that what a mutation is? I see a universe in which coming apart and recombining are the status quo. There is only the salmon run of survival, driven by will and passion. The stronger passions win; the weaker lose. The whole thing comes together under one altered mental state or another, and thus you have a new entity. Like genetics fusing two into one. Spiritual genetics. Did I make this up?

I've decided I have to communicate with them, because waiting is killing me. (Killing me!—God, I'm funny.) So last night I wrote a reply and left it on the computer screen, as if there are protocols for reaching through the ether. I had the good sense to feel silly about it afterward, because at least three of the nineteen don't need protocols. That would be Pastor Evans, Jerry Arnasen, and Alex Franke. How do they get through to me? How can I get through to them?

Greetings, your wretchednesses . . .

None of the normal physical barriers seem to apply, though what that means in terms of awareness is so inexact that I can only assume they are like drowning animals, thrashing against the ambient element of their death and struggling now and then to the surface. Forget RIP. They brood in the shadows of life, and when they see a sliver of light, they come for it. The light comes through me. Maybe when you subside into the energy of the universe there is oblivion, but short of that it must be anarchy. And I don't know exactly what I'm probing for here. An anarchy against the laws of life maybe, against God, against the notion of losing one's identity, against equilibrium in the cosmos. Lostville.

My note. I was writing about my note. It read:

I need to know what to expect. You won't succeed without communicating with me.

When I got up this morning, the star-field screen saver was on—those little pinpoints of light that rush out at you as if you were on a journey through space. My hand actually shook when I nudged the mouse and the monitor light cued from amber to green. Then Microsoft Word got brighter and brighter until I could see that my two sentences were still there, nothing below, nothing on the task bar, no scroll cursor to show there was something farther down. I am almost relieved. It was a stupid thing to write, an act of despair, like sprinkling salt and walking out of a deathbed chamber backward. It implies surrender. It makes the whole blasphemy a working hypothesis. Thank God I deleted it and came to work.

It's Friday, and with only a couple of customer interruptions, Sam and I had a long talk this morning. I told him everything that's happened between Beckie and me. He was visibly disappointed. Then I told him about the note I left on the computer.

"I guess you won't be stunned to learn that I didn't get an answer," I said.

He looked at me in that attentive, forthright way he has. "It wouldn't surprise me if you had."

"Meaning my alter ego would tiptoe out in the middle of the night and write itself a reply?"

"Meaning whatever. My jury is still out, Bowie." Soft punch in the arm; warm glint in his eyes. "You know that, don't you? Just because I think you should sift through the psychological issues doesn't mean I don't understand that what's happening to you is a real anomaly."

I like that. I'm suffering from a real anomaly. You can hide rotten bananas, and after a while they stop smelling, but real anomalies send messages back and forth.

"So where do I reach out to?" I asked.

"The bus."

"The bus?"

"Haven't you wondered where it is?"

"I don't think it's on my best-sites list, Sam."

"Okay. I just thought maybe you needed to put past traumas on your itinerary. The scene of the crime, you know? Check them out, see if they don't give you some closure."

"You're including the waterfall?"

"Yes."

"You really think that's a good idea?"

"I'll go with you, if you want."

"I'll think about it," I said.

And I have. He's right. I've been avoiding the whole north side of the mountain since I got back on skis. So, I suppose that says something about where my demons are hanging out these days. But the bus. That's just foolhardy, unless I really want to confront those obscenities in limbo head-on. And maybe I do now. I'm dead certain it won't be the way Sam has in mind, though. He's thinking I'll find a rusting wreck sinking into the elements and that it will help me come to terms with the reality. I'm thinking I'll find the reality of the surreal.

January 26, late night

I came back to The Ski Shop because if they catch me on the road, it will be like before. And they will catch me.

Six hours since I went to the bus, and it feels like six centuries. Time is irrelevant now, because the only thing that matters is keeping my identity. Losing your life is better than losing your identity. This is almost exactly what I wrote when I started this narrative, so I guess that much of me is still the same.

It's cold, and I've boarded up the front window. The gas that was leaking from the water heater when I arrived has probably aired out, but I can't bring myself to relight the pilot. It took me a long time to get up from the floor, where I sat shaking, and move to the computer. I need to stare at a twenty-first-century artifact from the planet Earth. I need to talk with my fingers on a plastic keyboard and forget what I just saw in a junkyard in Sheshebans.

From the beginning. When Sam finished grooming yesterday I told him I was going to do what he suggested. Revisit my stations of the cross. See if it didn't help sort things out. Only I told him I wanted to go alone, and he said he understood that. Then he said he thought B&D's Salvage in Sheshebans might be where the bus was. I knew then that he'd been thinking about this for a while, that he had scoped it out for me.

It was snowing and the light was failing, so I had a little trouble zeroing in on the location, which is fairly narrow where it fronts the sidewalk. The oldest thing at B&D's is its sign, and even if I could have read it in clear weather, the flakes coming down filled the air in front of my face like a game of fifty-two pickup. The place was closed—it was almost six o'clock—which meant you couldn't back a truck inside the fence and you couldn't go inside the office. That was fine with me. I didn't want to explain anything to anyone. I just parked on the street and slipped through one of the gaping separations in the chain link.

Except for the hardpack underfoot from human traffic, it didn't look like anything had been disturbed there since the Earth was formed. Lintels of snow, frost-etched facades, and grotesque arabesques of ice turned the mounds of blackened debris into a frozen ruin of a city. The lanes were irregular, winding past neighborhoods of similar objects strewn over an acre or more. In short, it was an archaeological dig whose parapets blocked my view, so that I had to go up and down its streets in dread of what I was about to discover.

But I sensed where the bus was before I finished the first row. It hung in my sense of space like a dead spot—and I can't do any better than that in describing it. Wherever I turned I knew its position: toward the center, toward the rear. At any time I could have gone straight to it. But I didn't. I crunched slowly through the crust snow back and forth, closer and closer. Those huge mounds of iron and steel and ceramic and tin were like sentinel outposts where I had to check in one by one. I surveyed dismantled furnaces and boilers and scaffolding and a tool-and-die stamping machine, as if they were the reasons I had come, but I was stalling. In my mind's eye was a yellow bus throbbing in its pocket of decay, a cenotaph for nineteen dead among rusting industrial pyramids and discarded corporate obelisks.

I was dead-on about the location, but it didn't throb and it wasn't yellow. It was just a blackened hulk in the twilight. I had to study the window frames before I could recognize the front and reconstruct the lines. The tires had melted, and the axles and transmission had fallen off. The shell was mostly intact, though leaning from the frame. I don't know why the idea of color was so terrifying. Thinking back now, I can recognize that the paint would have blistered off in the first moments of the fire. I walked around the bus end to end, still not trusting that a brake light wouldn't wink on or a headlight burst out of the blackened maw where the driver had died. But it was absolutely inert.

It had been just a mortal tragedy after all, I thought. The passengers were not lurking quietly in the shadows of their seats. I could go on board and perhaps sit among the traces of them, and it wouldn't mean a thing. They had perished. The bus stops here—ha, ha.

A single yard light from the tower above B&D's modest office came on in the deepening dusk, and though the illumination was reduced by steady snow, its sodium rays fell on the seat posts like a spotlight on a stage. My stage. Seized by a growing boldness, I went to the front opposite the driver's seat and put one foot on the step.

Solid thrum.

Another step, off the ground now.

The bus had me. Big deal.

One more step and I was standing next to where the driver had died. From there the gaping lozenges where the windows had been were relatively bright, but it was hard to make out the interior. The angle suggested something not very earthbound, because the canted shell was like a ditched fuselage or a submarine gliding obliquely to the bottom of an inky ocean.

I could go even farther, if I wanted. It was okay. That smell of carbonized matter was just a lingering history. I moved down the aisle. *This is a snap,* I thought, and it *was,* because there actually was a snap—as sharp and precise as a sprung steel trap. Simultaneously the ligaments in my crotch strained as if my right hip were tearing loose. My trailing leg flexed, and the fiery tracks of something ragged raked through my jeans. And then my left knee was in my face and I was sitting on the floor of the bus in pain and surprise.

The floor—what there was of it—had given way. I tried to stand, but stiff fingers pawed my thigh—the hard edges of the hole through which my foot had plunged. Two feet higher up my right hand rested on something yielding. Seat springs. This was where someone had sat while they died. Baked-on debris flaked off on my fingertips. I could smell the residue of a fire, no longer caked like weathered ashes but dry and powdery. Atoms of vaporized matter, some of it human, were in my nostrils, my body, and yet I was the same. Nothing had changed. Groping for leverage against the seat frame, I pushed myself out of the hole until I was standing level again.

Inventory: right leg raw and exposed, hip attached with Elmer's glue, nerves screaming. Mind screaming too (*Far enough!* . . . *Far enough!* . . . *Far enough!*). I had braved what I had to brave. Except that that was just the *physical* inventory. And my physical well-being wasn't why I was here. My psychological well-being was. Psyche says forge ahead. Psyche says never leave a haunting darkness unexplored. *Move to the back of the bus, please.*

This is so wrong!

Shut up.

Cautiously, gingerly, I resumed the long, long journey down the aisle. *Empty seat, empty seat.* I shuffled on, not sure who was in charge of my thoughts. Not sure whose voice was chanting: *All the way, all the way . . . step to the back of the bus, please. . . .* Clutching at stanchions. *Empty seat, empty seat . . .* Self-preservation countering: *Don't go, Bowie . . . do not do this—do not!*

I don't know why I couldn't have been satisfied. My body seemed to be changing shape, my weight draining from one step into the next, like a Slinky, like sand in an hourglass. Much too fast. *Stop. Help. For God's sake, help.*

And then I was standing above the long bench that spanned the back of the bus, blocking me. End of the line.

You made it, Bowie. Kind of nostalgic, huh?

I remembered reading that the three survivors had sat at the rear, away from the driver's side. But what about the doomed? Where had Franke sat? And the four sisters from Sweden? And Arnasen? And Evans? I pictured the pastor up front, keeping the driver awake with small talk.

And then, as if I had just given substance to the passenger list, the floor behind me gently sagged.

How much does a soul weigh? Nineteen souls? Sweat broke out on my brow, prickled under my cap. Something behind me had stood up. Or sat down. Slowly I edged around and surveyed what I didn't want to survey. If I tell you that my heart sank through my gut like dry ice, you will still not know how totally fracturing this was to my state of mind. I was moaning. My lungs were gasping like alien twins demanding air, and nothing was beating in my chest. Because there were stains in the air. Stains in the seats. A stain where the driver had sat.

It's easy to see how stupid I was. You or any rational person would not have taken that first step onto the bus, let alone continued into the very heart of a blasphemy. But how can you appreciate my desperate need to hang on to sanity, to refute everything, to grasp a single victory over the intense fear that going onto that bus represented? I didn't want to confirm it; I wanted to deny it. It was survival of self, literal salvation, everything or nothing forever!

That's how I felt, sinking down onto the rear bench. My leg burned; my hip ached; and when the ruined bus engine coughed and caught, my guts liquefied.

That was the moment when my scream of rebellion died and I began to take a cue from the silent shadows—shadows that were starting to look like passengers now. Not a limb twitched; not a groan escaped. The bus lurched and righted itself. I thought I glimpsed something crimson—the reflection of taillights—off the curtain of snow falling furiously outside. And up through the front, where the windshield should be, it was just a wall of light. How it remained so dead black inside is part of the mystery I don't want to explore. Everything seemed to have its own hue, and the hues didn't mix well, like a badly edited composite photo.

A little tug of g-forces, gentle swaying, and the bus began to move. The nearest figures to me were only three feet away, and there was one thing I could almost make out, even to the hint of color. And from that one thing, repeated in the profiles all the way up the aisle, I deduced with certainty what it was. Red scarves. They all had red scarves wrapped around their faces.

I knew where we were going. The destination if not the route. It snowed and snowed and snowed, but if that white curtain were suddenly ripped aside, I would see the cosmos instead of the mountain road. Only I would see it without mortal limitations. No vacuum pricked with stars—I would see what I see in dreams: writhing wastes of energy and fabulous agglomerations; cataracts of energy sweeping up all consciousness and individuality. I had to wonder if it was as terrible for the nineteen. Their infandous limbo was inside that bus, and if they left it— left the separate and seminal urges at the cores of their beings—without a mortal destination (read Michael Bowden Carmichael) they would cease to be individuals and become the ordinary dead. So we were riding toward a doom not quite finished that we all understood.

But that is where the kinship ended. If they weren't already a part of the hereafter, they were infinitely remote from me. I smelled their putrefying cerements and tasted their exudations and felt their clammy uncoffined forms, yet I was alive! A sulky silence underscored that separation, and the profundity of their silence was more disturbing than if they were chattering away, as they must have been on the afternoon of November tenth.

Too soon the engine began to whine as the speed of the bus exceeded its load and we went into free fall. We lurched left, then right, and I slid back and forth along the empty bench like a bead on a wire. There was an abrupt crescendo—if not voices, then emotion. The loss of control was palpable. First the brakes grabbing and howling. Then the sense that mass was shifting sideways. Finally the pent-up silence of the passengers bursting with recognition. I cannot find words to describe the screams. They were screams of imminent extinction. Only cats register torment with such unearthliness. The odd thing was that none of the nineteen moved. They must have been flung all over on November tenth, but as if they were confined to assigned seats as witnesses to a memory, they sat in collective stillness, waiting for me to catch up.

I didn't want to catch up. That much of me at least was still resisting the voyage of the damned. But there wasn't any choice. Whatever my need to know, their need to take the mystic ride to somewhere beyond a common purgatory was paramount.

The actual impact is confused. There was a concussion—there must have been a concussion—because I heard the echo of it, phantomlike, an underwater fade, a dull thud so jarring that I didn't register the initial sound. We had hit the bear, and a sickening centrifuge began to churn. I squeezed my eyes tightly shut, but the swirl kept accelerating. Part of me was being hurled free; part of me was being dragged down. And then it all stopped dead again, and I opened my eyes.

It was like the eye of a hurricane, an impossible equilibrium in the midst of impending violence. A few more ticks of grayness before the rupture. The explosion of the gas tank, when it came, seemed incidental. I never felt heat, never saw flames. It must have happened just like that for them—too quickly for anyone to react—because along with them, I was already past that, witnessing something on the very border of physical death.

It is like standing on the crest of a wave. Behind you is the order of the ocean; in front of you are the shores of Chaos and Night. And even if it's just an instant's aberration, it's an instant from which you can never fully recover, because it topples every reference point you have. Pure death, unredeemed death, is entry into disorder.

Do you think you can withstand that? To be conscious and nothing more in the howling abyss of formlessness?

Not possible. I rode with the nineteen, so I know. Anything more or less than that stitch in time and space, and we all would have been annihilated. Instead, a terrible friction ignited the air and filled it with light. Call it the fabled white tunnel. Call it whatever you want. It wasn't peaceful. There wasn't any serene passing. White light notwithstanding, something unholy was unfolding. Was and still is unfolding. Because that's when everything empathic stopped and shifted to me.

I am certain now that the alchemy of nineteen souls transmuting is suspended in me. I am the missing ingredient that they need. Specifically, they need my surrender. How this happened has to do with my physical death and resurrection in the waterfall. I died so slowly that the line between life and death became finer and finer, measured in degrees of falling core temperature. At 55.1 degrees my physical life was for all intents and purposes over, but there was still no fatal damage to my brain. I was conscious of my existence, if not in a wide-awake state then at least at the level of a dream. The old mammalian reflex—whatever the hell that really means—kicked in.

Has anyone ever defined the exact physiology of that? How do elements of matter sustain thoughts? Write me the chemical formula for a conceived abstraction. At some point the linkage is discrete and singular. One single tangible strand, one single intangible idea. Your life as a human—the idea of your life as a human—becomes indivisible. Body and soul meet at that point, part at that point.

And there I was . . . am.

And if this is too much intellectualizing, let me tell you what happened next. Because the reeking, clammy, uncoffined nineteen still hadn't moved. They just sat there facing forward in that lighted shell, bus or tunnel, their red plaid scarves wrapped tightly around their faces. And I rose to my feet—jerked to my feet like a marionette—and rolled forward with lunatic grace. I babbled. I believe I was apologizing. And I did something that was reckless in the extreme. Reaching out to the third figure I passed, I took hold of the fringe on its scarf and unwound it, layer by layer, like unwrapping a mummy. I did this trembling and with broken laughter, as if to deny what I was doing.

I don't know what I felt when I saw the face. I said something mildly exclamatory, as if it were a simple faux pas. And then I moved blithely on and undid another scarf, another face. And another. Each time miming surprise. *Oh, pardon me.* I don't know how many I did. Not nineteen. But enough—oh, God yes, more than enough!—so that I knew what they all looked like. But it didn't help. Where were the four sisters from Sweden and the boy who was recovering from Hodgkin's lymphoma? Where was Alex Franke? I should have unveiled at least one of them. But all I got was my own face. Over and over.

When I reached the front row, I stumbled off the bus. Actually, I must have fallen off, because I have fresh cuts and bruises on my face and hands. It was still snowing outside, but not the way it had looked from inside. Instead of the furious pelting curtain, a few flakes drifted down aimlessly, like misplaced benedictions. I stood there in the splintered light from B&D's single beacon and stared at the blackened hulk of the bus, lying like a leviathan on a white beach strewn with flotsam and jetsam. Thank God it was just the same as when I got on board. The past quarter hour had to have been a fantasy, right? Sam was on the money again. Revisit the traumas, put them to rest. Except that in my left hand I still held a red plaid scarf, like an outsized loose thread from a universe that was unraveling at the speed of light.

The scarf is still in the car outside. I don't want to bring it in, because it's like one of them, and they'll catch up to me soon enough. In fact, just as I got here I heard glass breaking. It was the front window of the shop. I thought that they were going to be inside waiting for me. But that wasn't it. When I came around to the front of the shop, I could smell natural gas. The window had been broken to let it vent before I could put a key in the lock and cause a spark. Whoever broke it was trying to save my life. Which probably means I wasn't the target of the intended gas explosion. Sam was.

Modus operandi: Sabotage the gas line to the water heater.

Target: Simota Ingmar.

Motive: Kill off the distractions, the stabilizing influences, the links that connect the candidate—me—to the secular world. Sam must be more of a liability now than an asset in maintaining me. Either that or I'm so close to breaking down that it doesn't matter. Isolate me. Drag me kicking and screaming over the edge. Did I hasten this by going to the bus?

Conclusion: If I hadn't come back here unexpectedly, Sam would have been the next one to put a key in the lock. The cabin would have been thoroughly saturated with gas by then. One spark—boom. No one would have broken a window to save him.

Too late to get hold of him tonight. I have to stay here so that I can warn him first thing in the morning. And this time I will convince him. When he sees the window, and I tell him about the loosened gas fitting at the water heater, and show him the scarf, he'll have to buy into it.

What can go wrong with my explanation? He'll play devil's advocate, of course. It may come down to whether I could have done this myself in an altered state, and whether or not he trusts my sanity when I say that there are no breaks in the continuity of yesterday.

One thing for sure. I'm not going to sleep much tonight, even though I'm exhausted. I can't remember when I've ever been this tired. Where's the can of Black Flag?

January 30, 2001

Leavethedrivingtous leavethedrivingtous leavethedrivingtous. Sam, Sam, get on board. You can ride forever from nowhere to nowhere.

I'm writing again, writing riding riding riding the damn bus.

Three days ago I burned this whole journal page by page in the wood stove in The Ski Shop. That was Black Saturday. The day after I returned to the bus. Then I deleted the copy on his computer. Two days ago I tried to delete me. I loosened the gas fitting on the water heater at the shop and went to sleep on the cot. I woke up in the middle of the night and found the gas fitting tight again. Then I tried to hang myself with the red scarf. Too short. A fiasco. So I'm still here. And the journal is still here, because I went and got the Zip disk that I had used to transfer the file to Sam's computer out of the glove compartment of my car. Then I printed it out, and that's why I'm back writing. Because if I have to live, then I have to fight. I don't want to be insane. Not for the next three hours anyway. I've got to get through what's coming this afternoon. Then I can go insane.

So let me get the facts down. Facts are like bread crumbs in a maze. I'm going to cling to the facts. Here a fact, there a fact, everywhere a fact-fact. *The Facts.* I'm going to document everything down to the time and the temperature. Idiot savants do that, don't they? Obsessive-compulsives and some autistic types do it. That's their security. That's how they inject order into mental chaos. Rain Man did it. Didn't I tell you that I thought Sam looked like Dustin Hoffman the night he picked me up from Mayo and we stopped in at Chili's? Yes, I did. That's a fact.

Here's some more. January 27, Saturday morning. Three days ago. Post–bus trip. I was at the shop, shivering and trying to get my head on straight. I had stayed there all night, and I sprayed Black Flag all over the place. I'm not going to look back to check what I wrote, because I don't want to reread this stuff, but I know I wrote all about my visit to the bus and coming back to find the broken window in the shop and that I was looking for the Black Flag. Small wonder I didn't pull an encore at Rush-Timmons, sick from all the bug juice I breathed. It gave me a headache, and I lay down on the cot. I was going to warn Sam in the morning that they were trying to get him. I kept forcing myself awake, imagining there were things crawling in my clothes, which I had not taken off. Even my shoes were still on. But the bugs were extinct, and there was no reason I shouldn't go to sleep, and finally I did—I fell into a really deep sleep. That had to be toward dawn.

It's unforgivable, but I never, ever imagined that Sam could come in and go out without waking me. The fact that I didn't hear him drive up in the snow is not surprising. Some traffic would have been passing in the night, maybe even a snowplow, and that hadn't awakened me. He must have seen my car and the broken window, so why the hell didn't he rouse me to find out about it?

But he didn't.

Cool, calm Sam. Probably a little cautious coming in, not sure if there had been a break-in or what. He would know I wouldn't smash the front window, even if I lost my key. So he came in as softly as the Indian he was, and saw that I was asleep in the back, and by then he had probably concluded that someone had broken the glass maliciously, and that I had happened along and decided to stay the night after boarding up the damage. He would see that the inventory hadn't been disturbed, which he could do pretty much at a glance, and then he might write me a note. He did write me a note.

When it's white, it's all right. Have gone out to groom and harvest.

I didn't hear him start the groomer, but that's not surprising either. He keeps it in a shed near the trailhead. I probably heard him when he passed close to the shop at the end of the trail check. Putting it together retrospectively, he was on his way to harvest when I came awake. That first sentence of his note is actually a line of groomer's doggerel they use to size up snow conditions:

> *When it's white, it's all right,*
> *When it's gray, it's okay,*
> *When it's blue, so are you,*
> *When it's brown, shut it down.*

If I wasn't wide-awake after reading the one line, Sam's second sentence iced my spine. *Have gone out to groom and harvest.* Harvest. That's when you collect a bunch of snow on a skid in order to fill in the holes and ruts on a trail. Sam has a harvester he built himself—a box with a blade that he drags behind the snowmobile. The blade kicks snow into the box, as much as five hundred pounds. The trouble isn't the harvester. The trouble is where he gets the snow. Because he doesn't like to harvest from the trails, which just thins them down as it evens them out. It's easier to get snow off the lake.

So, if the murderous bastard that loosened the gas fitting the first time wanted to get him, it knew precisely where he was going. That was the picture Saturday morning. That was why I rousted out in near panic.

Sam always goes the same route, even to keeping on the same tracks so that the rest of the lake snow isn't packed down. He goes to an inlet where other snowmobiles don't track, and he runs a straight course, branching off in fleur-de-lis patterns that go farther and farther out each time he harvests. You can predict the next arc with certainty. He runs the trails first. Packs it to see where it leaves holes and ruts. Then he goes to the lake.

I grabbed my skis, boots, and poles and was out the door. Forget gloves, hat, and windbreaker; I was in a full sweat out of sheer dread by the time my edges were carving through Sam's snowmobile tracks at the top of the runs. It wasn't going to be good enough. I wasn't going to overtake him just by following his tracks. If there was a way, I would have to leave the trail.

As soon as I hit the major switchbacks, I cut across the unbroken crust on the downside. There had been thaws and refreezes, and the fresh snow was thin and drifted, so I was skiing on ice, mostly, with here and there something that would take an edge and slow me down. When the trees closed ranks it got especially hairy. No soft evergreens to break a skid; all elms, oaks, and basswoods.

I managed to stay in sparse stands where tendrils whipped my hands and legs and nothing thicker than a clothesline looped into my path, but I didn't know exactly where I was. I just kept heading down until I shot across the regular trail and caught sight of the uniform ruffle left by the groomer's drag. The imperative of heading Sam off sang through me like the high note on a violin, while a drum beat steadily beneath it. I prayed desperately to the wizard divine of the universe, the green god of summer, the lord paramount of all things. My tips knifed like shark fins into a soft blanket in a high meadow with weeds all blown in one direction. I had to be gaining. But the meadow yielded purple shadows in the lee of a tree line, and I caught ice again.

I raced down the south side as recklessly as a snowball through hell, crossed the trail twice more, and came out not far from the inlet. There was a fierceness in me that wouldn't be denied as I charged and clattered along the ice on the inlet. Sam would not die. Would not! *Would . . . not!*

. . . and I wish to God *I* had died.

There would be that much expiation, then. Because I saw the fresh track of the harvester, and in that blinding white blaze of early morning—early mourning—I squinted and found the strip of black. Like a shadow it lay. A hole to the nether regions. And Sam, that very worthwhile human being I have only recently come to appreciate, maybe the best friend I ever had, Sam Ingmar, had already gone into it.

How could so commanding a mind be so easily destroyed? He can't be dead. He must be negotiated with. He must first see that he must die. Otherwise it's no deal.

They got his body out an hour later. A couple of scuba divers found him after only five minutes of searching. He was lying on the bottom in about fifteen feet of water not far from the snowmobile and the harvester, which had sunk upright. I saw his eyes when they brought him up, and the glittering obsidian that had absorbed the whole world was still absorbing it.

I am sickened by what he must have seen when he was going down. Did they watch him? Did they come out of the woods in a cortege with red plaid scarves hanging down like vestments as they gathered around the hole? Did they stand there while he tried to struggle up onto the ice? Did they push him down? I don't know how they cracked the surface, or whether he saw it coming too late to veer the groomer away, but it wasn't a merciful way to die.

What can make a wholesome church group who lived their lives under the banner of Christianity into demons? How could they devolve into something so uniformly ruthless? You've got all the answers now; tell me, Sam.

January 31, sometime in the A.M.

Sam in a box in the earth. I wish we hadn't done that. I wish I had had the wits to leave him in the lake.

A funeral is such a belated and misguided convening. Sam would have hated it. Metal casket, picked flowers, inactive friends, curious customers, distant relatives, old lovers. The minister didn't know him from Adam—though he did have the showmanship to keep it simple and general.

Sam's brother, or half brother, made the arrangements. Stalwart, big-boned, blue-eyed, somberly dressed, he inclines as much toward the Norwegian side of the family as Sam did the Ojibwa. The minister was Lutheran, a man with a slight lisp, delicately blotting his lips every minute or two. He sounded intelligent as he read something from Romans or Corinthians. Dominions and thrones. As if Sam has only cashed out his little skiing enterprise and moved on to better real estate.

The half brother's name is Karl. He glanced at me half a dozen times before the service and finally walked over and introduced himself. "They tell me you were a close friend," he said.

"I helped Sam with the shop."

"And you were there when it happened?"

"I didn't see it, but I called rescue."

He looked at me too long, and I thought he was more judgmental than Sam. There wasn't much about him I could relate to, except directness. He has Sam's good-listener quality and his hint of a smile, but not much sincerity.

"Sam was a good judge of people," he said finally. "You must be very dependable."

He was complimenting me with a purpose, and when I didn't help him, he went right to it.

"Hate to bring up the store in these circumstances, but I'm from Mankato, and I don't get up very often. There are legal formalities ahead, and after that I'll have to make some decisions. I understand there was some vandalism in the shop—a broken window or something like that?"

"It was an accident."

"Well, I don't think I want to just lock it up with everything he has in there. Would you consider keeping it going for a while?"

"The snowmobile is at the bottom of the lake."

"Do you need a snowmobile to keep it open?"

"If it snows, the trails won't be groomed."

"You could keep it open, though?"

I shrugged. "I could keep it open."

"I'll give you whatever he was paying you and, say, twenty percent of any profit?"

I stared hard at him for thinking money mattered, for talking business at Sam's funeral.

He thrust a card at me. "Look, neither one of us wants to talk about this right now. I have to go back to Mankato tonight, and I'm going to be in Chicago for ten days starting Thursday. How about running the store that long, and then we'll see where things stand?"

The minister spoke, and then the coffin went down the aisle of the small church, and everyone filed out into a motor procession that crept through Sheshebans's dreary streets toward the graveyard half a mile away. The antline of cars ate into me like I was on a chain gang. If I could have gotten to the coffin, I'm half convinced Sam would have escaped with me. I yearned to hit borders, cross boundaries, leave everything behind. Once, during my divorce, I did this. Two days of unplanned flight. There is something healing about new cities in the night whose names you don't know and whose emptiness soothes you as you cruise along under orange expressway lights. If I could trundle that ghastly box from city to city, keep Sam in transit, would it save him from terminal mystery?

The grave site was unbearable. Karl and a mix of Ojibwa and Norwegians trying to move gracefully through the snow with the black wooden coffin. The Lutheran minister with the lisp and the handkerchief started reading something final and comfortless. I kept flashing back to the pitiless hole in the inlet ice, so inert, so vacant. They were burying Sam too fast.

In the middle of the service, I turned and crunched off through the snow, making so much racket that I didn't hear steps coming after me. But when I faced around to open the driver's door of my car, she was there.

"Hello, Bowie."

"Beckie." My eyes swept the cemetery to either side of us.

"I'm sorry about Sam." She negotiated the final three yards of uneven snow without looking away from my face.

"You're tempting fate coming here," I said.

"I wanted to see you. I wanted to tell you you're not to

blame. The paper said he went through the ice in a snowmobile. That it was the third accident like that this winter. It happens."

"Sam groomed for probably twenty years. He wasn't about to misjudge an inlet in January."

"It could have been an accident," she insisted.

"How? Once the ice is frozen, it stays frozen until spring thaw. And it's been frozen since early December. Stay away from me, Beckie."

She never said another word. Just looked at me with a little hurt, a little confusion. I like that woman. She could have walked past all my totem poles and war masks at that moment. But I got in the car and never looked back.

January 31, late

There's a storm coming tonight, and after that the number of skiers willing to struggle through the drifts will fall off sharply. I'm trying to think past today, but everything has an endgame feel. Even the shrunken sun seems to be perpetually setting. My emotions have flatlined. I feel like a horribly wounded junkyard dog who might as well go down in his last fight.

This afternoon I tried to go back to the waterfall. What else is left? With about an hour till dark, I brass-brushed my Fischers, threw on some glider, and closed the shop. The long sunset met me at the trailhead just before four thirty, and the frozen tracks from my failed attempt to rescue Sam were still there, glaring silver down the slope. For the first time in nearly three months, I turned north.

There are no trails and no tracks in that part of the woods, so I moved slowly. Not far down I caught the pungent odor that should have stopped me altogether. It was too cold for such a strong reek to be decay, so it had to be something alive. And hibernating bears break down urine in their bodies, so it had to be something awake. Nevertheless, I let my skis wend on, waggling tips and sledding sideways to check my progress. There were no animal tracks. I was safe, I told myself. And that is why I skied between piles of brush and discovered too late that it was a blind alley. It looked like a den; it was a den. Which should have reverted my thinking to the hibernation theory. But the beast before me had not been informed of the season's policy for its species. It rose up on trunk-size hind legs and extended lethal high fives.

It should not have been there, but then the black bear was probably thinking the same thing about me. Given the effect I have on killer puppies, a fanged titan should have had me diced and on a bun before my knees knocked three times. Instead, it hung there, jaws open, cornered but undecided.

It's always funny when you think back on a dangerous encounter you survived. Shit. That's a Sam-ism. First night driving me back from Mayo he said that. Sam didn't survive, but I'd laugh my ass off if I could have that night back driving with Sam.

Okay, Sam. Today was funny.

Five hundred pounds of reared-up cutlery are a scream now, but I couldn't scream then. I've seen smaller pickup trucks. The pause was interminable. A Kodak moment, if not a Kodiak one. One of us should have been doing something. And in fact my skis, completely of their own volition, kept sliding and sliding. Ten meat cleavers were waving me off, but I was going to embrace Ursa Major.

The classic question "Does a bear shit in the woods?" is not my area of expertise. However, people skiing into bears is another matter. My bowels were asking permission as Smokey reared ever higher, drawing back enough so that it looked like I was going to pass right under his eating utensils. If I attempted to wipe out before I got there, odds were I would three-sixty into occupied space. Fact: The only way two animals can occupy the same space at the same time is if one eats the other. I had just eaten an apple, so I stayed on my feet, too petrified to raise the poles, and the bear, presumably confused by this odd tactic, let me sail on through.

I don't know how many style points I deserve for this maneuver, but it was too early to celebrate out there on the north slope. Twenty feet ahead of me was a solid wall of underbrush. The only way out was to sashay back the way I came in.

I can't remember if the bear growled as I reversed course, but its fetid breath washed over me from ten feet away, so it must have. And for the moment, that was all it did. Either I had chanced upon a stupid, cowardly, mute bear, or it was stunned by my audacity. This couldn't last. I foresaw massive forelegs shimmering with staccato slaps while screaming wounds increased by multiples of five all over my body. The blaze of white on the beast's throat craned higher as I came abreast until, unexpectedly, its front paws lowered a few inches and it closed its jaws and nuzzled the air. There is nothing more opaque than a black bear's black-glass stare, and yet I was sure this one was straining to recognize something. Very softly it came down on all fours. With more of a huff than a growl, it ambled off ahead of me.

The temptation to just blast up the trail was almost irresistible, but you don't outsprint bears any more than you should stalk them. So when the beast's pungency began to fade, I edged forward, ticking my poles cautiously off the crust a few inches at a time like a blind man with a cane. All I could think was that I was going to round a stand of trees and become bear confetti. Blessedly, twenty yards ahead, the paw prints turned down.

I beelined for the trailhead then. But with all the traversing, I had moved west, and now I was scampering along unfamiliar molten carpets unfurling in the last rays of the day. I never made it to the falls, but the listlessness with which I had started out was lifted. No more blue funk. No more Sam-is-dead fear of living. Oh, God, Sam, you would've loved it out there with me today. My senses were honed. The glare off glazed surfaces seemed to perform LASIK surgery on my eyes, and I saw every mote of woods and snow like an eagle. I could smell the cabin, smell the highway. At the top of the mountain I looked back in triumph. The snow in the reed beds is like foam, and the snow on the slopes is like orange sherbet, and in the woods the snow is like the pale thigh of a perfect lover. What's to fear?

Back here in the shop I've got a new answer to that question. Because it occurs to me that the black bear could have been the mate of the bear hit by the bus. In fact, it's likely, given the size of their territories. It scented me and turned away. What, exactly, did it sense in me? Fact: There is another way for two animals to occupy the same space at the same time.

February 1

The Sheshebans area was hit hard by the storm last night, and I took my chances with the spiders rather than drive home. I think I'm going to stay here from now on. Things breathe in the dark in my apartment, food rots in the fridge, the computer is infiltrated, and a snowman watches my window. Out here I'm close to the woods. It's natural. There are plenty of canned goods and cases of bottled water on hand.

The storm started about two a.m. Light, feathery flakes that got bigger and faster until by four or five a.m. they were like comets. But it was a soft bombardment, and it buried what was.

I'm out of Black Flag. Whatever isn't dead isn't moving, though. Probably not a whole lot of pupating larva is going to break out six-packs of legs anytime soon, and the eight-leggers aren't stirring either. They are all locked in egg cases, overwintering and down for the count. So, it's just me and the books.

I'd forgotten how a book can grab you when you read alone without distractions. No TV, no telephone, the computer off and a storm piling insulation on the roof. I read *Unnatural Beings: A History of Deviancy* all day during the storm. You might think that would be a P. T.

Barnum encyclopedia of freaks and anomalies, like Elephant Man, but it's almost entirely devoted to beings with deviant powers or who are spiritual vessels for corrupt forces. The names have a terrifying formality: *lusus naturae,* heteroclite, *rara avis,* teras. This should be required reading for the shrinks at Mayo—the new science of deviant forces: laws that violate other laws. Fields of study are just separate rooms. Too bad so many scientists never find the connecting doors. Charlatans and the truly ignorant have claimed the unexplored territory at the edge of the map and given it a bad rep. And I guess that's where I'm doomed to wander, because who is going to see me as anything but a psych case? But I'm still first person singular, and I've got to hang on to that. I can't remain "in process" indefinitely. That endgame feel I mentioned, it has to happen.

So tonight I went looking for it. I thought I might try the direct descent to the waterfall. That's the one that parallels the road. The one I took November tenth. But as I started out it occurred to me that if I waited for the predicted storm to pass, the added powder would take some of the dangerous speed out of the descent in the morning. So I ended up just skiing toward the highway. I thought I was postponing a reckoning, but I needed what came next. It reminded me of who I am and what I still have to do.

Not much traffic had been by last night, and it all looked very pristine. No snowplow grit on the embankments, no dog piss. The rounded drifts were strictly Walt Disney, as were the Christmas lights on the lone house up there at the corners. It's an old farmhouse, and the bulbs are the big old-fashioned kind that glow in blue and red pockets of snow along the roofline and on the porch rail. Red for Jessica, blue for Danny—that's the way we used to sort them out every year. Standing out there in the cold looking at that glow filled me with remorse for what my family has lost. Maybe it doesn't come through these pages, but that's still the number one thing for me. I remember my kids' elfin faces between the staircase balusters on Christmas Eve—as close as Dolores let them get to the presents. All the traditions were from Dolores's childhood. She was very exacting about that.

Once I tried to break the string. "Papa Noël has uncovered a long lost Christmas custom from his felicitous past," I told them.

"What's 'fish-fist-us'?" Danny wanted to know.

"It means Dad's gonna make this up," Jessica said.

"Make up the greatest Christmas adventure story of all time? Hardly."

There is an old-time radio show on WFAM that runs from Thanksgiving to Christmas Eve every year. Twenty-six episodes of something called *The Cinnamon Bear*, the story of Judy and Jimmy trying to recapture their silver-star Christmas tree ornament in Maybeland. They have all these incredible adventures with Paddy O'Cinnamon, the Crazy Quilt Dragon, and the Wintergreen Witch, to name a few. Dolores said it was too corny. She said the kids would rather watch *The Grinch* or *A Charlie Brown Christmas*. The kids listened with me to a couple of the fifteen-minute episodes, but after that Dolores always said they didn't have enough time. If there wasn't a "really worthwhile" special on TV, then they had to have baths, or go to bed early because they had been up late the night before, or practice something for something-or-other that was going on somewhere else. I never could compete. I don't know why I got so huffy about *The Cinnamon Bear*. Jessica was right. It wasn't even from my childhood. The year it debuted, 1937, my father was probably still crawling around on all fours. But I listened to it every night when I heard the re-creation on WFAM, and the next Thanksgiving I listened to it again. In fact, this is the first time in four winters I've missed it.

If you tell me that's just self-pity—okay, it is. But it turned into a fantasy of sharing with my children too. That was real. That was real.

So tonight I skied past the farmhouse with the red-and-blue Christmas glow, and then I skied across the field to a hill that must be a county park right-of-way, because there is a paved trail there and lampposts. I stopped at the crest and stared at the spangle overhead. Each star was like one of those magical Christmas lights I'd left behind. One of the trail lamps made my shadow seem to stretch toward infinity. Arms outstretched to the sides, palms resting on the ski poles as if they were wires controlling me from below, it was the shadow of a puppet. And that suggestion of orchestration together with *The Cinnamon Bear* contrived to put an idea in my head, because suddenly I felt an overwhelming dread that I was absolutely correct yesterday when I fled the bear and that I understood everything that is trying to take over inside me.

It *is* the bear. How simple. It wasn't just nineteen people who were killed in the bus. The bear was killed. A black bear. And the black bear in the woods, which had very likely been its mate, turned away from me. It sensed its mate.

The more I think about it, the more the links forge together. I couldn't stand the hospital confinement; and I was obsessed with the red columbine—with the dirt. They wanted to put canned oxygen on me, but all I wanted was to revel in the outdoors. And I took on three orderlies, and I got out of the restraining straps. The fact that I don't remember any of the aggression probably means that whatever is trying to share me was in control at that point. The other things—sensory acuity, heightened instincts, my changing perception of music, fits of temper, bashing the snowman—hint at something vaguely brutish emerging in my nature. This coup in my soul, this coming into being, starting from death, is profoundly wrong, profoundly threatening to the living things around me. And the simpler the DNA, the more violent the reaction, as if the gut reflex of life has been antagonized.

Maybe all altruism, all violence, all pacifists and predators, and every evolutionary direction, are fundamentally represented in each cell. And now, in the twenty-first century, I am resonating some dark atavism. Whatever triggered killer strains in the evolutionary spiral—that's what is trying to get into me. What if every form of organic life is a little bit of order introduced into chaos, and what if whatever I'm becoming goes against that and pushes the order back?

Tonight at the shop I went online until I found what I was looking for on something called Radio Spirits. I used the shop credit card number to make a purchase, and then I wrote this note in my journal:

If you are reading this, Jessica or Danny, I want you to know that first, last, and always I love you. In a way, I hope you never see this. Your mother was probably right: You would have been better off to just forget me. But if you are seeing this—if it somehow survives and is brought to your attention—then you must be grown-up. You will remember then receiving something in the mail, something I went online just a minute ago and ordered sent to you. The Cinnamon Bear *tapes. I hope those survived your childhood too, somehow. Maybe you'll play them for your children and tell them about their grampa. I sent them to you at the most dramatic hour of my life. That should tell you how I feel and, if personal identity is possible in eternity, how I will feel about you forever. . . .*

The waterfall. I'm going back to the waterfall. That's where I lost my sense of order. That's where I put one foot into chaos, while the other still drags on terra firma.

February 2

I awoke to a murder of crows. That's the correct term. A murder of crows began gathering at dawn. I heard them through the cabin walls. One at first—the alpha executioner—settled like a black stain somewhere outside in the mist and the snow. Most likely on that dead sycamore behind the shop. I knew from his first piercing caw that something bad was happening. Lord Death convening . . . something. My eyes shot open. *Just a crow,* I told myself. But the damn things have perfected that one note, haven't they? You've heard it—clarion, electric. And when it's directed at you, it stabs to the heart with accusation. No trial. No parliament of owls—to use another correct term, for the record—just the damning call to disorder by a murder of crows.

Then came the soft thuds. Snow falling off branches as they swarmed. A raucous crescendo to deafening in fifteen seconds. And finally the claws scrabbling on the roof and the sharp puncturing of beaks through ice crust and shingles. One hundred percent Alfred Hitchcock insane.

I knew Sam's shotgun was on the rafters in a carton that had contained skis, and I flung myself off the cot, barefoot to the ladder. In a moment I had the thing down, pulling off the plastic sheath, fumbling for shells. I levered the first one into the chamber and pushed two more below it. The window was still boarded, but I could see shadows flitting across the seam above the broken glass. I opened the front door.

Mist notwithstanding, the crows almost shut out the light. Those closest to the door just popped up and fluttered back on the snow a few feet away in that stately pose of the omnivorous and brassy felons they are. One of these vented a harsh cry distinct from the torrent above, and astonishingly the others on the ground immediately turned and walked toward me. Walked. How disturbing is that, even though crows do this by nature, instead of hopping or fluttering? These strutted toward me. Even when I threw the shotgun to my shoulder, they only hesitated.

The first blast took out three of them more or less in a line. Feathers exploded in the air, splattering gouts and gore all over the snow. I'm not ashamed to write that I felt joy. Red entered the spectrum of black and gray. Red, which must have been blood but may have been feral glints in their lethal black eyes. The concussion coiled off, leaving an uncanny moment of silence. In fact, the passerine gallery that clung to branches never moved until I edged out the door in my bare feet and, ejecting the first shell, gave them what-for in a second discharge. Then they lifted up and flapped leadenly away. They were only crows, after all, with the brains and instincts of crows. By the time I got off the third round, their dissonance was just a forlorn lisp fading through fog.

I have no idea where they've gone, or if they'll be back. I'm tired of theorizing. I want to hear Sam tell me that it was the kind of thing crows do, even though it isn't. This is the last day. I know that. Like I said, there's a terminal feel to everything.

The smell of spent casings and shotgun oil fills the shop, but there is another smell much harder to describe. It's like one of those ozone sprays, supposedly scentless, that makes you nauseous. If the hole in the air had a smell, this would be it.

I don't know exactly what I did for the next hour after the crows disappeared in the fog. Got dressed, I guess. I kept looking around at the rafters and the walls, waiting, listening. The temptation to phone Beckie was almost irresistible. But that would have been fatal to her. Let it be a romantic thing between us—this self-imposed distance. That will keep it idealistic. Besides, maybe she was only meant to show me that I'm not impossible to love. And I believe we would have loved, in different circumstances.

Out of sheer nervousness I began setting up the wax on my ski bottoms, and it was the brass brush removing plastic burrs that masked the sound I thought I heard creeping in from outside. It could have been the slow crackling of tires on snow, but I paused ten seconds, nerves tingling, and heard nothing more. I began another long, even stroke. The hiss of bristles on a ski base is like surf spending itself. It ends in a little rush as you lean down the ski, sweeping it free. But this time there was an added sigh, like the release of air through a piston.

Definitely from the parking lot. A die-hard snowshoer arriving, or a skier too inexperienced to know that the trails were nearly impassable. I put the brush aside and went behind the counter, thinking, How was I going to explain all the dead crows in the snow? *"The boarded window is because crows keep flying into it. I shot at a swarm to scare them away."* Lame. But it didn't matter, because the customer who opened the door wasn't a die-hard snowshoer or an inexperienced skier. He was a man whose face was wrapped in a red plaid scarf.

He glided forward a few slow steps and executed a purposeful shift to his left, like a member of a wedding party making room for the next one down the aisle. And then another came through the doorway. And another. And another. All swathed in the grave-shroud red scarf. Eighteen. One by one filing silently in, flanking in front of me and filling the room with that strangling ozone smell. Eighteen, not nineteen. I don't know why I counted — as if I were going to issue trail passes — except that I was in shock.

There were four sky-blue-and-white jackets with breast patches of the Swedish flag, and next to them a slight figure with sculpted hands who might have been the boy recovering from Hodgkin's lymphoma. One couple stood touching, the woman slightly in front of the man — the newlyweds. And Alex Franke's vacant eyes bore into me. Some of the passengers had ski boots on; others must have changed on the bus that day coming back from Mille Lacs. The room swelled with rustling fabric but remained somehow vacant. And into that crush came the nineteenth figure, a man wearing sunglasses, the bus driver, and when I saw the absolute emptiness in his face, I wished he were swathed like the others.

I could barely breathe. The air crawling over my skin felt as though I were standing next to a high voltage tower. Tears started down my cheeks. I kept repeating "Damn," each one shakier than the last. If they had swarmed over me, I would have been released. I would have fought. But the charade went on, because one of them stepped forward and with beguiling calm said:

"You really shouldn't go out today."

His eyes had an odd flatness above the scarf, like

grapes losing their symmetry, and I thought then that maybe the ability of this spectral troop to materialize was corruptible. That was why they kept the scarves on. Maybe the clock was running for them too.

"Pastor Evans, I presume," I grated to stifle the tremble in my voice. "I'll go where I please."

"It's very bad out there. Not a good day at all."

"It's a terrific day, and I'm going out."

"Believe me, it isn't."

"Why not?"

"It just isn't."

"Because of the bear?"

"The bear. And the woods are full of uneasy things. Dangerous, uneasy things. All of them."

"It's not me they hate," I said too loudly, trying to overpower the tremor. "It's you. You've infected me. I haven't changed."

"You've changed," he said softly.

For a minute there was just that, and when I spoke again, I was pleading, extending my hands. "Look... I'm the same. See? I could be the same, if you'd let me. All you have to do is go away and don't... don't insinuate yourselves in my thoughts, my feelings. It's not fair. You've had your lives."

"We're trying to protect you."

"I won't need protecting, if you go back."

"Go back? Where?"

What if they couldn't? What if they were as lost as I was?

"I don't care how many of you there are," I flared with great agitation, "or what you are. It's *my* life. Not yours. Yours is gone. So get the hell out of my way."

They didn't get out of my way, but they didn't stop me either. I don't think they can. They need my free will. I pushed my way past them and out the door, marching heedlessly through the bloodied snow, flecked with bits of crow, and away from the obscene yellow bus parked in the lot. I started to run. I ran to the highway and turned north. It was bitter cold out, yet somehow clammy, and the mist kept me from seeing anything but the frosted yellow line beneath my feet. The waterfall was miles away, and my jacket was back in the shop. I ran for a few minutes; then slowed; then stopped. Despite my conditioning, the sudden burst of activity had my heart detonating in the megaton range. Wearily, I turned back.

The bus was gone by the time I reached the parking lot. The shop was as empty as if it had all been a grim fantasy. No dollops of snow on the floorboards, no puddles or prints. I'm calm now. My skis are ready, and I am going to the waterfall.

February 2, 2001

If this hasn't been destroyed, it's probably being read by students and professionals as a model of paranoid schizophrenia in some college library. In that case, you won't be disappointed. Read on and I'll make it easy for you to disbelieve. Read on, Dr. Anthony P. Weibens, if you want to see how a personality under siege orchestrates his fantasies. But you should know, I'm rock steady right now. Despite what's happened—and what I know is going to happen—I'm as calm as paint on a wall. There's a part of me—of everyone, maybe—that recognizes a larger destiny when it comes. We are all trainees from an age we've forgotten, where the sum total of what we are is called to the front lines. I think a woman in childbirth knows this. Or a cancer patient. Or someone on a plane going down.

The early mist was interrupted by a storm, and what was white at dawn is now sickly yellow haze as I write this, as if the sun has been torn up and scattered horizon to horizon. I have yet to see the sky. Truly a day for an apocalypse.

Sometime in the afternoon I left the cabin and immediately sensed anarchy. In the words of Pastor Evans: *"Not a good day at all."* Things were moving in the woods that shouldn't have been moving. Everything was out in the open, and nothing was afraid. Nocturnal things—owls, raccoons, skunks, possum—were all up on deck. I've never seen a porcupine in the wild before. Today I saw two.

I made half a mile from the cabin before something swooped down and laid my left temple open. My hat spun to the ground, but the thick brow band kept the talon from raking higher. Even so, my blood spattered the snow. *Revenge of the crows,* flashed across my mind. Except it wasn't. The fantail of a hawk dipped past me and back up into the haze. I've never heard of a hawk doing this, and I've never seen birds fly in a fog.

That was the start of the gauntlet. I brushed the blood into my hair and adjusted my hat over the wound like a compress. Then I skied for the denser stands of trees, throwing looks back over my shoulder every other stride.

Stay in transit, and you are less likely to become a target. Like jogging through Central Park in the Big Apple. Like hitting the mean streets in a big-city riot. I didn't know what could attack me, but I knew almost anything would. Mad air. Fallen branches forced me to zigzag, and once I caught myself at the edge of the sinewy creek that flows unpredictably under gray snow. And when I came through an open corridor between some thinly placed hardwoods not far from the waterfall, I met an old nemesis. Thick-necked and huge, a stag with an attitude was suddenly there.

"Not a good day at all . . ."

The morbid manner of the buck in the road that night with Sam, and now this one with his flat, black eyes, as empty as decay, fixed me with the debilitating chill that they were one and the same. I wanted to reject that. It deepened the menace. It linked to a conspiracy. He lifted his foreleg in that peculiar way deer have—like a drum major lifting a baton—and stamped his challenge.

The ski poles were my only weapons, and I raised them almost reflexively. Immediately the stag lowered his bristling rack. That these formal signals were exchanged between a civilized man and a wild animal sent a thrill of recognition through me. With a flurry of diminutive steps, the stag charged. I braced like a two-fisted jouster, and he drew up suddenly, lightly parrying the poles. I felt as though we had touched boxing gloves in the middle of a ring. That thrum through the shafts and grips tested the mismatch of force and resistance. There would not be another feint. The next charge would knock me down, and then he would try to trample and gore me.

I must have looked like a stick drawing as I scuttled sideways toward the trunk of a basswood, skinny skis going like a bailer, narrow graphite shafts swinging every which way. When I was almost there the hollow, umbral eyes swallowed me with dead aim. This time I dug the poles into the snow and jump-turned like a downhill racer as he charged. But a matador I am not, and the broad curve of an antler drove me into the trunk. I rolled, got the pole up. When the haunch wheeled past, I buried the carbide tip. No longer than a fingernail, it barely penetrated before stopping like it had struck granite.

Blowing, slathering, and dull-eyed, the stag danced to a halt. I glanced up the basswood twenty or thirty feet to the first branches. No help there. But when I looked back, the buck's head was turned in another direction. He stood faintly phosphorescent, crowned majestically by a blue-tipped candelabrum. It almost seemed justified that he should win. No one will fashion lawn statues in my image.

And then, as the faint rush of breaking crust snow

reached me, I saw what had distracted him. A chain of silhouettes stretched through the mist. We were sandwiched by shadows, all darting in the direction from which I had come. I didn't understand what it meant, but the stag grasped a new imperative, twitched his white flag, and surrendered the stage in a single bound.

I sagged against the trunk and closed my eyes. Mass flight had saved me—a soft stampede I couldn't get alarmed over. It could be a fire driving them. That would explain the midday haze. But there was nothing acrid in the air. If it did turn out to be a fire, I would head for the road. Or maybe I would just stay here and let it purify the whole deranged world around me. Blood from my scalp wound trickled down. I tasted salt and opened my eyes to the same woods, suddenly silent and empty.

If you've read everything, and you think I'm just delusional, then you won't have any trouble explaining what took place next. As far as you're concerned, none of my ordeal really happened beyond the fact of an accident three months ago. It's all stress-produced and anxiety-fed. But you should know that at that moment, leaning against the trunk of a tree, I could not have felt more calm and resigned. Stress and anxiety had done their duty and now fell apart like worn out rags.

What I understood was that the stage had been cleared for me. I had ignored the warnings of nineteen lost souls and put myself in harm's way, but something potent had rescued me. I had an appointment. Exhausted, drained, bleeding, and bruised, I skied slowly toward the waterfall. And even though I knew that whatever was waiting for me had driven the animals away, I felt serene, detached, worshipful.

Winter's light was having its hour. It has always been a source of fascination to me that on an absolutely gray day, with the sky as opaque as a mattress, there is incredible light at ground level. It rises out of the snow in hues of yellow and blue and white—white especially—so pure that your eyes water. And if the sun makes a cameo appearance low on the horizon, like a cheap bulb lit in a distant room, the grandeur and remoteness are complete. You get to see the glazed orange lake to the east, and the blue plains with the goddess tree, naked and multi-sceptered, to the west, and the silver slope of wrinkled snow to the south, and to the north—today—I found the font of my second baptism.

The waterfall sighed and hissed as I homed in, a thing of enchantment, though I had expected horror. I did not remember the intense cascade of white over ice-encased rocks. Or that it boiled with cold and spume. The wind, which had flatlined, was stirred again by the movement of the cataract and the chill of a crystal basin. And there was a kind of nether gloom, a remnant of the haze, churning out from behind the veils, that remained on the forest floor while shafts of yellow and white struck high up the trunks of stately trees.

I stared mesmerized into the heart of the falls. It was like one of those kaleidoscope tubes you look through into mirrors that multiply fragments of colored glass. Velvet jets of blue and blue-black drapes and purple nebulae reconfigured over and over against a deep-violet spectrum. But for all its beauty, it had an emptiness that sucked vitality into it. Or maybe that was attributable to *him*. Because very gradually it came to me that I was not alone.

Enter violet incarnate. Mr. Freeze. He wore a dark, heavy coat instead of the pin-striped suit, but everything else—the great sad eyes and expressive lips, the large, doughy hands and gold ring, the mimelike whiteness, the waxy scar across his eyebrow—was the same. He stood in the snow as serene as a statue, and I thought of the snowman I had battered apart.

"Are you God or Satan?" I asked dully.

"Dear me," said the voice, whose mellow inertness had never left me. "Let's not anger either one of them. I'm merely the indentured help."

"Jesus, you *are* Satan."

"A challenging syntax, but wrong."

I hung on my poles and studied him. "No matter how you cut it, you're the dark side of the apocalypse."

His thin lips puckered thoughtfully. "Whatever that means. I'm here to give you the answers you want. You really are in an extraordinary situation, Mr. Carmichael."

"I don't want to be in an extraordinary situation."

"But you are. Absolutely unique. In fact, to put it in the terms you favor, your circumstances have shaken heaven and hell. That is why the kingdoms of the Earth despise you. They sense that you are a new order. A challenge to the rules, in fact."

"God wants me dead."

"God may want you dead, but He won't *make* you dead. That would break the rules. *His* rules. And that would mean God isn't perfect, wouldn't it? Tsk, tsk. Can't have that. That would upset everything—the foundations of the universe. No, no, the primitive life below man is acting on its own, as it always does. They are just plants and animals, Mr. Carmichael. Their reactions are a little more visceral than theological. Surely you've felt the chaos, the primal rage that flows through the corporeal world. You didn't invent that. That's what life is like below man. There is no conspiracy against you, Michael Bowden Carmichael, just a lust to kill you because you are such an extraordinary thing."

"Quit saying that. I'm a blasphemy."

"You're a circumstance. We'd love to make you a blasphemy." He locked his hands behind his back and strolled three steps. "Whose terms would you like it in—Christ's, Muhammad's, Buddha's? Actually, you'd probably like Manes, though the ancient Egyptians said it best."

"I don't want anyone's terms. I just want to quit playing a bit part in the drama of my own life."

His face became absolutely unreadable then. "The mechanism of soul transfer in this vaporous little world has never changed," he began. "Upon physical death, the anima of a human spirit moves up or into an equivalent being. But not the beast. The beast must not rise. You've read Solomon's words in Ecclesiastes. And you know who *he's* quoting."

God. He was telling me that Solomon was quoting almighty God—. . . *the spirit of the sons of men, which goes upward, and the spirit of the animal, which descends.*

Suddenly the cold being before me grew horrifyingly mechanical. He spoke rapidly in a drone, lining it out, as if reciting a legal abstract. And I was dismayed, shocked, shaken. I don't want to know the politics of power in the universe. If there is a war in a heaven, do not make me choose sides. Do not turn me into a casualty or, worse, a prisoner. I do not need to know that a fallen angel assigns the souls of the dead along their paths of reincarnation. Or that he is forbidden to move humans lower or animals higher in the order of life forms. Or that I am the test case that can tear that edict asunder and desecrate the word of God. If the war is between God and Satan, then why are the battles always between Satan and man?

Everything vile Mr. Freeze expounded on sounded

like a cosmic variation of free will and disobedience, or like religious versions of matter and energy. I still don't know what he is—Lucifer's butler or Old Scratch himself—but evil exudes from him as subtly as the violet tint he gives the air. I saw the intensity of something monumental vitrify in his eyes, and it is that look that connects him fully with what I saw three months ago.

I experienced the same perverse triumph then, only it was coming from another entity—the hole in the sky—as I hung half-dead in that waterfall. An absence of light had found me; a pure silhouette had rushed into my face radiating malevolent joy. In a bus twenty yards away the mother lode of death was being delivered on a raging pyre, and still that feral presence had been fascinated by *me*—just me. And now I understood why. It was because it had just discovered a staggering opportunity. Nineteen souls—twenty, because how can you omit the primal essence of the bear—were suddenly cast into darkness, and the Prince of Darkness was on hand to orchestrate the transmigration. And there I was, sustained by only a primitive mammalian reflex, a living thing that was still a man but was ebbing by degrees into something less than that. Less than human. And that is the key. Because it meant that the nineteen latent human souls thrust into me also flowed downward into something less than human, if only for the brief ride toward yet another physical death. We should all have died. Cells doomed; spirit evicted. But we didn't. In fact, we took on another passenger. The bear. The beast. The spirit that descends. All very kosher for the animal—so to speak—because it was descending according to divine plan into the remnant of undead cells I had become, preserved in the icy womb of a waterfall.

Only, I was coming back. Cells reviving and still up to

code; spirit rehomesteading. Life thereby flowing upward again with me, *not* according to divine plan for the animal. I had taken the spirit of man down and the spirit of the beast up. And to top it off, they were together inside me. And they still are, as they have been since November tenth. Only they are dormant, because thus far I have blocked them from sharing conscious control.

It shouldn't have happened. No human has ever recovered intact from being so clinically dead. Certainly not with collateral terminal events at hand. Perhaps without the alien souls from the bus my technically living tissue could not have revived. I don't pretend to know. But my guttering spirit had caught again, just as that coherent and utterly commanding presence had hoped. And by then he had assigned them all to me: the humans . . . and especially the bear. The whole species miscegenation implanted itself inside me as if I were a fertilized cell with a revolutionary number of spiritual chromosomes. Revolutionary number and variety. A full load of latent blasphemy as I ascended back to human life, bearing the brute soul with me.

The hard excitement went out of the eyes of the figure in front of me. As abruptly as he had begun, Mr. Freeze stopped speaking. Silence fell on me like a mandate.

"So, if I do this," I weighed in numbly, "if I accept what you want me to be, all this turmoil inside me goes away?"

"Yes."

"And all the fauna and flora love me again?"

"I haven't the faintest idea."

"I don't think they'll love me."

"You'll be a new order. Can you imagine what that means?"

"It means you'll have won a coup against God. You'll

have taken a vessel of lowered resistance—me—and forced a change in the divine plan."

"A change?" he spat out in derision. "The Creator of the universe sets His perfect rules and leaves the stage. How defeating is that? But now they are not so perfect. That is what is ramifying through the foundations of all consciousness."

"I guess it must be a particularly stinging humiliation when you can't engage your adversary directly," I said slowly. "And the bear. What a colossal corruption that would be—an animal's spirit ascending into a man, and man devolving to his brutish nature in one steep step. All contrary to that page from the Bible you spiked to my wall. 'The Lies of Solomon,' as you put it. I can see why you're thrilled."

The light in his eyes banked at my sarcasm. "You aren't culpable, if that's what's troubling you, Mr. Carmichael."

"No, but I'm expendable, once I quit resisting. Everything takes effect when I quit resisting, right? That lets them share control."

"You have no choice. It's a matter of time."

"Is it?" That was the lie. Time. I am mortal; I have enemies. How long can they go on protecting me? (*You will have to guard the lie of your existence. But you can't do that forever, can you?*) "Then why are you trying so hard to convince me?" I said. "How much time do you have?"

He stood so still that for a moment I thought he had become inanimate, a mime-faced effigy bathed in a faint violet haze. And then, as if changing tactics, he said: "I never would have suspected your altruism if you hadn't tried to protect Rebecca Franke, Mr. Carmichael."

"Altruism? I don't mess with husbands who aren't totally dead."

"Mr. Franke is quite conflicted. It's hard to tell which one of you is being nobler: you for giving her up, or Alex Franke for being willing to share his wife. It would be delightful to test the limits of that."

"If you think you're going to get to me through her, you're wrong. I'm not going to become a martyr to save her."

"No. Not her, Mr. Carmichael. But I believe altruism is the chink in your armor. How I hate to stir mortal virtue. Have you noticed the storm?"

I jerked around, saw that the woods beyond the waterfall were grayed. Snow was pelting down and ice was flowing—flowing, that's the only word—from trunk to trunk. I looked back at the source of these accelerated effects, but Mr. Freeze had vanished. And as if on cue, I heard the cry that is etched on every father's reflexes.

"Daaa-dy!"

Jessica. My little lost girl and her Limberlost cry. And dogging her last syllable, Danny's frightened and impatient, "Dad-*dee!*" Implicit in that was that I *could* rescue them, that in the ultimate disposition of our family I would always be there for them.

The storm swept into the basin area before I could move, stinging me, trying to build a wall. I kicked out in the direction of the shouts, but after only a few feet, the voices came again from another direction. I hollered that I was coming, but a few seconds later Jessica made a third even more plaintive cry, and it wasn't from where she had cried before.

It occurred to me that they weren't really there. How could they be? Why would they come? But I knew *he* had the power to do it. And to kill them as he had killed Sam.

It was a blinding storm, a succession of scrims that presented me again and again with precious silhouettes, only to reveal them moments later as stumps or stubby pines. I flailed urgently up the mountain, shouting for my children in the silences. The wind circled, playing the ventriloquist. And then I saw them. Unmistakable figures huddled under a bough.

"Don't move!" I ordered.

I never took my eyes off them as I clambered and poled against a driving snow. But coming through the final curtain of branches, I felt my dismay return like a slap in the face. The figures stood and separated into four. Their offset crosses emerged first—yellow crosses on blue patches—the Swedish national flag. Then the sky-blue jackets and the shroud-wrapped faces came clear. Their eyes were fixed on me, four young sisters who could have been pleading with a gatekeeper to let them board a flight for home as they spoke:

"You're not going to leave them in the storm, are you?" . . . "Aren't you their father?" . . . "Poor things—they won't last much longer." . . . "For God's sake, save them!"

My skis slid backward on compacted wet snow, and another man—the man who had survived the earthquake in Latin America a year ago, I think—was in my way.

"Which one do you want to lose first?" he demanded.

Dogging his question came Jessica's scream and the roar of the bear, both bursting out of the haze.

I twisted in the brute's direction. Glazed snow crust flew up like chunks of Styrofoam as I blindly charged. There were green flashes deep within the storm and a steady crackling of ice and more roars as overburdened branches splintered and fell. Disoriented, I paused.

"You're going wrong," came a woman's voice.

I knew it was the newlyweds, but I never looked straight at them.

"Please don't let your children die," the man pleaded.

"They're not here!"

"Pastor Evans picked them up coming home from school."

"They wouldn't have gone with him."

"It was your secret code that got them in the car. He told them it was from you."

"Liar!"

"White Room..."

I looked into his vacant eyes now, and my blood blanched whiter than the snow, whiter than the White Room.

"Which one are you going to let die?" badgered the woman.

And then I heard the bear again, and Jessica screaming, and I shouted her name, and Danny answered, and the newlyweds were gone, and there was this eerie silence except for the crunching of my skis as I slew-footed up the mountain. Jessica—my beautiful Jessica—had finally gotten her starring role. Center stage. But, alas, it was in a tragedy.

When I saw the glow coming from a level break in the trees, and a dozen figures encircling something on the ground, my heart tore loose.

The periphery is lost to me now, because I was focused on the hole in the snow. The break in the trees wasn't a clearing. It was ice. A pond on a plateau. And the figures in the circle were staring down at a perfectly black ring of water. That was the ghastly fascination that drew me, held me, until at less than a dozen feet away I saw the bubbles and understood that it wasn't yet aftermath. *Jessica was drowning now!*

I flung myself forward, but the hole was too small for me to squeeze through. Throwing off the poles and gloves, I plunged my arm into the icy blackness. Bubbles streamed up my sleeve. So many bubbles—more than my clothes could have held. Lungsful of bubbles.

The intense cold dulled the contact when it came. It was just a reverberation through my shoulder, like a buzz of electricity. But then I had her hair, and I willed my fingers closed.

Her body was waterlogged and, despite my frantic upward lunge, it rose with agonizing slowness. Why wasn't she grasping my arm? (*Grab my arm, Jessica! Grab it this instant!*) And then I had my knees under me, the skis twisting awkwardly, and most of my arm clear of the water. Up came the hair wound around my fingers, then the head, and . . .

. . . it was Sam.

Can I lie to myself now and write that I was only shocked and repulsed? I was relieved. Shocked and relieved. Revolted and relieved. Sickened but relieved. It wasn't Jessica. I was holding the corpse of my best friend by the hair, and the only thing that flooded through me was that Jessica had not drowned.

Only secondarily did I react with horror. I tried to let go, but my fingers wouldn't uncurl from the intertwined hair. I pumped my arm up and down. Sam's eyes were open and hard as pearls. His lips were blue and puckered as if about to speak—"*. . . you should have let me know they were after me, Bowie. You should have stayed awake and warned me!*" One final mighty fling, and he slid like a stone from my grasp.

I staggered to my feet. The figures shuffled back. Slowly I raised the ski poles to the storm. "All right!" I bellowed hoarsely. And again, softly in surrender, "All right."

Sealed.

Done.

Doomed.

The snow stopped immediately. I felt the polar air lift. Ice tinkled and clumps of sodden snow calved off branches. When the air cleared, he was there again in his violet haze.

"It's your destiny, Mr. Carmichael," he assured me.

"Where are they?" I croaked.

"Your children are safe. I'll see that they return home."

"I want to call them after they're with their mother."

He strolled around me, stopping behind my line of sight. "Considering the stakes, I've been rather patient with you. Don't imagine you can secure your children beyond my reach."

"I want to call them when they're home."

"And then you'll cooperate?"

"I'll come back here. I'll quit resisting. I'll think what you want me to think. I'll stop thinking." I sagged against the poles. "I'm very tired. . . ."

"We'll be waiting, Mr. Carmichael."

So that's why I'm here, back in the shop, trying to get this down. I don't know why that's important. Except that I've never completed anything in my life. Fatherhood, marriage, friendships. I've had a hundred jobs, a thousand dreams, and except for notoriety, I've left my mark exactly nowhere. And I guess I can't really finish this journal either. . . .

I'm stalling to make sure they've had time to get my kids back home. The worst thing would be to have Dolores answer the phone while they're still missing. What would I say? *Hi, hon. Guess what? A zombie minister is bringing the kids home in an LTD. And—oh, yeah—I'm going to become the Antichrist.*

Anti-Adam, anyway. The rules are about to be broken.

That's why I have to do what I'm going to do. One thing, though. One doubt. Am I just trying to redeem the mess I've made of my life? Am I copping out of that? Children I can't see; a sister I never talk to; relationships I leave hanging? When you look at it that way, this whole thing really *is* suspect. I can hear Sam speculating on whether or not this proves that everything that's happened to me isn't a deliberate psychological ploy after all. Me versus me.

Either way, it's a done deal. I want to make clear that I'm not trying to be a martyr. That crucifixion shadow I saw of myself up there by the farmhouse with the Christmas lights—that wasn't my imitation of Christ. And my exit stage left isn't the redemption of mankind. Or if it is, it's beside the point. I actually considered what Mr. Freeze said, you know. What's in it for me? There is nothing in it for me. No Faustian deal. So, don't impart any noble motives to me, even though I now realize what I must—*unalterably must*—do. If they ever put a sixty-seventh book in the Bible, it won't be the one Mr. Freeze envisioned. The Book of Bowie has a new ending. I'm going to be famous.

Hard to stop writing when you know what happens next. I am going to play host for the dead, and it may kill me. So be it. Because if it does, it will kill them too. Kill the host, kill the parasites. It will be spring soon, and I don't want to experience it with a viper's touch, withering every flower and blade of grass. I want to die in the snow. Now that I think about it, almost everyone I've ever admired is dead. Elvis, Einstein, Jackrabbit Johannsen, Margaret Mead, Abraham Lincoln, Gandhi. My parents are dead. Sam is dead. One and all, they've beaten my record of 55.1 degrees.

* * *

I called the kids just now—called Dolores actually. They were there, and she was fit to be tied. I guess I can understand that, but she wouldn't let me talk to either one of them. You can imagine: "What's going on?" . . . "Where are you?" . . . "The police want to talk to you."

"Please, I just want to talk to the kids," I said.

"You're not answering me. What did you do with them?"

"Did they say I did anything with them?"

"They said a minister dumped them in the frigging woods. They said they could have died! Bowie, if this is one of your crazy ski things, and you've bribed them to cover up for you—"

"I never saw them."

"I was going out of my mind—"

"I never saw them. They never saw me."

"But you know something happened."

"Please, Dolores, let me talk to them. Give me five minutes on the phone alone with them, and I won't ever call again."

I could hear her weighing it. "Don't do this to me, Bowie. I made the decision once. They're better off if you just leave them alone. Let's stick to the script."

"It's not my script."

"It's your children's script. If you love them, let them go."

The outrage inside me knows there's an answer to that, but my mind can't quite frame it. I ended by asking if they were okay—I made her go look—and she came back and said they were okay, refraining from adding, *No thanks to you.*

"Tell them I love them," I said, knowing she wouldn't for the same reasons she wouldn't let me talk to them. "Tell them I'll see them in the White Room."

* * *

I don't know what comes next. Or rather, I do, but I won't know exactly how it feels until it starts. My sense of self is a barrier to the victims from the bus. They want me to want them. My will is essential. Welcome them in and they will come. But who exactly will share control? All of them? Do I become a patchwork soul, a spiritual chimera, or is it like sperm, with the winner contributing half the characteristics of the new me? Do I get to choose? I'll take Alex first. Last would be the bear. Doesn't matter, though. Because I'm going to make sure that by the time they get promoted it will be too late for any of us. There won't be a body left for any of us to inhabit. It's going to be hell, and that's the way I want it. I'm going back to the waterfall like I promised in order to save my kids. But I'm going full throttle. And when I get there, it's going to be "all aboard."

February 3, 2001

How exciting!

I know I shouldn't feel thrilled, but I do. It's fitting that Bowie's journal should end with hope. After sitting up all night reading everything he wrote, I think that seems right. There's been enough horror. And I don't feel the least bit presumptuous writing this last entry for him. After all, he wrote about how we would have been lovers in other circumstances. In a way, I'm going to give him that.

Right after I got here yesterday evening, I read the part he wrote in the afternoon, and as soon as I realized where he had gone, I dashed out to the car and drove down the mountain toward the waterfall. It wasn't hard to pick up the trail. You couldn't miss the destruction. It looked as if that cannibalistic Windigo Sam told him about had roared through there.

Bowie must have started skiing down and surrendered to all of them right where the road gets steep—right where he lost control on November tenth. And he must have been in an agony of pain—but triumph, too!—because clearly they fought. Whether they were fighting with him because he was going to ski into the waterfall again, or with each other for possession of him, I don't know, but it became the Armageddon he wrote about. I know it was his intention to take all of them with him to an absolute death. He was willing to commit suicide to prevent them from sharing his identity, because he was afraid he'd turn into a blasphemy of man and beast. He was wrong, of course.

It was Alex, that was all. My beloved Alex. Whatever else was inside Bowie, it was only Alex he would have had to share with. That's what I believe. And I know just what Bowie would say—that I'm in denial over what death means, because I want my husband back—but it's Bowie who couldn't accept the truth. How could he? What with Alex's spirit inside him all those weeks since the accident, trying to exert his will, trying at the very least to become what Bowie insists on calling a hybrid or a mutation.

At first I was sickened as I drove, and I hated Bowie for what he had done. The carnage was awful; a terrible trail of dismemberment. There was too much gore—too many body parts—to be one person. I don't really understand that, because all the bodies from the bus are cremated or in their graves, aren't they? But they must have vessels of themselves somehow—a semblance of themselves anyway—just like Bowie said. I kept stopping the car and jumping out for a better look. Horrible. But I was relieved as well, because none of it was Alex. I'm sure of that. The scattered remains were being torn apart and eaten by crows and animals that were acting strangely—also like Bowie wrote. I'm sure there will be nothing left to find when the birds are done out there and winter does its cleansing. *But I found the prize!* Miracle of miracles, Bowie's body—alive. Again.

It's because he never made it to the waterfall this time. I don't believe he was entirely in control. Alex, of course, didn't want him to make it to the waterfall. And if Alex was even partly in control, then that explains why they didn't get far enough to have a fatal crash: because Alex can't ski. My dear husband never learned to ski! Isn't that a laugh and an irony for Michael Bowden Carmichael—Mr. Ski himself? And it proves my point that even if all the other souls are lying dormant inside Bowie, it's only Alex who will share his will. Not that I believe for an instant that all those remains on the mountain really represent some kind of plot against God. I go to church. Would I risk letting something hellish into the world?

The body was suffering hypothermia, and delirious, but I got it into the car and up here to the shop. It's lying on the cot, asleep. The color and pulse are coming back. I can't wait!

About the Author

Thomas Sullivan has been a gambler, a Rube Goldberg-style innovator, a coach, a teacher, a city commissioner, and a born-again athlete. His short stories have been published in every magazine from *Omni* to *Espionage*. He lives in Minnesota.

*In the beginning there was life.
And death...*

DUST OF EDEN

by
Thomas Sullivan

Before the world was born, there was the Dust of Eden—blood-red earth from which all else was created. A bit of Eden found its way into the hands of Ariel Leppa, an embittered elderly woman unaware of its ferocious power...for a time.

Soon she discovers enough of its power to create a place called New Eden—a place where she has control over everyone and everything—so she thinks.

0-451-41138-2

Available wherever books are sold or at penguin.com

Ⓢ SIGNET BOOKS (0451)

"A master of the macabre!" —Stephen King

Bentley Little

"If there's a better horror novelist than Little...I don't know who it is." —Los Angeles Times

The Resort 212800
At the exclusive Reata spa and resort, enjoy your stay and relax. Oh, and lock your doors at night.

The Policy 209540
Hunt Jackson has finally found an insurance company to give him a policy. But with minor provisions: No backing out. And no running away.

The Return 206878
There's only one thing that can follow the success of Bentley Little's acclaimed *The Walking* and *The Revelation*. And that's Bentley Little's return...

The Bram Stoker Award-winning novel:
The Revelation 192257
Strange things are happening in the small town of Randall, Arizona. As darkness falls, an itinerant preacher has arrived to spread a gospel of cataclysmic fury...And stranger things are yet to come.

Also Available:

THE WALKING	201744
THE TOWN	200152
THE HOUSE	192249
THE COLLECTION	206096
THE STORE	192192
THE MAILMAN	402375
THE UNIVERSITY	183908
THE DOMINION	187482
THE ASSOCIATION	204123

Available wherever books are sold or at penguin.com

S413/Little

New York Times Bestselling Author
PETER STRAUB

Houses Without Doors　　　　0-451-17082-2
This spectacular collection of thirteen dark, haunting tales by bestselling author Straub exposes the terrors that hide beneath the surface of the ordinary world, behind the walls of houses without doors.
"STRAUB AT HIS SPELLBINDING BEST."
—*PUBLISHERS WEEKLY*

Koko　　　　0-451-16214-5
The haunting, dark tale of a returned Vietnam veteran and a series of mysterious deaths. A *New York Times* bestseller, this is considered by many to be Straub's scariest novel.
"BRILLIANTLY WRITTEN...AN INSPIRED THRILLER."
—*WASHINGTON POST*

Mystery　　　　0-451-16869-0
Characters in a world of wealth, power, and pleasure fall prey to an evil that reaches out from the abyss of the past to haunt the present and claim the living.
"MESMERIZING." —*CHICAGO SUN-TIMES*

Available wherever books are sold or at
penguin.com

S411/Straub